ABOUT THIS BOOK

A CHILD has often been made the confidant of his elders — sometimes with hilarious, momentous or devastating results to the latters' lives. The young boy who is the chief character in this novel becomes involved, without realizing either his power or the implications of adult behaviour, in an emotional tangle between the three daughters of the schoolmaster in whose household he has been placed for a year by his parents.

The setting and period of the story are both unusual and fresh. Its events take place in a seaside town in New Zealand at the outbreak of the 1914 war — a war that perhaps brought the first signs of disintegration into a long-accepted code of moral behaviour prevalent in Britain's colonies no less than in Europe.

THE YOUNG HAVE SECRETS

THE YOUNG HAVE SECRETS

A NOVEL BY

JAMES COURAGE

JONATHAN CAPE

THIRTY BEDFORD SQUARE   LONDON

FIRST PUBLISHED 1954

PRINTED IN GREAT BRITAIN BY BRADFORD & DICKENS, LONDON
BOUND BY A. W. BAIN & CO, LTD., LONDON

The Story is in four parts:

7

Part One

ON THE BRIDGE

CHAPTER I

SELDOM or never in the history of Longmeadows, Walter read, *had a whole form been condemned to spend an entire half-holiday shut in their class-room under the stern eye of that stern master, the Professor. The Lower Fourth, in fact, was not only alarmed at the prospect but thoroughly disgusted. Even the cheerful mug of Magpie Melkington drooped like an unset jelly.*

'It's an insult,' he raved to Plunk and the Hon. Tristram. 'It's terrible. It's practically rotten.'

They banged their fists on the walls of the corridor to express their dismay at the dreadful punishment.

'We'll starve,' squeaked little Plunk.

'We'll simply fade away,' murmured the Hon. T., languidly.

'And all because some lowly bug from the Third threw a squib on Pop-Eye's desk,' Magpie shouted. 'It's not fair, it's a swindle.'

'We must fight, you fellows,' hissed the Hon. Tristram. 'We must devise —'

They cowered together against the wall as a dark figure appeared behind the swing-doors. With his black gown swinging, the Professor . . .

THE tram stopped abruptly on the bridge. For a moment, brought to himself far from Longmeadows, looking up from the paper-covered book on his knees, Walter was uncertain of where he was or of what had happened. He raised his face to the level of the window of the trailer, staring, now with all the absolute absorption of his ten years, through the dusty glass at the bridge and the mud-flats of the estuary beyond. The wintry yellow sky of the evening was reflected in the deepish water under the bridge.

The tram, he discovered, had run down or over a small black

and white dog, a young collie. The driver had already climbed stiffly from the seat of his cab and had dragged the yelping, writhing animal from under the wheels, holding it up by the scruff of the neck, where there should have been a collar to grasp. And now the conductor came running from the rear of the trailer — the second coach of the long green tram — to stand with the driver beside the iron railings, the balustrade of the bridge. Walter saw them argue together with puzzled but not alarmed faces, the coats of their blue uniforms pressed against their bodies by the wind from the open estuary. The dog, held up by the driver, was dying in convulsions. Its back was broken. The conductor glanced at the cowcatcher of the tram, shrugged a shoulder, and pointing with his ticket-punch at the waters of the Heathcote below the lattice-work of the balustrade made an outflung motion with his arm. The driver stepped to the railings; still holding the frantic screaming dog he seemed to study the slow flow of the river towards the half-tide now coming in over the mud-flats and sand-spits of the estuary under the hard yellow cold of the sky. For a few seconds nothing happened.

Walter, almost alone in the trailer, watched the two men and the writhing dog. The English school-story he had been reading on his way back from his own school had fled from his mind, the lads of Longmeadows vanished. His fair-skinned pink face was close to the window, his thin body slightly raised from the slatted seat, his attention wholly on the action of the tram-driver. He held his breath.

And now the driver, perplexed, touched the dog on the spine, shrugged, leant back and flung the dying young animal in a wide arc over the railings of the bridge. The dog hit the water with a scattered flower-like splash, fought for a moment on the surface, then disappeared below the brownish stream. The driver, wiping his hands on the thighs of his uniform, climbed back to his cab. The conductor followed. There was a whisper of released brakes and the tram started forward, drawing its green caterpillar of a trailer, over the bridge and along the road below the low hills on the further banks of the estuary. A cold wind blew up the water, from the sea ahead.

The boy slid back from the window on to the firm wooden seat of the trailer. He was shivering with a kind of fear or excitement, the yelpings of the dog that had been thrown to drown still sharp in his ears. The eight-mile ride to Christchurch in the mornings, the eight-mile ride back to the seaside township of Sumner in the evenings — these were usually the dullest stretches of his day, only to be endured if he spelt out a story to himself, talked to other passengers on the tram or munched sweets which he could not often afford to buy. Now, however, something had happened to break the staleness of the long journey: something, all the same, which had shocked him and which he wanted to talk about.

He glanced round him at the faces of the few other travellers in the trailer. Somebody besides himself must have seen the dog flung from the bridge, somebody must have been as struck by the incident as he had been himself. But no: nobody else had raised a head to stare from the windows when the tram had stopped or had caught the sound of those agonized yelps from the bridge. A man bent over an evening paper, two women spoke quietly together above the shopping-baskets on their fat knees. Walter was disappointed, as though with a secret nobody wanted to share. And he wondered now whether Mr. Garnett himself, who sat always in the main coach of the tram and not in the trailer behind, would have lifted his head from the correction of his school's exercise-books to notice so strange an accident as a dog running forward to be caught under the wheels, a dog with its back afterwards broken and bloody, a dog cruelly thrown to drown. Mr. Garnett was the headmaster — the only master — of the preparatory school Walter went to in the city of Christchurch: he was also the head of the household in which the boy was a boarder — the only boarder — in Sumner. The two of them travelled, separately, to and from school on five days of each week.

'I'll ask him,' Walter said softly to himself. 'I'll ask him. And if he didn't see the dog, I'll tell him.' And he stuffed the school-story, *The Boys of Longmeadows*, into the canvas satchel beside him and began to form in his mind the words he would use to the old man at the end of the tram journey, when they reached the terminus. Some of his excitement, even his fear, died down: he stopped shivering and turned up the collar of his Burberry against the draughts in the trailer. Yes, he would tell Mr. Garnett.

The estuary beside the road and the tram-lines broadened out towards the sea, then narrowed towards the bar of the spread river, with low yellow sand-dunes on the far side of the water. On the near side bluffs and cliffs of volcanic rock began to over-shadow the roadway, reddish in the western light. Ten minutes later there was a salty acid smell of the sea itself: the tram rounded the last bluff, rattled over a causeway and was suddenly and at last among the little houses on the crescent bay. The town was shut in its valley by high wrinkled hills on either side; a U-shaped valley open only towards the beach and the dunes, with, at the eastern end of these, the tumultuous bar of the river-estuary. A pier ran out a small distance towards the bar, over the flowing deep water. Close to the ramp of the pier an immense rock, some volcanic afterthought, stood up from the floor of the beach, one hollowed side open towards the esplanade: this was the Cave Rock, a landmark to the township.

Walter and Mr. Garnett, pupil and master, left the tram at the far side of the town, where the line ended against the flank of Scarborough Hill. Usually Walter did not wait for the old man but ran on ahead, up a side-road away from the sea, towards the Garnetts' wooden house. Tonight he stood on the footpath, anxious for the master to join him, watching the stout seal-like figure approach without hurry over the grit and shingle of the road in the evening light.

'Did you see the accident, sir? The dog on the bridge?'

'Yes, Blakiston.' The old man began to walk beside him,

taking small deliberate steps on feet laced into black boots. Under his overcoat he wore a moss-green suit, baggy at the knees: in one hand he carried a dispatch case of parched brown leather, in the other an unfurled umbrella. His beard, the white-pepper colour of a fleece, came trimly down to the buttons of his waistcoat. Set squarely on his head was a dusty Homburg hat with a black band. 'Yes, Blakiston,' he repeated, in bland answer to Walter, 'I saw the accident. I don't see, however, what else the driver could have done. It was a matter of expediency.'

'But he let the dog drown —'

'The tram, you may not have been aware, was already late.' Mr. Garnett walked on with ponderous step, his umbrella trailing. 'Expediency,' he said again and glanced aside, smiling with his eyes, at Walter. 'Do you know the derivation of that word — where it comes from?'

'No.' The boy wished he had not spoken. He disliked Latin. 'I was sorry for the dog,' he said awkwardly, shut in himself now, hearing again the yelps on the bridge. 'I was sorry it got run over.'

The old man nodded. 'Yes. And the dog must have an owner who will also doubtless be sorry. But, singularly and sadly enough, life is plentiful on this planet, plentiful and brief.' He sighed.

There seemed no more to be said. Walter, embarrassed, looked ahead, along the road bordered with half-grown macrocarpa hedges and wooden palings. The street-lamps were already lit in the twilight. 'Do you mind if I run on, sir?'

'Run on if you want to, yes. Tell my daughter I'm on my way; she can set the dinner-table in advance.'

Walter hurried ahead, his satchel bumping against his shoulders. The Garnetts' wire gate — the back gate he used — led to a cinder path between dark green shrubby plants. Now he ran up the path, seeing the light in the kitchen window of the house, his pulse throbbing somewhere in the roof of his mouth.

The handle of the door turned under his cold fingers.

'Miss Muriel,' he cried, forgetting as he always did to wipe his boots on the scraper beside the step in the yard. 'Miss Muriel....'

He would tell her of the accident, the dog, the odd mixture of excitement and agitation in his heart.

CHAPTER II

'THE poor thing,' said Muriel Garnett evenly. 'Though of course if it really ran straight under the tram . . .' She shut the oven door with a click of the latch and turned her face towards Walter in the kitchen lamplight. She was a brown-haired woman, brisk, slender, not yet thirty, the eldest of Mr. Garnett's daughters and the only one of the three of them now left at home. 'Take off your coat,' she went on in the same soft clipped voice, and turned up the wick of the lamp a thrifty fraction of an inch. 'Take off your coat now you're in. Are you hungry?'

The boy drew in a breath of the roasting mutton, the roasting potatoes. 'Fairly,' he answered.

'You didn't buy chocolate to eat in the tram?'

'No, Miss Muriel.' In the dark scullery off the kitchen he hung up his Burberry behind the door and slung his red cap with the white star over the peak — the cap worn by the thirty boys of Mr. Garnett's school — on to his own special hook. He came back to the kitchen swinging his satchel against his bare knees. 'Would the dog float out to sea?' he asked, as though from a distance. 'Would it float down the estuary?'

'I've no idea, Walter. It might sink at once.' Miss Muriel wiped her hands on a cloth, then with two fingers brushed the forelock fringe of almost yellow hair from his forehead. 'You didn't actually see the dog run over, did you?'

'I was reading . . . one of my school-stories, the Longmeadows ones.'

'You ought to have been doing your homework.'

He did not listen. 'The tram stopped, I heard the brakes — the air-brakes —'

'Yes, well, don't worry about it now.' Her voice was kind, comforting. And returning to the range, she lifted the lid of one of the saucepans on the top. Beneath her apron she wore a high-necked cream blouse, above a nurse-grey skirt that almost touched the linoleum of the floor. 'Don't think about that unfortunate dog any more,' she said, through the steam about her head.

'The tram-driver might look for it on the mud. Tomorrow he might. Mightn't he?'

'I don't suppose he'll want to . . . Where's father — was he on the tram with you?'

'He said to tell you he was coming.' The boy could hear precise steps on the cinders of the yard, a cough, then a dragging sound as the old man drew the soles of his boots over the scraper. 'He's here.'

'You're both of you late. It's almost seven.' And before her father came in she asked: 'How did you get on at school today, Walter? Did you behave yourself?'

'I was all right. Miss Threplow took us for drawing.' He looked under the frame of the kitchen scales on the table. When a letter came for him from home, from his mother, Miss Muriel placed it under the iron base of the scales to await his return in the evening. The letters usually came on a Monday: today was a Friday and the table was bare. 'I'm drawing a tulip from a picture on a card,' he went on. 'The tulip's got a curved stem because Miss Threplow says there aren't any straight lines in nature, not really straight.'

Mr. Garnett pushed open the back door and edged his stout body, his dispatch case and umbrella, sideways into the kitchen.

'Ah,' he greeted his daughter. 'Well, Muriel, my dear.'

'Well, father.' She pecked at his right ear with her lips, then placed his umbrella in a corner. 'Are you tired?'

'A long day, a long day, you know. Is mother well?'

'Very bright. She's by the fire in the dining-room.'

The old man slid out of his coat, sniffing at the smell of the roast in the oven. 'I'll be glad of my dinner. Very cold on the tram tonight.'

'Walter's been telling me you ran over a dog on Heathcote bridge.' She brushed her father's coat then placed it, folded, over a chair. 'Did the dog delay you?'

'A little accident . . .' The old man glanced at the boy who stood in the shadows of the room. 'A little affair,' he added in a voice very like his daughter's, 'demeaning to those concerned . . . Now I shall wash before my dinner.'

Walter sprang forward to the door leading to the dining-room, the living-room of the house. 'Shall I help lay the table, Miss Muriel?'

'It's ready, dear, except for the knives. You can take those out of the drawer if you're careful with them.'

'I will be.' He let himself quietly into the other room, walking on his toes lest he disturb a person he feared, Mrs. Garnett herself.

The old woman sat pinched into a basket-chair before a smoky fire. To Walter she seemed as ancient as a bone on the beach, and as bleak: the knuckles and tendons of her thin hands gleamed like knots of fencing-wire. The meagre greying hair of her skull was scraped back into a bunch above her nape, exposing a high forehead, an arched nose, and eyes as hard as the steel spectacles in front of them. She was, Walter suspected, older than Mr. Garnett: in fact, when he had first come to the house as a boarder, six months before, he had taken this formidable woman to be not the wife but the mother of his schoolmaster. Now she twisted her head to face him as he tiptoed into the room behind her.

'Oh,' she said, 'it's you. Have you shut the door?'

'Yes.'

'You're improvin' then.' Her hands moved over the tangle of knitting on her lap. 'You're very late, aren't you? What have you been doin'?'

Walter took the knives from the drawer of the sideboard, looking at her over his shoulder. 'The tram ran over a dog, Mrs. Garnett.'

'A dog? What kind of a dog?'

'A collie pup, I think. The driver let it drop in the water and it drowned.'

'Why was the dog on the bridge?'

He set the lemon-handled knives on the table, one to each of the four places. 'There's a farm there, along the estuary,' he told her. 'Not a sheep-farm, a sort of cow-farm. You can smell it from the tram.'

Mrs. Garnett sniffed: she no longer frequented trams. 'People have no sense, and no sense of property; they haven't had any for years, not in this country.' She crouched to the fire. 'Have you washed your hands since you came in from the tram?'

'Well . . . I haven't yet.'

'Do you know what I used to say to my son Mark when he was your age?'

'I dunno. What?'

' "Wash your hands before you handle clean knives and forks." Are you listenin', young man? That's what I said.'

'Yes, Mrs. Garnett.' Walter stared. 'And what did he say?'

'It wasn't for him to speak. He did as he was told.'

'Yes, Mrs. Garnett.' He shut the knife-drawer. 'Is it — is Mr. Mark the one in the lighthouse?' he asked as he always liked to ask whenever the only son of the Garnett family was mentioned. Mark Garnett, whom he had never seen, was a legend, a wonder — and a disappointment to his mother.

'He's a lighthouse keeper,' she said shortly. 'You've a bad memory and you're not a clean boy.' And now she turned her head as her husband entered the room. 'This child ought to wash when he comes home, Arthur. Remind Muriel.'

Mr. Garnett showed no outward sign of attention. His bearded mouth barely touched his wife's brow. 'How's the rheumatism, mother?'

'Painful.'

'A cold evening. Frost.' The old man looked about him at the warm room, the curtains drawn across the veranda doors, the glass dishes on the sideboard, the lid of his roller-top desk under the window. 'Snug enough in here,' he remarked, sitting to rub his knees. 'Singularly snug, in fact.'

Walter, ignored, ran back to the kitchen. He washed his hands under the scullery tap and dried them on a damp towel behind the door. He could hear the faint sleek roar of the sea in the distance, the murmur that always sounded, like the whisper in a shell, over this town wedged into a valley between headlands. He thought of the beach, the breakers, and of the dead dog floating out to sea: he stood quite still in the dark mice-smelling scullery, listening, his face lifted to the lace curtain of the window over the sink. Presently he heard again the clang of the oven door in the kitchen.

'Walter,' Miss Muriel's voice summoned him, 'don't dawdle, dear. Be quick.'

'I was being as quick as I could,' he said moodily, returning.

'Now that's no way to talk. Dinner'll be ready before you are.' She bent to the oven, her apron hanging in front of her knees, her cheeks reddened by the fire. 'How much homework have you to do before Monday?'

'Some. I've got to read about bread-fruit.'

'Bread-fruit?'

'They grow in the South Seas, like pineapples only higher up. There's a picture in my Reader . . . I've got sums to do too.' He stood beside her at the range, watching her baste the mutton with a tin spoon. 'Would a dog drown in five minutes or ten or half an hour?'

'That dog. I can see you'll dream about it. I'll hear you crying out again in the night, across the passage.' She straightened herself and touched a small brown mole that grew beside her soft upper lip. 'I saw my sister Hilda today,' she remarked; 'she asked after you, Walter. She's bought herself a gramophone, one

23

of these new English ones with a horn or a trumpet-thing on top, like the advertisements.'

'Would she let me play it?'

'If you go to see her perhaps.' Her sister Hilda, Walter knew, was Mrs. Geoffrey Macaulay, a pretty woman who lived with her husband in a newly built bungalow on Scarborough Hill, above the township. Mr. Macaulay, a young Scotsman, was an architect. 'She and Mr. Macaulay are coming down to see us tomorrow,' Miss Muriel informed Walter. 'You like them, don't you?'

'I don't know them much.'

She fetched a tray from the dresser and took a cloth from beside the range. 'Which do you like best?'

'Mr. Macaulay's got a motor car,' he said evasively.

'Do you like him for that?' She laughed. 'You shouldn't like people simply for what they own, you know.'

'*You* like him, don't you?'

'I?' With the cloth she lifted the sizzling roast from the oven to the tray. 'A great deal,' she said, 'but not for his car. And now I think we might have dinner at last. Father'll be famished, and so am I.'

CHAPTER III

'For what we are about to receive,' said Mr. Garnett, 'may the Lord make us truly thankful.'

'Amen,' murmured his wife. Miss Muriel did not speak.

Walter sat himself down opposite to Mrs. Garnett, feeling the cold white table-cloth slide against his knees. The first time he had heard grace spoken in the Garnett household he had not understood what was expected of him — his own parents invoked no such blessing — and had not even stood up for the ceremony. Only a stiff reminder from old Mrs. Garnett had brought him to his feet. 'We always stand, young man.' Walter had blushed and had not since forgotten the hint.

Now there was a silence as Mr. Garnett, his napkin already tucked into his waistcoat, carved the mutton. The lamp threw a creamy bubble of light against the ceiling.

'Walter,' said Miss Muriel presently, 'will you pour the water, please?'

It was his dinner-time task. He went round the table, clasping the curly glass handle of the jug against him. Unless he poured the water boldly the lip of the jug dribbled on to the cloth and down the side of the tumblers. With Mrs. Garnett's glass he was especially careful. When he had finished she took a small box from her lap and dropped a pinkish pill into the water, a pill that misted the surface with bubbles. Walter thought the pills might be sherbet.

'Knife sharp enough, father?' Miss Muriel watched the old man as he carved. 'I did run the steel over it.'

'This colonial mutton . . . not like the English Southdown . . . it wants consistency.' He grunted, breathing heavily, his beard trembling a little, 'One would think, in this land of sheep, the farmers might breed meat of a closer texture.' He passed a plate to his wife, then handed Walter a helping. 'Do you know what the words "consistency" and "texture" mean?' he asked the boy absently, without looking at him.

Walter hesitated. This was a test because he had failed with the word "expediency". 'Do they mean a sort of thickness?' he ventured. 'Do they, sir?'

'He hasn't the least idea.' From across the table Mrs. Garnett drawled her comment. 'He's only a colonial.' She took a sip of the misted, pinky water before her. 'Besides, he never remembers anythin'.'

'I do,' Walter retorted. 'I remember nearly everything.' He looked morosely down at his plate. 'I do remember things.'

Mr. Garnett smiled at the boy's bent head. 'Well, you made a good guess at "consistency". Almost an alpha for that.'

Miss Muriel interrupted: 'Let him alone, father. He's hungry, he's been at school all day.'

'I questioned him only from academic interest, my dear.' The old man, ruffled, attacked his mutton. 'And the son of a farmer, even here in New Zealand, might be expected to show some knowledge of the classical rudiments of his own language, after all.'

'Yes, but not now. Let him eat.'

The meal continued. Under the meat and potatoes, under the brown gravy on his plate, Walter slowly uncovered a picture, a pattern, in which a young Chinaman was for ever bent forward in flight across a bridge. Three birds flew perpetually over the sky, between blue pagodas and darker blue trees with rigid branches.

'I met Hilda at the store this morning, father.' Miss Muriel placed a rice pudding on the table. 'She and Geoffrey may drop in for tea tomorrow afternoon, if Geoff gets back from town in time. Or on Sunday perhaps.'

'And how is Hilda?'

'A little plumper than she was, I thought.' Miss Muriel glanced at Walter. 'Decidedly plumper ... Walter dear, you're not eating.'

'I like eating slowly sometimes.'

'You're too thin; you might be a sparrow. And you must sit up straight too, not crouch.'

'All right,' he said. 'All right, Miss Muriel.'

'Hilda hasn't been here for so long,' old Mrs. Garnett reflected aloud. 'She's gettin' to be as much a stranger to us as Rose.'

Rose, Walter was aware, was the third Garnett sister: a photograph of her, in the uniform of a hospital nurse, stood on the mantelshelf. A delicate oval face, surprised under a starched cap. Walter thought her more beautiful than Mrs. Hilda.

'Hilda has her house to look after,' Miss Muriel reminded her mother, 'though, goodness knows, she's slack enough at it ... She was even carrying a basket today — there's domesticity for you.' She got up from the table, hurrying the end of the meal. 'Will you be at home tomorrow, father?'

'Yes, Muriel, I shall be at home, though I'll be taking a choir practice in the evening.' Mr. Garnett wiped his mouth and beard. 'No sign of Rose honouring us with a visit, I suppose?'

'None, that I know of. She was looking after some patient in Timaru last time mother had a letter.'

Walter had not taken his eyes from the photograph of Miss Rose, across the room. Not only was she beautiful, he thought, but mysterious — this young nurse whose eyes gazed past him out of the picture. Her hand rested on the edge of a table supporting a small palm tree; from the tight belt of her uniform hung what seemed to be a watch and a key. Her lips were partly open, as though about to call somebody or to laugh. He had never met her. 'Does Miss Rose like dogs?' he asked suddenly.

Nobody replied. Miss Muriel cleared the table.

'That boy has dogs on the brain,' said old Mrs. Garnett presently. Her stiff black clothes creaked as she moved towards the kitchen. 'I'll help you with the dishes, Muriel.'

'Very well, mother. Walter, you can do your homework in here tonight, it's cosier than the kitchen.'

'If I work for an hour can I play with my stamps afterwards? Can I? If I'm quiet?'

'I suppose so. But don't disturb father.'

He sat over his books for an hour by the clock, his elbows on the bare table, his hands shading his eyes from the lamp. In a chair by the fire Mr. Garnett corrected the day's dictation exercises with a red pencil, his dispatch case planted across his knees. From time to time he muttered to himself or the pencil stabbed a note in the margin.

'Your spelling, Blakiston,' he commented once to Walter, 'is atrocious. "Tell" has two "l's", not one. Will you make an effort to remember?'

'Yes, Mr. Garnett.'

'Good. And you must improve your Latin.'

Presently a soft honking sound, regularly repeated, told Walter that the old man dozed. His beard, ash-grey in the lamplight, heaved and settled against his chest, the red pencil slipped to the carpet. At half past eight Miss Muriel returned from putting her mother to bed. She touched her father on the shoulder, took off her apron and folded it, then rattled at the fire with a poker.

'You look like a bear when you're asleep, father.'

'I was thinking, my dear, not sleeping.' The old man stirred, groping for the pencil on the floor. 'I was thinking, singularly enough, of Homer's description of the dawn.'

'You were dreaming, father. You'd better follow mother to bed.'

Mr. Garnett peered at the gold watch tethered to his waistcoat. He wound the spring slowly. 'I'll stay up a while as tomorrow's Saturday. No early start.'

'You're getting old, father, that's the trouble with you. Rust in the works.'

'We're all getting old, Muriel. Or older, at least.'

She shuddered and glanced aside at Walter under the lamp.

'Not Walter,' she said. She came across to the boy, touching the little mole beside her lip, looking down at his stamps spread on the table, splaying the fingers of her soda-roughened hands. 'Well, have you found a stamp with a dog on it?'

'No,' he said, astonished because he had again been thinking of the accident on the bridge. 'There's only a Newfoundland one and I haven't got that yet.'

'Only that one in all the world?'

'I haven't got all the stamps in the world.'

'Well,' she teased, 'there's time.' And she picked up his stamp catalogue from beside the album. 'Stanley Gibbons. Nineteen-thirteen,' she murmured aloud the words on the red cover.

'It's last year's,' he said. 'I haven't bought the new one, it's too dear.'

CHAPTER IV

'YOUR bath, Walter.' Miss Muriel tapped on his door. 'Are
you awake?'

He had been awake since six o'clock, reading again of the boys
of Longmeadows, the book spread open on the pillow. Now he
sprang up, wrapped his thin body in an overcoat and ran across
the landing to the bathroom. Cold blue tank-water lay still in
the blistered tin bath under the window. Miss Muriel's own
early morning splashings darkened the cork mat on the floor.
Her bedroom was next to the bathroom, which opened off the
small dim landing at the top of the stairs.

Walter slid out of his pyjamas, dabbled a toe in the chill water,
then lowered his ribby body into the bath. Shivers ran up his
spine. He hated this daily plunge into wintry water: only Miss
Muriel's example had shamed him into a custom that nobody in
his own home had ever suggested. It had been one of the greatest
shocks on his first arrival as a boarder with the Garnetts — this icy
baptism at seven o'clock in the morning, with the warmth of
sleep still upon him. Even now, almost six months later, he
occasionally imitated the sounds of deep bathing to fox Miss
Muriel's ears next door: splashing with his feet and hands only,
supporting himself on the sides of the bath, gasping and whistling,
keeping his body clear of the water.

'Are you washing your neck, Walter?' It was Miss Muriel's
voice through the wall.

'And my ears.' He shouted back the expected answer.

'That's a good boy. I'm going downstairs now.'

This morning he sluiced himself all over — his chest, thighs,
arm-pits: the boys of Longmeadows, he had read, did not shrink
from cold water. His shivering body trembled against the thin

30

towel; the veins in his wrists were like the blue rivers on a map; his teeth chattered together without control.

'As it's Saturday you can have bacon.' Miss Muriel placed his breakfast before him ten minutes later. 'Would you like an egg with it?'

'Yes.'

'Yes, *please*,' she corrected him lightly.

'Yes, please. And an egg.'

He ate his breakfast at the kitchen table, the wintry sun shining on the yard outside and on the bare sticks of an apricot tree against the fence. There were frost-flowers on the lower pane of the window. When he had finished his egg he slipped the bacon-rinds from his plate into the pocket of his green Norfolk jacket. Miss Muriel ate her own breakfast standing beside the range, one foot on the fender.

'What are you planning to do today, Walter?'

He thought of the possibilities of the day — a visit to his friends the Nelsons, a fishing expedition to the pier, his stamps, his books. 'I'll explore the Cave Rock, I think,' he decided aloud.

'Don't get lost, by yourself.'

But he never got lost. 'I'll take my compass.'

'That won't help you, if you don't know north from south.'

'The mountains are north, and west.'

'A long way off. I'm not sure,' she mused, 'that your mother and father would like you to go wandering off by yourself. After all, I suppose we're in charge of you here.'

'I'll be all right.'

An hour later, self-reliant, he left the house and swung off down the straight road to the sandhills and the beach, his cap pulled forward over his forehead, his compass in his pocket, his overcoat unbuttoned.

'Walter, wait!' It was Miss Muriel, closing the gate behind her. 'You can come shopping with me.' She wore a grey mackintosh, a hat like a black mushroom. 'Here, you can carry the basket.'

He took the basket, regretfully.

31

'You should walk on my other side,' she told him. 'A gentle-man walks on the gutter side, always.'

'Why?'

'I don't know, dear, it's just the custom. In England, at least.'

He kicked at the grit and shingle of the footpath. 'Is England twenty thousand miles away? Is it, Miss Muriel?'

'Not twenty. About twelve, perhaps.'

'Have you ever been there?'

'None of father's children have. Only father himself, and mother of course. They came from a place called Winchester.'

'When?'

'Oh, before we were born. Thirty years ago, nearly . . . But I've told you all this before, often.'

'I like hearing things, if they're interesting.'

'Curious Walter,' she teased him, 'Mr. Curious Blakiston.' And she touched him on the ear with her woollen glove. 'The trouble is,' she said, 'you dream all the time and never listen. I could tell you things . . . many things. . . .'

'Nice or nasty?'

'Worse than a dog being run over, Walter. Worse than any-thing you'd hear at school.'

'About you?'

'Some of them, yes,' she said. 'But you're too young, much too young.'

They had turned into the main road, beside the tram-lines, and now walked along the footpath until they reached the red wooden front of the general store. Inside the window a few flies, left awake from the autumn, crawled sleepily up cliffs of tinned fruit and packets of oatmeal. The doorway was shadowed by the corrugated iron roof of a veranda. Walter followed Miss Muriel into the shop. And at once a large stout woman — the only customer beside themselves — detached herself from the counter to greet the boy in a voice as large as herself.

'Well,' she said, 'if I don't see Walter!' And she gave a second, tighter smile over his head at Miss Muriel. 'Good morning.'

'Good morning, Mrs. Nelson.'

'A nice day,' confided the other. 'Saturdays always get round to being fine, somehow.'

'Yes.' Miss Muriel took the basket from Walter.

'Where's Jimmy, Mrs. Nelson?' the boy asked.

'Well, he's in school this morning. He'll be home at lunch time.' With one eye she winked at him solemnly. 'Why not trot along and see us this afternoon? You and Jimmy can play, out the back.'

Walter glanced at Miss Muriel. 'Could I?'

'I'll look after them, Miss Garnett,' Mrs. Nelson broke in. 'I'll keep them out of mischief and give them tea.'

'My sister and her husband — the Macaulays — are coming to us,' said Miss Muriel doubtfully. 'I think Walter hoped to see them.'

'I'd rather go to the Nelsons',' he said.

'Well, good Heavens, let him come to us,' cried Mrs. Nelson. 'He can always leave if he wants to get back early.'

'Very well,' Miss Muriel said. 'It's kind of you.'

'Not *kind*,' the other objected. 'I like Jimmy to have kids in.' And she threw at Walter: 'He's got a bike now. You must see that. Before he kills himself on it,' she added, laughing.

'What time shall I come, Mrs. Nelson?'

'Any time after lunch. We'll expect you.'

She gathered her parcels into her broad arms and waddled from the shop. Miss Muriel, in her turn, bought baking-powder, soap and pickles from the storeman.

'Do you really like this Jimmy Nelson?' she asked Walter as they reached the footpath.

'Yes.' Apart from a boy named Marriner at school, Jimmy Nelson was his best friend: more, Jimmy Nelson was the only friend he had made since his arrival in Sumner. They had encountered one another fishing on the pier. 'I like him a lot,' he said.

'A pity his mother doesn't send him to father's school. The

local children here'll turn him into an absolute larrikin . . . Not that Mrs. Nelson seems to care.'

Walter sensed a criticism. 'You don't like her, do you?'

'It isn't *her* I object to really, Walter, though she's a little common perhaps . . . You never see the father, I suppose — Jimmy's father?'

'No.' Mr. Nelson was a mystery, an absence, a conjecture. 'He's dead, isn't he?'

'None of us know, exactly. And that noisy, undisciplined little boy. . . .'

They walked on, up the road towards the butcher's shop and the Post Office.

'A curious woman.' Miss Muriel had returned to Mrs. Nelson. 'I think she has an idea we're all freaks of some kind, simply because father's a schoolmaster and we've not much money.' She shook her head. 'Not that she's well off herself — I mean, having to do laundry-work to keep that child at school.'

Walter's attention had wandered. 'Can I go off for a walk by myself now?' he asked presently. 'Can I go on the beach, Miss Muriel?'

She took the basket from his hand. 'If you want to, I suppose. But don't talk to everyone you meet. And don't be late for lunch.' She straightened his cap. 'There, now you look like a little gentleman.'

CHAPTER V

THE compass was a small one, the size of a penny, with a steel pointer wavering beneath the glass: a Christmas present from his grandmother. Now he consulted it importantly, chewing the bacon-rinds he had taken from his dusty pocket. The sand dunes were ahead of him, at the end of the road, almost due north-east. If he had been an explorer, he thought, he would have made a note of that, like Captain Kettle, in a log-book. The compass was meanwhile a treasure, and, though he used it only on Saturdays and holidays and though its rather unreliable information led to nothing of practical use, a companion in solitude. And, carefully, he blew on the glass, rubbed it, and replaced the compass in his pocket.

At the top of the dunes, away from the houses on the sea-front, the wind from the bay struck cold on his face. Beneath him was the wide yellow crescent of the beach, enclosed at one end by the headland of Scarborough Hill, at the other by the isolated pyramid of the Cave Rock and the waters of the estuary flowing to the sea. The sands themselves were bare save for a straggling wrack of dark kelp, driftwood and a few shells. The tide was coming in: the wet shore reflected the jagged blue gleams of the sky. A soft breathing roar from the breakers reached him on the wind.

He ran forward to the water's edge, looking vaguely about him. If he found the drowned dog, he thought . . . but there was no sign of the dog, nor was he sure that he wanted to find it. The dog had vanished and he would — he must — forget about the accident. Meanwhile, in a sudden spasm of loneliness and anxiety he spat the bacon-rinds from his mouth, shivering on the deserted beach.

35

But the beach, he saw now, was not wholly deserted. A figure — a young man with a walking-stick, a stroller in a grey-brown knickerbocker suit — was approaching from the Scarborough end, his chin lowered, a tweed cap folded under one arm. When he came closer Walter recognized the reddish-gold hair bright in the sunlight.

'Mr. Macaulay,' he called into the wind.

The young man, the husband of Miss Muriel's sister Hilda, seemed surprised at the interruption to his thoughts. His handsome pink face, with a sandy wheat-coloured moustache on the upper lip, came up sharply as he stared across the beach at Walter. 'Hullo there,' he called back. 'What are you after?' His voice had a faint burr, even a lilt, which the boy had been told was Scottish. 'Looking for wrecks? Or shells?'

'No . . . Only wandering about.'

The man approached lazily over the beach. 'Maybe you're just getting away from the sight of houses, as I am,' he remarked. 'I don't blame you.'

He waved his walking-stick thoughtfully towards the red roofs of the town beyond the dunes. 'Any decent architect's nightmare,' he grinned.

'I've been out shopping with Miss Muriel,' Walter contributed.

The other's eyes met his for a moment, keenly. 'Aye,' he said, as though lacking an answer. 'She's all of a busy woman, your Miss Muriel.'

'She says I'm not to say "woman", only "lady",' Walter laughed. He pretended to look for shells on the sand at his feet: he was apt to be a trifle shy of Mr. Macaulay. 'You haven't seen a dog washed up, have you, Mr. Macaulay?'

'A dog — why a dog?'

Walter blushed. 'They do get washed up sometimes, if they drown,' was all he could find to say.

The other poked at the seaweed, licking the broad lips below his moustache, puzzled. 'I've seen no dog.' And he nodded with his chin towards the Cave Rock and the far end of the shore.

'Walk along with me a while, Walter. Isn't Walter your name?'

'Yes . . . Walter Henry Blakiston.'

'I see. Well, as we both seem to have a morning off, let's go as far as the pier.'

Walter fell into step beside him. 'You and Miss Hilda are coming to tea this afternoon, aren't you?' he asked. 'At Mr. Garnett's.'

'Why do you call my wife Miss Hilda?' the young man laughed. 'It's as bad as "lady".'

'Mrs. Hilda, then . . . I'm going to tea with the Nelsons.'

Mr. Macaulay accepted this in silence. 'It's lonely for you, maybe, boarding at my father-in-law's . . . Do you enjoy school?'

'It's not bad,' Walter murmured, loyally. 'I'd rather be at home though.' And, watching the thin waves of the tide reach out towards their feet, he added: 'I had to come and live with Mr. Garnett because there's no school near us at home, see, and I'm not old enough to be a boarder at College . . . I didn't go home last holidays because Mum's been ill.'

'Aye, so I heard . . . And I suppose you get homesick?'

Walter looked away: the question hurt him. 'Sometimes . . . Not much, if I don't think about it.'

'Well, I hope our Miss Muriel's good to you.'

'She gets a bit ratty if I'm late or if I don't eat all my dinner. Otherwise she's not bad.'

The young man smiled. 'I'm glad to hear that.'

Walking together over the heavy sand they came to the end of the beach. Beyond the high black bulk of the Cave Rock the pier jutted forward over the deep water of the estuary; and on the approach to the pier, overlooking the sand of a smaller beach beyond, stood a wooden tea-room. The tea-room window on the pier side was full of red- and lemon-coloured bottles holding fizzy drinks and of larger bottles containing chocolate, caramels and acid-drops. For a moment Walter lingered as he and Mr. Macaulay passed the window.

'Are you hungry?' the man asked.

'No,' Walter said, and hesitated, glancing back. 'Well, I am, a bit.'

Mr. Macaulay pushed open the glass door of the tea-room with his stick, nodding for the boy to follow him to the counter. The room, after the dry sea air outside, smelt closely of washed floors and damp sponge cakes. Overhead, paper festoons, fly-blown and faded, waved in the draught from the door.

'What would you like, Walter?'

'Do you mean I can choose?'

The young man hung his stick over his elbow and produced a purse from his jacket. 'Well, I will not buy you the shop, but choose something.' His warm lilting voice was lowered as though in conspiracy. 'Maybe there's something you'd . . .'

At the back of the counter was a long cardboard box, lying flat but piled with shiny black straps. Walter pointed.

'Liquorice. Can I have one of those?'

'Take a handful.' The man grinned. 'By the sheen on them I'd say they'd been licked already.'

Walter took four of the straps and thanked him.

'Roll them up and pop 'em in your pocket.' Mr. Macaulay paid the girl across the counter. 'And you'd best keep mum about where you found 'em', he added to Walter. 'All this wouldn't go with the blood of the Highlands, you see,'

'I won't say anything, Mr. Macaulay. Honest, I won't.'

They strolled back to the beach the way they had come, the wind in their faces, the boy's mouth now full of the black sticky liquorice.

'You eat a strap too,' he suggested to Geoffrey Macaulay. 'It's tough at first, till you chew it.'

The other accepted the liquorice. 'A long day since I've tasted this stuff.' He touched his fair moustache, chewing with a kind of wary relish, his eyes teasing Walter. 'It might be worse . . . Right enough for a desert island.'

The boy felt that some remark was expected of him. 'Do you like being an architect?' he ventured at length.

'I? Too many people want bungalows, Walter.' His blunt, wind-reddened face became serious, his lips twitched. 'All these damned tin roofs and verandas and back kitchens designed to fit a section . . . There's money in it, all right, but I'm after more than that. If you've got talent, maybe — '

'I can draw things too. Houses and engines.'

'You stick to farming, when you grow up . . . How many sheep does your father stock?'

'Dunno really.' The boy's mouth was full. 'Six thousand, about. They're a special kind of sheep — Corriedales.'

The other was silent. As they paused under the shadow of the Cave Rock he prodded at the sand with the ferrule of his stick as though loath to move on, as though taken now by some recollection hidden from Walter. 'Do you ever see Rose at the Garnetts' — or Miss Rose, as you'd call her, Walter? The daughter who's a nurse?'

'She's away, always.'

'You'd like her. She's the . . . rather like my wife in some ways.' He watched Walter's face closely. 'Muriel doesn't speak of Rose?'

Walter shook his head, thinking of the photograph on the mantelpiece. 'Not often,' he said, with full mouth.

'She nursed my mother, you know, before she died.'

'When?'

'When? Before I married. Last year.'

'In Christchurch, you mean?'

'Aye.' Mr. Macaulay nodded, in thought. They walked on along the beach. 'Aye,' he repeated slowly. 'Never get yourself mixed up with too many women, Walter. Not if you want a quiet conscience, maybe.'

Walter felt uncomfortable. At the same time he was being treated as an equal, a pleasing sensation. 'Do you want another piece of liquorice?' he asked.

'What?'

'Another strap?'

'Better not.' The other's voice changed: he gave Walter an open attractive grin. 'As it is, I'll have my wife asking at lunch why I've a black tongue.'

'Is mine black too?' Walter extended the end of his tongue between his lips. 'Is it?'

'Black as the hole of Calcutta. Clean your teeth when you get in.'

'I'll keep my mouth shut, then nobody'll see.'

Geoffrey Macaulay glanced up and down the beach. 'You'd best take yourself off home now, Walter. Maybe I'll see you later this afternoon if Hilda and I drop in on the family.'

'I'm going to visit Jimmy Nelson,' the boy reminded him. 'Thanks again for the liquorice.'

'And thanks for the walk.' He patted Walter's shoulder, with an almost tender, physical warmth. 'I wasn't feeling so cheerful, in myself . . . Can you find your way home?'

Walter pushed a hand into his pocket, then showed his compass. 'It's for when I get lost.'

'Good. Then you'll know your way ahead a sight better than I do.' And he gave the boy a playful shove in the direction of the sand-dunes and the town. 'Don't forget now — keep your mouth shut.'

CHAPTER VI

MRS. NELSON, one hand stroking the back of the tame rabbit crouched on her lap, lounged amply forward at the kitchen table. 'The way these animals breed,' she said to Walter, 'you wouldn't hardly believe it really. Worse than humans. Jimmy bought a couple last Christmas and now the whole yard's crawling. You ought to see the creatures.'

'I've showed him, ma,' Jimmy Nelson told her. He was a compactly built small boy, a year or so older than Walter, with black curly hair and eyes the colour of prunes. Walter and he sat at opposite sides of the table, a loaf of brown bread and the remains of a yellow seed-cake like a ruined haystack between them. Tea was almost over. 'I've showed him, ma,' said Jimmy. 'We cleaned out the hutch and raked the straw.'

'Good boys.' Mrs. Nelson, placing one hand firmly on the rabbit's back to steady it on her knees, leant over, opened a drawer of the dresser beside her and raked out a packet of cigarettes. 'Keep still, you,' she said to the rabbit and glanced round the bright warm kitchen. 'Jimmy, have you sneaked off with the matches? . . . This kid of mine,' she confided to Walter, 'doesn't like his ma smoking cigarettes.'

'It makes you stink when you kiss me.' Jimmy got up. With a slice of cake in one hand he plunged the other into the pocket of his short blue trousers and pulled out a box of wooden vestas. 'Here,' he said, 'and don't ask me to light one for you. You might kiss me afterwards.'

His mother's wide brown neck shook with laughter. 'You go and kiss your rabbits,' she said. 'And a fat lot of good they'll do you.' She lit her cigarette, threw the match at the coal-scuttle, blew a stream of smoke from her mouth and glanced triumphantly at Walter. 'Well, smoking's a vice like any other . . . I'll bet your Miss Muriel doesn't smoke, does she?'

Walter shook his head, watching the rings she blew from her lips. 'She hates it.'

'Ah, well, she's one of these ladies . . . she's got to think of her class.' And she lifted the rabbit suddenly from her lap. 'Here, Jimmy, take this animal and put him back outside. He doesn't know his manners, any better than you do.' She brushed at her dress, clicking her tongue. 'Take him. Quick.'

'You shouldn't blow smoke over him,' Jimmy said and seized the rabbit. 'It upsets his bowels.'

'It wasn't bowels,' Mrs. Nelson sniffed. 'Never mind.' Again she quivered with laughter, this time at Walter. 'You're well brought-up,' she told him. 'You ought to teach Jimmy to speak politely.'

'I talk all right,' Jimmy said. 'You shut up, ma.'

'Take that blasted rabbit out . . . No, don't give him caraway seeds, take him out. I can smell him from here.'

'It's not so bad as your cigarettes, anyway,' Jimmy retorted, and departed to the back yard, hugging the rabbit to him.

Ruffled, Mrs. Nelson snatched up the tea-pot and poured herself a last cup of the now treacle-brown tea, her cigarette stuck upwards from her lips. The fire in the kitchen range fluttered behind Walter's chair. 'Well, how are you getting along with those Garnetts?' she asked him presently.

'All right, Mrs. Nelson.'

'Feeling more at home with them?'

He nodded vaguely, fingering crumbs on his plate.

'Little liar,' said Mrs. Nelson evenly. 'You're scared stiff, it's easy enough to see that . . . Oh, I've nothing against the Garnetts — except the one that married that Macaulay boy — they're a nice enough lot as families go, here in Sumner. A bit stuck-up perhaps, a bit too English. That Muriel was a bit short with me in the store this morning . . .' Brooding, she leant her elbows on the table, pushing up her sleeves to rub her freckled forearms.

'Still, they're an odd crowd to stick a young nipper of a kid like you into. Too old for you, for one thing.'

'Miss Muriel isn't old.'

'Well, she's younger than I am,' Mrs. Nelson laughed, 'whatever that makes her. Too old for you, anyway.'

'The other boys at school,' he said, 'are the same age as I am, mostly.'

'Yes, but you don't live with them.'

She stared past him, at the clouds of the winter afternoon beyond the window and the half-grown pine tree in the yard. 'Do you know Geoff Macaulay?' she asked at length. 'The bright lad Hilda Garnett caught — married, I mean?'

'Yes.' Walter was a little confused. 'He's decent . . . He bought me some liquorice on the beach.'

'He's a good-looker, is Geoff Macaulay . . .' And she went on in her smooth comfortable voice. 'Both those younger Garnett girls set their caps at him — Rose and Hilda.' She laughed. 'You won't have heard about *that* pickle, I suppose?'

He looked at her blankly. 'Can I go after Jimmy?' he asked.

'Jimmy'll be back in a minute.' She piled another slice of seed-cake before him. 'No, but listen, Walter,' she went on, 'you take a warning from me — don't get yourself entangled.'

He had no idea what she could mean. 'Where?'

'Well . . .' She flicked cigarette ash towards the coal-scuttle, defensively. 'Though I don't know why I shouldn't tell you. Never too young to learn . . . Those Garnett girls — or rather, Rose and Hilda, until Geoff Macaulay came along last year — they'd neither of them met a man they could marry, or thought they could marry. That old tartar of a mother, she wanted a lord or something for her damn daughters. And a fat chance they had of meeting one here . . .' Mrs. Nelson scratched her nose reflectively. 'Anyway, it wasn't till Rose brought home this Geoff Macaulay — she'd been nursing his mother before the old girl pegged out — '

43

'Miss Rose?' Half-listening, Walter repeated the name absently. 'She didn't kill her, did she?'

'God, no, I don't think so!' Mrs. Nelson got up, her cigarette waggling in her mouth. 'Don't you go saying things like that or the police'll be after you with a Black Maria . . .' She grinned to herself. 'Anyway, I was telling you: Geoff Macaulay should by rights have been Rose's beau —'

Walter had drawn back. He left the seed-cake, went to the window and looked into the yard. Jimmy was closing the door of the rabbit-hutches against the paling fence.

'Go on,' said Mrs. Nelson, disappointed, to his back. 'Go out to Jimmy. I'll tell you the rest some other time . . . As it is, I might as well talk to the back of my neck.'

At this moment, however, Jimmy returned to the kitchen. 'Can I finish the cake, ma?' he asked and banged the door.

'Yes, finish it. And then give Walter here a ride on your bike. The two of you and your blasted rabbits've given me a headache.'

'Come on.' Jimmy seized the cake and beckoned to Walter. 'You can ride a bike, can't you?'

In the yard Walter looked dubiously at the bright nickel handlebars and spokes of the new bicycle leaning inside the coal shed. He envied Jimmy. 'Of course I can ride,' he boasted, though in truth he always — somehow — managed to fall off. 'But couldn't we play battles instead?'

'Those are kid's games,' scoffed Jimmy, the elder. But he agreed to play nevertheless. 'Battles' was satisfactorily noisy.

Across the road from the Nelsons' bungalow, behind a few strands of rusted wire-fence, was an empty section with a jungle of lupins straggling thickly over the uneven soil. It was one of the back-road plots that had not yet been built upon; still a kind of inland sand-dune. From the footpath outside the fence the two boys surveyed the ground.

'We haven't got our guns.' Jimmy ran back to the house and presently reappeared with a short curtain rod and an umbrella-handle without spokes. He gave the curtain rod to Walter and suddenly, startlingly, let out a loud war-whoop, smacking the palm of his hand against his pouted lips: 'Wa-wa-wa! Now you do it,' he instructed Walter.

Walter lowered his voice to the depths of his chest. 'Wa-wa-wa,' he bayed delightedly into the chill evening. Somewhere, far away at the back of the township, a dog barked in answer.

'An Indian squaw's dog,' Jimmy grinned. With his dark skin and eyes, he might have been a young Indian himself: the faint scent of wood-smoke in the twilight might have drifted from a savage stockade, so arched and alert were his nostrils as he turned to Walter and instructed him in the rules of the battle game in the section.

'Each of us goes to an end of the forest — see? — then we creep towards each other — see? — and the first one who sees the other fires his gun and wins. We crawl on our bellies, see?'

Walter saw, and was anxious to begin. And, tucking the curtain rod against his body, he ran to the further end of the section.

'If we miss each other or come across an enemy tribe or get lost,' Jimmy called, 'we sound our war-whoop and the battle's off. See?' He vanished into the lupins at his side of the forest.

Walter hopped through the strands of rusty wire, forced his way into the lupins then lowered himself to the ground. Under the rank sour-smelling bushes the sand was dry and soft; it clogged his clothes as he crept forward clasping the brass rod. Rabbits had scratched shallow pits in the sand. After a time, finding himself held up by the clutching bushes, he lifted his head and shuffled forward on his knees, thrusting the rod among the branches and gorse-like lupin-boles. Twigs whipped at his face. It took him ten minutes to struggle across the width of the section: in his absorption with the hazards of the ground and the game he had altogether missed Jimmy. They had passed one another in the forest.

'Wa-wa-wa,' sounded Jimmy's voice from the fence on the

45

far side, behind him. Jimmy too had got through the lupins without a sight of the enemy. His high war-wail echoed like an owl's cry in the falling night. 'Pax now,' he called.

'Wa-wa-wa.' Walter took up the cry. 'Pax to the war.'

Both boys stood up. 'It's a truce, see?' Jimmy yelled. 'Nobody's won. Come out in the road.'

They fought their way out of the lupins to the grassy verge of the road. A last ray of sun shone, frostily red, on the rocks and shoulders of the hills above the township: smoke rose straight up from the chimneys of the bungalows. Walter's knees, stockings and elbows were crusted over with whitish sand; Jimmy's shirt hung crookedly below the belt of his trousers. The faces of both boys were sticky with sweat, their mouths gulped at the air like the gills of stranded fish.

'Gosh, it was a good game,' Walter panted.

'Better next time. That forest was too bloody thick.'

'I couldn't even hear you.'

'It was like the Maori war.' Jimmy waved the umbrella-handle in triumph. 'Wa-wa-wa,' he shouted.

'Wa-wa-wa,' echoed Walter. Jimmy and he would be friends for ever, he was certain.

Across the road Mrs. Nelson came out to the veranda of the bungalow: with her big arms warming her bosom against the chill air she stood looking over the scrubby veronica hedge at the road and the peace conference.

'What are you kids up to?' she called. 'You'll have the policeman here, with that shindy. Come along in now.'

'Five minutes more, ma.'

'You come now, when I tell you! My heavens,' she exclaimed as they dawdled nearer, 'you're both filthy. Like monkeys. I thought I told you to stick to biking, Jimmy.'

'Well, Walter wanted — '

'Never mind what Walter wanted. He's not such a larrikin as you are.'

'Oh hell, ma.'

46

'And don't swear, either.' She snatched the umbrella-handle from her son. 'Playing about with that rubbish — you're not a savage — come in now before it gets dark — '

Walter glanced along the road. 'Is it late, Mrs. Nelson? Is it six o'clock?' The Garnetts' house was in the same road, two hundred yards away, towards the end where the hill began.

'About six.' Mrs. Nelson began to brush at his knees and elbows. 'What your Miss Muriel's going to say to your clothes — '

'I said I'd be back,' he broke in. 'I told Miss Muriel — '

'All right, but come inside a moment first.' She drew him into the passage. 'Listen, Walter, don't you pay too much attention to what I told you at tea. I run on sometimes — '

'I don't remember what you told me,' he said, surprised into shyness.

'That's all right then. Go now. But come again.'

'Come again tomorrow, Walter,' Jimmy said.

'I can't. They send me to Sunday school.'

'Cripes,' murmured Mrs. Nelson, 'they would.'

'Cripes, they would,' echoed Jimmy. 'Cripes.'

'You shut up,' said his mother. 'A dose of Sunday school wouldn't do you any harm either.'

Walter backed away down the path to the gate. 'I'll come again,' he called. He waved at Mrs. Nelson and Jimmy, then hurried down the straight gravelled road towards the Garnetts'.

CHAPTER VII

'WHAT I don't understand, father dear,' said Hilda Macaulay, 'is why you don't sell the school and retire. Instead of that you go so far as to take on a boarder — this child, Walter — to add to your burdens. He even stayed here through last holidays.' She smiled past the lamp at her father's broad face and beard at the end of the table. 'I'm only thinking of your comfort,' she added. 'I'm not really criticizing — '

'No, Hilda. But now you're married, and with Rose and Mark both away, the house is half empty . . . Besides, the boy's parents are well-off, much better than I am. His fees — '

'Oh, if it's money . . .' Hilda began. She threw her furs back from her shoulders and again uttered her tender laugh. 'You're a funny old stick, father. I should've thought you saw more than enough of boys during the day without having a half-grown child about the house — '

'Muriel takes him off my hands here.' Mr. Garnett grunted. 'He's no trouble.'

Hilda glanced along the table. 'Oh, Muriel loves trouble,' she said lazily. 'She dotes on it.'

'Hilda, what utter rubbish you talk!' Muriel straightened herself and looked hard, with a flicker of pain, at the handsome Hilda. 'I simply try to take life as it comes . . . And, in any case, I like having a young person about the place . . .'

A silence fell over the table.

'Noisy,' said old Mrs. Garnett suddenly. 'Young people are either deceitful or noisy. Often both.' She sat before her empty tea-cup, her twisted hands in her lap. 'You wait, Hilda,' she murmured warningly to her daughter, 'till you have a child of your own.'

'Well —' and Hilda laughed across the table at her husband ' — talking so aptly of the devil . . . Shall we tell them, Geoff? Has the great moment of revelation come so easily?'

Geoffrey Macaulay lifted his head. 'Tell them now, Hilda, by all means.' His blunt face regarded her coolly. 'I don't see why not.'

'Father,' said his wife to old Mr. Garnett, 'hold your breath. 'Your first grandchild has decided to signal his appearance.' She threw back her head, laughing helplessly. 'How funny it sounds — how completely pompous . . . Do I surprise you all?'

'A very pleasant surprise, Hilda my dear.'

'And you, mother?'

The old woman's dry lips plucked at her daughter's cheek. 'Yes, Hilda, yes. Don't listen to my crotchets.'

'Thank you, mother darling.' Hilda looked towards her sister. 'And Muriel?'

'I think I'd guessed the news already, Hilda.' She straightened a knife on the cloth. 'And of course I'm glad you're so happy —'

'Oh, I'm happy all right,' Hilda crowed. 'Happy as the day's long except when I get this awful itch to throw up my breakfast most mornings.' Her flushed face glanced across at her husband. 'Geoff of course, with his usual ancestral Calvinism, says it's guilt for woman's original sin in the Garden of Eden.'

'That's no way to talk, Hilda.' Old Mrs. Garnett frowned. 'No way at all. Children have to be born into the world —'

'I know, I know, mother dear.' Her red lips mocked the old woman. 'In any case, I shall bring up my baby nearly as strictly as you did us. Oh, don't I remember —' and pushing up her auburn hair from the creamy skin of her forehead she again glanced, laughing, at her sister. 'Muriel,' she teased, 'is staring at Geoff as though he couldn't possibly have begotten any child of mine.'

'I was doing no such thing.' Muriel flushed at the suddenness of the attack. 'That's almost a wicked thing to say, Hilda.

Certainly uncharitable.' She recovered herself. 'It's no concern of mine — '

'Goodness, I was only making a joke.'

'Then I think it was in rather poor taste.'

Mr. Garnett interrupted calmly: 'You haven't informed us yet when your child's to be born, Hilda.'

'When? Donkey's years yet, father — or at least months. About Christmas or just before, to be exact. Isn't that so, Geoff?'

'November.' The young man's brown eyes swept the table with a hunted embarrassment: he fingered his collar and green knitted tie. This afternoon visit to his parents-in-law was trying to his patience. 'Dr. Thomson's keeping an eye on Hilda's progress,' he said to nobody in particular.

'Have you thought of a name for the baby?' Mrs. Garnett unclasped a hand from her lap and jogged Hilda's elbow. 'Don't go callin' him somethin' new-fangled.'

'I thought "Malcolm", if he's a boy, mother . . . If it's a girl, Geoff has some ghastly plan for "Millicent", after his mama, or even "Muriel".'

'Oh, no,' cried Muriel. She shot up quickly from the table, seized the tea-pot and tested the warmth of its side with her fingers. 'I don't want her called after me,' she said in a kind of anguish. 'You must think of some other name, Hilda.' She went rapidly out of the room to the kitchen, her chin lowered.

'*I* didn't think of it,' Hilda called after her. 'Oh, hang,' she sighed to the table, 'now I've upset her. Geoff, my pet, you'd better go and comfort the silly creature.'

'Ah, you're just tactless, Hilda.' And with an effort Geoffrey Macaulay turned his fresh face to his father-in-law, changing the subject. 'I was talking to your boarder, that young lad, on the beach this morning, sir. He struck me as intelligent enough — '

'He has good manners, Geoffrey, even some sensibility. But at his lessons, rather backward; doesn't concentrate . . . And of course, like most boys of his age, he lives rather in a world of his own, apart from us.' The old man slewed himself round in his chair and gazed at the fire in the grate. 'The mother is very beautiful,' he said slowly, 'though I've seen her only once, when she brought the boy to the school for his first term. She seemed much affected in parting with him to us — singularly so, I considered. There may have been some family trouble.' He shook his head. 'Every family among my pupils, I find, has trouble of some kind . . . But Mrs. Blakiston — yes, very much what we'd call in the old country a lady.'

'We're all ladies, father.' Hilda's careless laugh rang along the table. 'Don't insult us.'

'I was speaking more particularly of young Blakiston's mother, my dear. I insulted nobody.'

Hilda leant forward. 'She was a Grace, wasn't she? One of that family from Mount Sterling?'

'I haven't your acquaintance with the landed gentry of Canterbury, Hilda.'

'Now you're being sarcastic, father. I only see their names in the paper, at race meetings and things like that: I don't *know* them, except a few of the more colonial ones Rose and I met at school — the ones with accents like tin cans.' She shrugged her shoulders. 'Oh, dear . . . it's so silly — why do we always have to compare everything with England?'

'Because we're English,' said Mrs. Garnett. Her eyes narrowed behind the steel frame of her spectacles. 'Why should we get away from England, Hilda? Our roots are still English — your father's and mine, at all events. It's no use your complainin' — '

'Oh, mother, I only meant . . . anyway, I don't care. Mrs. Blakiston was a Miss Grace from Mount Sterling, I'll bet on it.' With her tea-spoon she dug childishly at the sugar in the bottom of her cup. 'Wealthy sheep people,' she mocked. 'The squattocracy — '

'Does the Kaiser want a war with England, sir?' Geoffrey Macaulay readdressed his father-in-law. And his slightly Scottish voice added hesitantly: 'The papers don't seem to have much notion of what's brewing in Europe.'

Mr. Garnett drew himself up. 'The Kaiser is related to the English royal family,' he propounded. 'And, short of internecine suicide, Teutons do not fight Saxons... All the same, Geoffrey, I did not like Agadir, I do not like this enlargement of the German Navy, nor do I care for the backbiting of Vienna towards central European minorities.' His ashen beard dropped to his chest: the warm room was making him sleepy. 'The Prussians,' he brooded suddenly, 'are like the Fabians in England, always nagging at the *status quo*. Boys of a similar temperament at school are invariably a nuisance.'

'You men,' shrugged Hilda Macaulay, 'and your dreary world of politics.' She turned as her sister rejoined them from the kitchen. 'I thought you'd run away, Muriel — run off with the old man of the sea.'

Muriel carefully placed the refilled tea-pot on the table. 'Do you want a basket of apples to take home with you, Hilda?' she asked with reserve.

'I don't know, pet. What sort of apples?'

'Father's Cox's Orange. Walter gathered the last of them from the orchard a week ago.'

'Geoff likes apples — yes, Geoff can eat them, pips and all. By the way, Muriel, wasn't that boy's mother a Grace from Mount Sterling? Wasn't she born a Grace?'

'I've no idea, Hilda. Ask him yourself.' She glanced at the clock. 'I let him go to the Nelsons for tea.'

'*That* awful woman,' Hilda said abruptly, 'with that grubby little half-caste boy! Ugh! I could tell her what I thought of her for marrying a Maori... Really, she's the worst woman in Sumner — smokes, doesn't wear petticoats, gossips like a house on fire, *and* overcharges when she washes my laundry....'

'You're unjust to her, Hilda,' Muriel said.

'Am I? Well, my dears, I wouldn't care to get into her power, that's all. She knows too much.' Hilda stretched her arms above her head, yawning. 'When's Rose coming home?' she asked her mother.

'She so seldom writes, Hilda.'

'She'd better come and nurse me when I have this kiddie.' Hilda pointed a lazy finger at her husband. 'Shall I write to her, Geoff?'

'Who?'

'Rosy, rose-bud, Rose,' she sang at him. 'Sister Rosy?'

'No,' he said. A raw colour darkened his face. 'Dr. Thomson says you should have no difficulty, Hilda, if you look after yourself.'

'Oh, I never look after myself. Never. Life's too short!' Hilda dropped her arms. 'I can't be bothered... No, but seriously,' she said, 'Rose has done maternity nursing, I know —'

Geoffrey Macaulay looked at his watch. 'We should be going, Hilda. In any case, I must run out and light the lamps of the motor.'

'If there's one thing that gives me real heart-trouble,' laughed Hilda, 'it's the smell of acetylene from those lamps. If you want to stifle me with an anaesthetic on baby's arrival, darling, refrain from carbide.'

'Hilda —' old Mrs. Garnett limped rheumatically towards her chair by the fire ' — be quiet. You're too free with your tongue.'

'All right, all right, mother. I'll be as English as a muffin from now on. Not a word of slang, even, shall pass my lips.'

The door from the kitchen creaked open. 'I'm back from the Nelsons,' Walter announced himself to Miss Muriel, blinking in the lamplight.

'The boy whose mother was a Grace,' cried Hilda, 'in person. The boy with the violet eyes.'

'They're not,' he said, overcome with shyness, 'they're blue.'

'How are you, Walter?'

Miss Muriel interrupted: 'You look as though you'd been dragged through a gorse-bush backwards,' she scolded, brushing at his clothes. 'An awful mess. Sand too....'

He sat himself down beside Mr. Macaulay. 'I saw your car outside,' he said in a whisper.

The young man winked, then, shielding his lips and moustache with his hand, poked out the end of his tongue to show the boy that the black stain of the morning's liquorice had not faded. Walter, in turn, displayed a flicker of his own tongue. A glow of conspiracy passed between them at the table: a secret laughter.

'Well, I suppose it's home to Scarborough Hill for the Macaulays,' said Hilda meanwhile. Humming to herself she stood smiling at her reflection in the mirror above the mantelpiece, tying a veil round her big hat and under her chin. 'I think I really look rather elegant today, don't you, Muriel? Striped material always suits me — thins me down.'

'I'll fetch your apples, Hilda.' Miss Muriel went to the kitchen and returned with the basket. 'Walter, you can carry it to the motor for them.'

'Come on, Walter. We'll nip ahead.' Geoffrey Macaulay drew the boy out of the room. In the hallway leading to the front door he paused to search for his cap among the coats hanging thickly against the wall. 'My wife can never say good-bye,' he murmured. 'She's a chronic lingerer.' The soft lilt of his voice had an edge of bitterness in the dark passage.

Walter stood waiting in the small glass porch beyond the door; the pots of geraniums, the mottled dying leaves of the chrysanthemums, gave out a musty scent, mixed with the smell of damp from the concrete floor. The porch had a few ruby and sapphire panes of coloured glass, low down, their tints almost extinguished now in the dusk. Only the geraniums, still flowering in the lateness of the year, shone like nuggets of crude vermilion out of a paint-box, against the pale upper glass of the porch.

'Take yourself an apple from the basket, Walter.'

'But they're for Mrs. Hilda —'

'I rather fancied they were intended for me,' the young man said evenly. As the two of them crunched down the cinder path to the gate his warm tweed coat-sleeve brushed Walter's cheek.

'Go on,' he said. 'Muriel won't mind. You look a wee bit thin to me.'

'Thanks, Mr. Macaulay.' He stuffed the apple into his jacket. 'Thanks awfully.'

The white-painted car, high in the body, stood like a ghost in the evening. A single street-lamp wavered its gaslight at the corner of the road, ten yards away. Walter ran towards the car.

'It's a Rover — it's written on the front. How many horse-power?'

'Six.'

To Walter the number seemed immense: he saw the horses — cart horses — straining forward, prodigious. 'How do they measure?' he asked.

'Ah, the makers have ways . . .'. Geoffrey Macaulay opened a box on the step of the car: his shoulders bent over, his strong sandy-haired fingers twisted a butterfly screw. 'Now, hold your nose while I start this contrivance. . . .'

Walter swung the basket of apples on to the seat, then watched the other presently light a match in front of the car. The matches reminded him of Jimmy Nelson. 'Mrs. Nelson smokes cigarettes,' he confided after a moment. 'Do you like Mrs. Nelson?'

'I can't say I've much of the woman's acquaintance . . .' Mr. Macaulay, absorbed in his priming of the lamps, spoke slowly. 'I believe Rose used to know her a little.' A spurt, a fan of yellowish-blue flame sprang up in the jets. 'People talk too much in this town, Walter,' he said a minute later. 'They're as full of inflammable gas as these lamps,' he grinned, 'and by God some of it's no less dangerous.'

CHAPTER VIII

O N this fine winter day Walter and the boy named Marriner ate their separate lunches between two of the stone buttresses in the playground. The buttresses, flanking a sheltered corner, were those of the tall bony Anglican church in St. Mary Street against which, or rather behind which, sheltered the wooden buildings leased by Mr. Garnett as class-rooms for that preparatory school he had founded some ten years earlier.

Walter's lunch was wrapped in newspaper. From the stains on the paper he could tell, before he opened the picnic-like package, what particular filling Miss Muriel had used for the sandwiches she squeezed into the mouth of his satchel each morning before he sprinted to catch the tram from Sumner. Jam always oozed through in a red smudge. Today the stain was an acid orange colour.

'Pickles again,' he told Marriner, wrinkling the skin of his nose. 'What's yours?'

'Meat.' Marriner's own sandwiches were neatly wedged into a superior lunch-box of tan cardboard. 'Cold mutton.'

'Want to swop a pickle for a mutton?'

'No fear.' Marriner's enormous sunken eyes, in a round head too like a skull, turned away from Walter's newspaper spread on the asphalt between the buttresses. 'Pickles only make you hungrier.'

'She never gives me enough, anyway. There isn't time after breakfast . . .' Walter spread out his four triangular sandwiches. Today, however, there was a surprise underneath: a sodden slab of madeira cake. 'Gosh,' he said, delighted. 'Look. A find, a treasure.'

Marriner was not impressed. 'When your belly rumbles,' he remarked, 'it's a sign you're growing. My uncle told me.' He spread out his own sandwiches, in which slices of pinky-brown mutton showed cleanly between the brown crusts at the edges. His nails were gnawed down to the quicks. 'Has your Miss Muriel got a husband?' he asked Walter presently.

'No.' He tried to think of something fresh to tell Marriner about the daughter of their schoolmaster, much talked about already. 'She's got a little mole above her lip,' he said after a moment. 'When she's — you know — nervous she touches it with her finger — like this — '

'Why?'

'Well, she does.'

'Like when you pick your nose.' Marriner's skull-like face grinned.

'Yes, only . . .' Walter wanted to say that the mole was almost pretty, an asset. 'It's the same colour as her hair,' he finished.

'Women are barmy,' said Marriner. 'All grown people are barmy.' 'Barmy' was the school word of the term. 'Swop you a meat sandwich for half your cake,' he proposed now.

Walter looked reluctantly at the cake then at the succulence of the slightly larger sandwich. He was hungry. 'All right,' he agreed. 'I'll give you the bit the pickles haven't marked. . . .'

'Does old Garnett make you do homework all the time in the evenings?' Marriner resumed. The question was not new. 'If you live in the house — '

'Not if I want to do stamps. I've got a Meccano too — a small one.'

'What number set?'

'Only the First. The others are expensive . . . Pounds.' Walter munched his meat sandwich sadly. Mr. Garnett, by arrangement with his father, allowed him a shilling a week for pocket money. The money vanished on sweets, on foreign stamps, on comic papers, on nothing. The shilling was paid to him on Sundays after supper: by Thursday it had gone. 'How much spending money do you get?' he asked Marriner.

'Mum gives me half a crown if I chop the kindling. I'm s'posed to put sixpence in my Navy League box but I don't always if I'm broke.'

'What's the Navy League?'

'Well, it's for ... it's to build dreadnoughts to scrap with Indians and Chinamen,' Marriner explained easily. 'A dreadnought costs a million pounds.'

Walter couldn't believe it. 'More than a motor car,' he said. 'Much more.' He watched the bicycles passing in the street beyond the iron railings of the playground. A cold wind blew round the corner of the church, raising eddies of dust against the grey stone and greenish mortar, sweeping under the boys' legs as they sprawled on the asphalt, swaying the upper branches of the huge tree, a Douglas Fir, that grew beside the entrance-corridor to the school building. Across the playground other boys were eating their lunch in the shelter of the open bicycle shed. A scatter of lean sparrows squabbled for crumbs on the gravel. The sky had the harsh burnished blue of the southern winter, ravelled with cloud from the coast.

'Mr. Macaulay's got a six horse-power Rover,' Walter told Marriner. 'That means it can pull against six horses.'

Marriner did not know anyone who owned a car. 'Who's Mr. Macaulay?'

'He's sort of married to Mrs. Hilda — she's another of Mr. Garnett's daughters.'

'Is she barmy too?'

'Fairly ... Mr. Macaulay's an architect, he designs houses and tram shelters ... I'd like to build submarines.' And he began to tell Marriner of the boys in one of the school stories he was reading: boys who had constructed a submarine from an old boiler, with a couple of yards of rubber tubing attached to the plug-hole for breathing. 'They tried it in the school baths but it exploded or something and this boy — the one who'd made it —

he was brought up all wet in front of the Head . . .' But he would lend Marriner the story to read for himself. 'It isn't as good as the Longmeadows ones though.'

Marriner sat picking at the white knuckles of his knees. Like Walter he wore knitted stockings, leather boots, short trousers, a jacket pulled out of shape by bulging pockets, and the red white-starred cap of the school. Even now, in the second term of their friendship, he couldn't get used to the fact that Walter was a boarder, while the rest of the school were day-boys like himself. It set Walter apart, a country boy. 'I'm glad I don't have to live in the old cock's house,' he said now, reverting to Mr. Garnett. 'Doesn't he ever let you go home?'

'Mum says it would only unsettle me,' said Walter, hearing the tone of his mother's voice as he had wept on her shoulder at parting. 'She says I can go home for next holidays, or anyway for Christmas.'

'Do you ever find any birds' eggs on your farm?'

'Thrushes and blackies — ' Walter felt a twinge of homesickness in his heart '— and, golly, once I found a weka's nest — '

'A weka's?' Marriner was immediately interested. 'What kind of eggs?'

'Like hen's a bit, only with freckles. The female — you know, the mother — can't fly, they're like kiwis and moas, so she only sort of grunts at you and flaps her wings — '

'I wish Mum and I lived on a farm,' Marriner blurted out in envy. 'We've only got a back yard with a cabbage-tree in it.' He lived in New Brighton, at the end of a different tram route from that taken every morning and evening by Walter.

The two boys finished their lunch, stuffing the sandwich papers into a cranny of the buttresses. To leave paper in the playground was a caneable offence: dirty paper, declared Mr. Garnett, gave the school a bad name among the Sunday church-goers.

'Come on,' said Marriner. He got up, patting his thin hams. 'My bum's cold, sitting on asphalt.'

Behind them the boys from the bicycle shed had begun to kick a dishevelled tennis-ball across the playground. Others were returning from their lunch in the town or from their homes in the suburbs: bicycle bells shrilled at the gate. Shouts and whistles echoed against the high flank of the church: the squabbling sparrows flew into the dusty cone of the fir tree.

'See you after school,' Walter said to Marriner, joining the others. 'See you on the way to the tram.'

Ten minutes later Mr. Garnett, his hair white in the hard daylight, his watch clasped open in his hand, appeared in the doorway of the corridor leading to the main classroom. 'Two o'clock, boys, two o'clock,' his voice called to them in mild asperity. He rang a small bronze bell with a flick of his wrist. 'Collins, Marriner, Bascomb, Blakiston . . . and you, Macdonald . . . two o'clock.' The thirty boys were shepherded, disconsolate, into the corridor, the door was closed, the playground empty.

This afternoon Walter's class, the Second, had recitation as a first-hour subject. Miss Threplow was on the dais.

' "Last, loneliest, loveliest, exquisite, apart . . .",' she read aloud from the green-covered book before her. Her voice was gentle, even flat. Today she had a cold: bruised blue rings surrounded her eyes, she kept a handkerchief tucked in her dress, her yellow-brown hair curved limply above her ears. ' "Last, loneliest, loveliest . . ." ' That's Kipling's description, boys, of our own country, our islands, as he saw them down here in the Pacific. Last week I asked you to learn the whole verse by heart.' She coughed. 'Marriner, can you get through it for me now, please?'

Marriner chirped through the verse with only one hesitation.

'Ye-es,' brooded Miss Threplow, 'though Kipling might wonder what had happened to his commas. Space the words more, don't rattle them.' She blew her nose. 'Overton, will you try?'

Overton stood up; Marriner sat down. Presently a pencilled note reached Walter under the desk.

'She's barmy too,' Walter read, in Marriner's scrawl.

The class-room had high windows facing the west and showing the tops of a row of plum trees in an orchard behind the church. Narrow aisles sloped down the room between the two separate classes, from the windows towards the raised platform and the blackboards. A smell of chalk, of boys' clothing, and the fume of a kerosene stove thickened the air.

'For next week,' said Miss Threplow at last, disposing of Kipling for the day, 'I'd like you to begin a poem by Matthew Arnold, father of the famous Dr. Arnold. It's called 'The Forsaken Merman', and you'll find it in your books, page twelve. Do all you boys know what the title means?' Her bruised gaze dwelt on them without extravagant hope. 'Collins?'

Collins's pale crafty eyes inspected the scrubbed floor. 'A sailor who's been left behind?' he ventured.

'Not quite.' She laughed lightly, smoothing her forehead. 'Well, no matter. The poem itself'll tell you. So, learn the first twenty lines for me, please, boys.' She shut the book, sneezed and glanced along the platform. 'Now I think Mr. Garnett is ready to take you in French.'

'Thank you, Miss Threplow, thank you.' The old man exchanged places with her on the platform. He settled his waistcoat and faced the class with a sigh. 'Now — '

'Please, sir, can I leave the room?' Marriner thrust up a hand. 'Please, Mr. Garnett, can I?'

'I daresay you *can*, Marriner, short of a paralysis singular at your age. The question is, *may* you leave the class.'

'May I then, sir?' Marriner stood fidgeting.

'Go,' said Mr. Garnett and wiped chalk-dust from his fingers with a pink cloth. 'Why you boys can't see fit to empty your bladders in the lunch-break is beyond me,' he confided to the blackboard.

The French lesson began. 'Sir,' presently interrupted Collins, who knew that syntax and verbs could be sidestepped. 'Sir, didn't the Frenchies nearly conquer New Zealand once? Didn't they land at Akaroa?'

The master considered the bait and decided to grasp it. 'They sent a ship, yes,' he affirmed, 'intending to colonize. That was fifty years ago — more. The British, however, had got here first, Collins. In the name of Queen Victoria — a very great woman, all of you — the Union Jack was planted on the beaches. The French, for better or worse, were a few days too late.'

'If they'd got here first, sir, would we all be Frenchies now?' Collins had prepared his innocent joke. 'Would we have used French letters?'

'I doubt it, Monsieur Collins, I doubt it very much. And the French are an elegant race who don't encourage lubricity in young boys.'

The class, puzzled, shifted their feet, suspecting a jest beyond them. Walter opened the flap of his desk, thrust his pencil-box inside, and glancing with longing and excitement at the pages of an adventure story he was hiding, decided to leave the book until his tram ride of the evening. Meanwhile, Marriner had sidled back into the room.

'Now,' said Mr. Garnett and stroked the white sporran of his beard, 'now, with our ancient mariner among us, we shall open Siepmann's *First French Course* at page ten. In view of your guttersnipe blushes, Collins, you will wait after school.' His shrewd eyes swept the class with authority. 'In the meantime, we shall pass on to your prepared homework. Bascomb, will you begin the translation at "Le jardin . . ."?'

At four o'clock Walter waited for Marriner at the gate of the playground: with satchels swinging from their shoulders, with overcoats unbuttoned, they dawdled together towards the Cathedral Square to catch their separate trams for home.

'Why did Collins cop it?' Marriner asked as they came to the bridge over the Avon. 'Did he fart or something?'

'Dunno,' said Walter vaguely.

'You don't know anything. You're a fool, man.'

'You're another, man. A big one.'

They grinned at one another, making affectionate faces, then spat over the balustrade of the bridge into the water.

'Come on, man, we're late.'

It was cold in the streets: the asphalt pavements were like gritty lava: bicycle bells tinkled with the crispness of frost: the wind hummed in the telegraph wires overhead. The two boys walked close together, like orphans.

'I've got sixpence,' Marriner said at length. 'We might buy some Tobler chocolate. I'm collecting the cards.'

They were both, it turned out, collecting the cards. Walter had an album already half full of the glossy small pictures of animals, of famous men, of Swiss chalets, of railway engines. But certain of the cards were rare, nobody ever found them in an ordinary packet. 'Have you got Animals No. 5?' Walter asked. 'It's a peccary, I think.'

Marriner was scornful. 'They only put one of those in every ten thousand packets. The woman told me in the shop.' His skull of a face was pinched with anger. 'It's a swiz,' he grumbled.

They reached the Square; both gazed hungrily into the window of the sweet shop, saliva moistening their lips. The packet that Marriner bought held only a picture of a lion, a common lion.

'Still,' Walter comforted him, 'it'll do as a swop.'

They ate the chocolate. Behind them the street lamps, just lit, threw a yellow glare on their red caps. The trams, long pea-green caterpillars, circled the shelter and grass in the middle of the Square. The cathedral spire pointed to the clouds racing across the flat city and the plains beyond. Like a moon in the blue air hung the face of the Post Office clock.

They turned from the window, the wind stinging their bare knees. Marriner asked: 'Do you have to wait for old Garnett before you catch your tram?'

Walter shook his head. 'I don't sit with him, either. It's better in the trailer, anyway.' And for the first time that day he thought of the dog that had been run over and thrown to drown. He shivered; it was as though he himself . . . and he opened his mouth to tell Marriner . . . to explain. But there was no time. An elderly stoutish man in a grey Homburg hat, carrying a coat and a dispatch case, had approached, walking as though his feet hurt him. He glanced at the dawdling boys and passed on in silence.

'I'm off,' Marriner whispered, 'or the old cock'll tell Mum I've been loitering. See you tomorrow.' He ran across the Square.

'See you tomorrow,' Walter waved.

He walked after Mr. Garnett to the place where the tram for Sumner, its motor panting, stood under the glare from a high iron lamp-standard in the middle of the Square. The old man was already seated in the tram, an evening paper shielding his face, his umbrella propped against his knees. Walter climbed into the trailer, undid the strap of his satchel, and with the taste of chocolate in his mouth settled down to read the adventure story that the day at school had interrupted.

CHAPTER IX

'A LETTER from your mother, Walter.'
The day was a Monday. The kitchen smelt cleanly of washing, of warm lather and of the flat-irons upended on top of the range. Miss Muriel pointed to the envelope weighted down by the base of the scales on the table. 'You'd better wash your hands before you read it.'

Walter dropped his satchel to the floor and grabbed the letter. His mother's writing was sloping and rapid: dark indigo ink on paler blue paper, with a long straight line dashed below the address. He longed to read the letter at once.

'I spoke, Walter. Did you listen?'

'I've been wearing my gloves, Miss Muriel,' he frowned. 'My hands are quite clean.'

'Fingers have all day to get dirty.' She gave him a slight push towards the scullery and the sink, calling after him the question she asked every evening at this hour: 'Was father on the tram?'

'Yes, he was. I ran on.'

He propped the letter on the window-sill while he rinsed his hands. The letter seemed to watch him — a tender face in the chill shadows of the scullery, his mother's face, her eyes the same azure colour as the envelope. On his fingers, as he shook the freezing tap-water from them in drops, were the raised red lumps and weals of the winter's first chilblains. The letter seemed to watch these too, distantly . . . He seized the envelope in his damp grasp and ran back to the kitchen, to the lamp on the dresser and to Miss Muriel.

'Let me look at your boots,' she said from the range. 'Not wet?'

'They're all right.'

'Yes, dear, but they'll dirty the floor. Take them off.'

Impatient, he attacked his muddy boots, unlaced them, kicked them under the table. At school it had been the day for football practice: between four and five o'clock twenty boys — ten a side — had fought and pinched one another across a soggy paddock in the Park, interrupted by blasts from a whistle blown by Mr. Garnett. During the game the old man had stood huddled under an oak tree, his eyes watering in the wind, his beard untidy, his dispatch case leaning against his boots. Both he and Walter had missed their usual tram homeward.

'Now for your slippers.'

'Oh — ' the boy blew out his lips, exasperated.

'You've all night to read your letter.' She pushed the irons to the back of the range. 'Your mother wouldn't want you to catch cold, would she.'

His slippers were upstairs. He stumbled through the dining-room — Mrs. Garnett, knitting by the fire, did not look up — into the hall and stumped his way up the stairs. The landing was almost dark, his room only a little less dusky. The chipped edges of the wash-basin under the window gleamed like teeth: the tilted dressing-table glass showed the varnished timbers of the ceiling. Walter lit the candle at his bedside, watched the flame flutter and settle, then flung himself on the grey blankets of the bed, swung his stockinged feet up beside him, and tore open his mother's letter. The letter was an answer to a scribble he had written to her three days before.

Dearest Walter,

Thank you for your note (it wasn't much more, was it?). I do hope you have no chilblains yet and that you have enough warm clothes for the winter. I don't like to think of you travelling by tram so much and not being quite warm in this beastly arctic weather. Here it has been cold too, the oaks behind the house have lost all their leaves, and I shiver as I do the housework in the mornings.

66

Your father has been very busy with the shepherds. He had an accident one day when he was oiling the windmill in the gully, the windmill you always wanted to climb as a little boy to look for a hawk's nest which wasn't there. A gust of wind spun the vanes round and cut his head open, not a deep wound but it certainly bled and I was frightened when he came swearing in to me with a gory handkerchief round his brow like a pirate. I bathed the cut and now it is only a scar on his temple which will heal and vanish in time. But I have been upset and nervous, as I do get whenever I have a moment to think in this big house without you here.

I hope you are not as homesick as you were last term, Walter. I haven't been at all well — I'll tell you one day — and have no help at present in the house. Servants are hard to get, they always have been, in this isolated place four miles from the village with so little amusement for them. You ask about coming home next holidays, but as things are at the moment, one way and another, I think it is better if I ask Gran to take you at Mount Sterling. I know she would like that, and you always enjoy staying with her and father, don't you. I hope you will not be disappointed, darling, with this arrangement. And don't think I have forgotten you — very far from it.

I cleaned out your room one day this week. Do you really want, I mean WANT, all those odd things in your museum in the cupboard — the seaweed and dead ferns and all those flints and skeletons? There was a deceased starfish I had to throw away as it had bred insects. But what you want with four moabones, a piece of coal — or is it jet? — a coin with a hole in it, and a tin full of dusty birds' eggs, I can't imagine. Haven't you outgrown these sacred trophies? Perhaps you'll decide when you at last come home, I'll leave them meanwhile.

You don't say much, dear, about your work at school, except that you've been learning the Merman poem, which I used to know by heart. Your last term's report said Weak in Arithmetic and Tries in Latin. You must work at these subjects without impatience, as you used to at home when I tried to give you lessons myself. I also want you to lose your shyness with *people*. You must forget that you're an only child, Walter, and make friends. I babied you too much here, perhaps, as your father said so often and I disagreed.

I am writing this by a fire of fir-cones I've lit in the drawing-room, the paper on my knees, with the magpies making that strange crazy noise in the trees in front of the house. The hills are still very dry and burnt here after the dry autumn, and as usual we need rain. My poor garden has no flowers.

I will send you a tin of biscuits and cake, as you ask, dear. I am glad Miss Garnett gives you a hot dinner in the evenings after school. You are growing and need food.

Love now and as always from your mother.

Walter tucked the letter into a bundle of others beneath his handkerchiefs in the stiff upper drawer of the dressing-table. He would read it again, he promised himself, when he came upstairs for the night. Now he shuffled into his slippers, snuffed out the candle, waited a moment to sniff at the whiff of the wick on his fingers, then slid down the banisters to the dark hall below. His mother's letters always gave him a mixed feeling of sadness and excitement: he re-read them frequently, puzzling over certain of the words, repeating phrases to himself when he awoke in the early morning. They were his only connection with that other life he had left behind on his arrival at the Garnetts' and to which he longed to return.

In his rush upstairs he had left the door of the dining-room open behind him. Now, as he hesitated in the hall, scared of a rebuke from Mrs. Garnett, he could catch the old woman's voice droning to her husband by the fire.

'This man she's been lookin' after seems to be convalescent. At any rate, if the hospital or the Federation hasn't another patient for her at once, she wants to come to us for a time.'

'Where is her letter?'

'There, by the clock. It came this afternoon. She says she's in need of a holiday.'

Mr. Garnett's milder tones remarked: 'She was never very strong perhaps.'

'Rose? She's strong enough — it's nothin' but these silly panics she gets herself into. Nurses shouldn't panic or worry . . . What Rose needs is to find a husband worthy of her and to settle down.'

'Marriage, my dear, does not solve everything in this world.'

'Better to marry than to burn.'

'You forget, she had some cause, poor girl — '

'No cause sufficient to keep her away from her home all this time, Arthur.'

Walter presented himself in the room. Old Mrs. Garnett, turning, bunched herself forward in her chair.

'Ah,' she said with satisfaction, 'the young man who leaves doors open.'

'Sorry, Mrs. Garnett.'

'Born in a tent, die in a tent.' She beckoned him to her. 'Doors were built to be shut. Do you see?'

'Yes, Mrs. Garnett.' Walter looked from her face to that of his schoolmaster. The old man's head was bent over his daughter's letter. 'Is Miss Rose coming home?'

'What were doors built for?'

Walter was caught off his balance. 'Doors?'

'You see, Arthur?' The old woman waved a knitting-needle for her husband's attention. 'The child's practically an idiot. Never listens. Might be a young bed-post.'

'Is Miss Rose coming home?' Walter repeated.

'Yes,' said Mr. Garnett. Absently he folded the letter and replaced it beside the clock. 'Yes, Blakiston. So she says.'

Walter, shifting his feet, stood awkwardly by the table. He must get himself back into favour. 'Shall I make up the fire, Mrs. Garnett?' he asked.

'You give your mind to doors, not fires.' But her voice had thawed; she even gauntly smiled. 'Rose'll have to teach you your manners, young man. You wait.'

'Are you washed, father?' It was Miss Muriel at the door. 'Shall I dish up the dinner?'

'Yes, Muriel. I am indeed washed.' The old man sighed, lowering his body to a chair by the table. 'Serve the repast to the hungry.' A moment later he was again on his feet: he had forgotten to say grace. 'Rose's letter,' he excused himself.

'Which is Miss Rose's room when she comes?' Walter asked, after the blessing. 'Which, Miss Muriel?'

'Next to yours. The door along the landing. She and Hilda used to share that front room together.'

He went round the table, pouring water from the glass jug into the tumblers. His eye lingered over the picture of Miss Rose on the mantelpiece. 'Does she always wear a nurse's uniform?'

The question had been addressed to nobody, and nobody answered. Presently, looking quickly from one face to the other, he sat himself down, biting his lip. In the silence a wind from the sea rattled the doors leading to the veranda; the wooden house seemed to heave in a slight convulsion as though the hills above the township, once the outriding flanks of an active volcano now long quiescent, had woken to a sudden tremor, a hint from the geological past. At the dinner-table Mr. Garnett raised his head, caught Miss Muriel's eye.

'An angel passing,' she smiled and touched the little mole above her lip. 'Rather a rogue angel.' A moment later she had turned to Walter: 'Sit up straight, child.' She straightened her own thin shoulders. 'Or do you want your back to grow more like a C than an L? Which?'

'An L.' He drew an L surreptitiously on the cloth with his thumb-nail, thinking of the capital letters in the Line-upon-Line his mother had given him when he was learning to read and when the capitals had somehow stood for the whole words themselves. 'L stands for Love,' he said now, half-aloud. 'L-o-v-e,' he spelt it to his plate, frowning.

'And W stands for Waste.' She pointed a warning finger at his dinner. 'Are you leaving that good meat?'

'It's gristle.' He pushed at the brown muscly lump with his fork. 'Must I, Miss Muriel?'

With an unfamiliar mildness Mrs. Garnett said across the table: 'Think of all the poor boys in London who'd be glad of it, young man.'

He attempted to think of them. But the boys — romping in gutters, standing under lamp-posts, sleeping in the illustrations to English magazines — were of no help. They seldom were. He picked up the gristle and stuffed it into his mouth, holding its toughness between his teeth and cheek, pretending to chew. A moment later, as though in carelessness, he had dropped his fork to the floor. He bent down and with his head below the table-top, shot the gristle into his hand and thence into his trouser pocket. With his mouth working innocently he emerged to straighten his back. He gave a false swallow.

'Gone,' he said, and helped Miss Muriel to remove the plates to the kitchen. 'I'm getting better at gristle,' he told her. 'Don't you think?'

'Much better. Exemplary.'

They returned to the table, Miss Muriel bearing, high before her like an evening sacrifice, a dish of stewed plums.

'Your favourites, father. The yellow ones. . . .'

The old man's eyes glistened. 'Ah,' he said contentedly and poked the corner of his napkin deeper into his waistcoat. 'I have a weakness for food, my dear, a singular weakness, not to be confused with greed.'

Mrs. Garnett, in her turn, inspected the plums. 'You'd better tell Hilda that Rose is comin' home, Muriel,' she said unexpectedly. 'When you see her.'

'No, mother.' Miss Muriel served the plums in silence. 'Rose can announce herself, if and when she does appear, I think.'

She took off her apron, blushed and sat down without a glance at her parents. 'As far as Hilda and Geoffrey are concerned it's far better that way.'

Walter piled the plum stones round his plate, counting them. 'This year, next year, sometime . . . When nurses get married,' he asked Miss Muriel, 'can they go on being nurses, if they want to?'

'I suppose so, Walter.' She waited a moment. 'What did your mother write to you about in her letter?'

This was a weekly question, not easy to answer. 'She wants me to go to stay with my grandmother next holidays,' he said at last.

'Oh.' Miss Muriel looked quickly at her father and away. 'I see. Well, you'll enjoy that, surely?'

He thought of his grandmother's house among the foothills of the mountains, a hundred miles away. 'I can catch trout when I'm there,' he remarked. 'Rainbow trout in the creek.' All the same, the reminder that he was not yet to see his mother saddened him: he wanted to read her letter again, to make sure. . . .

'Can I go upstairs to get a handkerchief?' he asked after dinner.

'You're not catching a cold, are you?'

'No.'

'Very well. Take the candle in the hall, and see that you don't let the grease drip on the carpet.'

He went carefully upstairs. But when he reached the landing it was not the door of his own room that beckoned: for the moment it was the door further on, the door of the room that was again to be Miss Rose's. Holding the candle high, he pushed the creaking brass door knob and peered into the room. The blinds were drawn down over the windows, the heaped-up mattress lay under a counterpane sprinkled with a pattern of carnations. On top of the high wardrobe stood a cardboard hat-box, tilted forward. Carpet-fluff stirred under the dressing-table . . . The air was close, long unused, yet mysteriously living. Miss Rose's room.

He shut the door and tiptoed to his own room. His letter lay snugly where he had left it under the pile of clean handkerchiefs.

'You ask about coming home next holidays,' he read again in the rapid writing that, for the minute, was his mother's speaking-voice, 'but as things are at the moment, one way and another. . . .'

He wanted to cry.

CHAPTER X

'AND did you cry?' asked Mrs. Nelson, some days later.
'Of course not,' Walter defended himself. Nobody must know.

She flicked the ash from her cigarette on to the linoleum of the kitchen floor. 'All I can say is that Jimmy'd howl his eyes out if he couldn't be with me in the holidays. Too right, he would — wouldn't you, Jimmy?'

'What, ma?'

'You can be a real grizzle when you want to be.'

Jimmy twisted round from the window. He opened his right hand and thrust a new shilling under Walter's nose. 'I'm saving up for a bike lamp. Then I can ride at night, see?'

'You don't leave this house after dark,' his mother warned, 'unless I'm with you.'

'You can come too, on the bar.'

'A fine sight I'd look, twelve stone of me, on the bar of a kid's bike in the dark.' She took up a rolling-pin from the table and pushed it fiercely across the dough lumped on a sheet of news-paper before her. 'I'd look better on the seat of that old tricycle Mr. Garnett rides to his choir practices,' she laughed. And she pointed with the rolling-pin at two cups of milk on a corner of the dresser. 'Drink up your milk, both of you.'

'I don't want no milk, ma.'

'All right, Walter can have it. He's skinny enough for a farm-bred kid!' Her brown forearms were smudged with flour. When loose ash from her cigarette fell on the pastry before her she brushed it off impatiently. 'I can see myself going back to a pipe,' she remarked.

'She did smoke a pipe once,' Jimmy informed Walter, grimacing. 'Like a Maori woman does.' And holding the silver shilling against his lips he hallooed at his mother: 'Wa-wa-wa, wahine, wahine, wahine!'

'The only Maori word he ever remembers,' said Mrs. Nelson. 'And God knows where he picked it up.'

'My Dad's a Maori,' Jimmy sang at her. His small sallowish face screwed itself up; his mouth broadened. 'I bet he is.'

'You young tyke, shut up.' She took the cigarette from under her nose and shrugged at Walter. 'This kid of mine . . .' she gave Jimmy up, lazily.

'Wahine, wahine, wa-wa-wa!'

'The Maoris are a fine race, and don't ᵧou forget it. Hard muscles and good white teeth — '

'So have I,' Jimmy retorted.

'You've got everything but sense, you have,' she said evenly. She roofed the pale wad of pastry over the top of a pie-dish full of apples and with a bread knife began to slice at the rim. 'There might be worse than Maoris,' she remarked, 'even on a dark night in the country.'

Walter put down his cup, carefully wiped the milk-moustache from his lips and glanced from the window at the Nelson's rabbits in their hen-house hutches across the yard. The yard was criss-crossed with clothes lines and leaning wooden props. Somewhere, from a nearby section, a dog let out a high forlorn whine like a yawn directed at the empty afternoon sky above the hills. Softly in the distance sounded the sea on the beach.

'Miss Rose is home,' he told Mrs. Nelson. 'She's staying with the Garnetts.'

She gathered up the tails of pastry from the paper under the pie-dish. 'You kids can eat these if you like . . . So Miss Rose is home, is she?' she took Walter up, dusting her hands, searching about for the yellow packet that held her cigarettes. 'When did she turn up?'

'Yesterday. She was there when I got home.'

'Who's she been with, nursing?'

Walter was vague. 'Some people called Fitch, I think, near Timaru.'

'Oh, them.' But Mrs. Nelson looked up sharply. 'I know that family . . . sheep-people . . . or I used to know them years ago. A funny thing, that.' She was silent for a moment, then slammed the oven door on the imprisoned pie. 'Jimmy, I thought you promised to fill me more coal?' She shook the scuttle at him.

Jimmy pocketed his shilling. 'I haven't had time, ma.'

'Well, you've time now. Skip to it, or no apple-pie for you.'

Jimmy trailed out, banging the scuttle against the door to the yard. 'Coal's dotty,' he flung back. 'Maoris cook with hot stones.'

Mrs. Nelson turned to Walter. 'Rose hasn't got herself another beau, I suppose?'

'I dunno,' he said, watching Jimmy in the yard.

'Well, Heavens, she has or she hasn't!' Mrs. Nelson snorted. 'Mind you,' she went on, 'I like Rose. She's got style, not the common type. Came through the old mother, I shouldn't wonder — her with her dropped 'g's'.' She gave a loud squawk of laughter, her blouse bulging and wobbling over her breasts. 'Well,' she said at last, more calmly, 'tell me something about Rose now she's brought herself to come home.'

Walter had seen Miss Rose only twice: he sought in his memory. 'She uses scent,' he said slowly. 'It's like a magnolia.'

'Well, that's something. Though nurses aren't expected to doll themselves up with perfume usually.' Mrs. Nelson folded her arms over her bosom. 'Still, I like expensive scent myself — adds something to a woman if she needs it. Go on.'

'I heard her playing the piano last night, and she sang a bit. I liked it.'

'That's Rose, all right. Cheerful one moment, down the next.'

Walter was silent. From the yard came a distant clatter and banging from the coal shed.

'Well,' Mrs. Nelson brooded, 'fancy Rose at home again,

with that stuffy lot . . . I suppose young Geoff Macaulay hasn't dropped in yet, by any chance?'

'No,' said Walter, surprised.

'He will.' She nodded. 'He married the wrong sister, you know, as I once started to tell you. Hilda, not Rose.' She swept the floury newspaper from the table, crunched it into a ball and poked it, reflectively, into the stove. 'They say women don't make mistakes that way, Walter, but men do — or they can . . . Oh, I hear things. It's not so hard to catch what's going on in a town like this — I go round, you know, doing a bit of washing and ironing in the week, it's my living partly. And I hear things. Mrs. Bristow and Mrs. Jack Peak — Eve Dunn that was — and Mrs. Pascoe on the hill, all clients of mine, and of course I do the sheets for the Andersons, friends of the Garnett girls or used to be, so I hear things all right . . . Anyhow, it was Rose who brought Geoff Macaulay home here to Sumner after his mother's death, poor old girl, wherever she went as a Presbyterian after she passed over. I don't know where they do go unless it's back to Scotland. But it was Rose invited him home — he used to come down in the tram or on a motor bike he had then — and of course, being lonely, he was taken up by all the Garnett daughters, Muriel included . . . If I'd been Rose I'd have announced the engagement while the iron was hot, so to speak, but she didn't do that. Or there was some hitch or the chap was cautious — the Scots are canny — I don't know. But Rose loved him all right. And everyone thought he was set on her, all good and proper.'

Mrs. Nelson paused, pushed up her hair and continued: 'Anyhow, what I was coming to, Walter, was that your Miss Rose took herself off on another nursing job, Waimate way, with a young cripple she'd been to before called Costello or something, an Irish name, and within a month her sister Hilda had hooked young Macaulay for herself. Of course Hilda'd been after him all the time — any donkey with half an eye could've seen that. She's smart, Hilda is, and knows how to put her clothes on. And once Rose was away she caught him. She got him, too right she did. But Lord knows what Rose made of the news when she heard it. I was told she went queer in the head for a time — neurasthenic, they call it nowadays — she's the sensitive kind and took it badly, as she'd a right to. Anyway, she didn't come home for the wedding. Nor has she been back since, till now.' Mrs. Nelson lit a cigarette. 'A lot of people blamed young Macaulay of course. There may've been something odd, something none of us found out. But there it was, he'd given his Rose the slip. Hilda was Mrs. Geoff Macaulay and no mistake.'

Walter had stood by the window, his fingers fidgeting against the sill while he watched the rabbits' scuts bounce behind the wire of the hutches in the yard. He had heard only parts of the story Mrs. Nelson had told him at such tedious length and had not been particularly interested.

'They're scared,' he said now and pointed to the rabbits. 'The noise of the coal's scared them.'

Mrs. Nelson, coming up behind him, banged with the flat of her hand on the window. 'Jimmy,' she bawled to her son through the pane, 'come along! Bring the slack if you can't carry big lumps. God Almighty,' she exclaimed to Walter, 'what's that young devil up to? He's had time to hop to hell and back.'

Jimmy staggered in, his face almost as smudged as though he had returned from a coal mine. 'Great chief Tangi,' he announced himself, baring his white far-apart teeth at Walter as he planted the scuttle beside the range. 'I put on some war-paint, ma. Like it?'

'That's enough of your Maori nonsense. You go wash your face at the sink. And don't blacken the towel either.' She swelled towards him menacingly. 'Making a savage of yourself before Walter.'

'Maoris aren't savages. You said so, ma.'

'No matter what I said. I say a lot of things.' She gave a glance at the clock and another at the sky above the yard. 'If you boys are nippy,' she said, 'you could get to the Post Office before it shuts.' Her fingers ran along the mantelpiece. 'I want some stamps,' she went on, finding a few dusty pennies among the canisters. 'Jimmy, you go buy me some ha'penny stamps.'

'Ma's going to write a letter,' Jimmy teased her from the sink. 'Who're you going to write to, ma?'

'Never you mind. You sluice your face.'

'You're going to write to the copper about me not having a bike lamp.'

'No copper's a friend of mine.'

'Well, you're going to write for tickets for the circus.'

Mrs. Nelson did not answer. 'Go on now,' she said, tipping coal into the stove, 'and Walter with you. You can take your bike; it's not dark yet.'

The two boys left the kitchen. Outside, the air pierced their clothes with a soft pricking of frost. In the yard the rabbits had retired to the back of their hutches for the night: quiet thumps came from the straw.

'The black one's had four babies,' said Jimmy. 'Ma says if she has any more she'll make a pie of them.' He fetched his bicycle from the shed. 'A Maori pie,' he shouted towards the back of the house, provocatively. 'Wa-wa-wa.'

At the gate Walter hoisted himself on to the bicycle's cross-bar. With Jimmy on the seat they wobbled up the empty back-road towards the far end of the town.

'Why does Mr. Garnett have to ride a trike?' Jimmy asked. 'I've seen him go past in the evenings. Gosh, it's funny.'

'He's old,' said Walter. The bar cut coldly into his thighs, through his trousers.

'Couldn't you steal the trike some night?'

'Well, I might,' Walter pondered, 'but he'd find out. Or Miss Muriel would.'

'What'd she do? Slit your gullet?'

'No, but she'd be angry.'

'I'd soon settle her. All ladies ought to be scalped. Who's Miss Rose?'

'Well, she's — ' Walter shifted his legs uncomfortably. 'Your mother knows her,' he said.

The Post Office stood at a junction of roads and tram-lines. On either side, verandas of shops arched over the footpath, making caverns of the windows beneath. A greenish glow of gas-mantles fell upon the tins of the grocer's: the herrings on the marble slab of the fishmonger's winked in the swinging gleam from a ship's hurricane-lamp. Eddies of grit blew along the dry gutters at the foot of the veranda posts. The boys glanced about them like spies. Only a few late shoppers were abroad, walking with heavy baskets in the dusk now settling down from the hills.

Jimmy bought the stamps for his mother. 'It's the same face,' he said, disappointed, his dark eyes examining the stamps in the road. 'It's still King Edward.' The late king's bearded features regarded them distantly above the braid of an admiral's uniform. 'He was head of the British Navy,' Jimmy said.

'And the Army.'

'I bet he was as rich as billy-oh.'

'It's King George now, and Queen Mary.'

With Jimmy's bicycle propped against the wall of the grocer's shop behind them they gazed at the green stamps, turned them over, breathed upon them.

'Three-cornered Cape of Good Hope stamps are the rarest,' Walter said. 'There's only four in the world. They're worth thousands of pounds each.'

'What's worth thousands of pounds?' The question came from a young woman — pretty, even beautiful — who had passed them, hesitated, and now touched Walter's cap lightly with her glove. 'Tell me. Or is it a secret?'

Walter took a step back. 'Miss Rose,' he greeted her, his voice coming out in a shy stutter of embarrassment as he looked at the feather curled round her hat. 'I didn't see you.'

'Oh, I'm just a moth — I came fluttering out of the air!' She laughed gently, then looked past Walter at Jimmy. 'I seem to remember you — ' she teased him with her eyes '— or to have seen you before somewhere.'

'It's Jimmy Nelson,' said Walter.

'He doesn't recognize me.' Her laugh was nervous, even a little wild, as she drew her long coat more closely about her. 'I've been away so long. How's your mother, Jimmy?'

'Ma's all right.'

'I'm glad to hear that.' She glanced up and down the road, stroking her cheek with her glove, as though on the verge of retreating into some trance or mood from which the sight of the two boys had for a moment roused her. 'I've been taking a little exercise after tea,' she murmured. 'A little walk to the places I remember best. I don't know that it's been a great success — everything looks so ordinary!' And she smiled down at Walter and Jimmy as though only they had saved her from the boredom of the solitary expedition. 'Are you boys walking too?'

Jimmy indicated his bicycle. 'It's new,' he fidgeted, and even rang the bell for her. 'Ma gave it to me on my birthday.'

'A lovely bicycle, very smart.' She tilted her head to one side, eyeing it with an air of distinction. 'I suppose,' she teased, 'you've quite given up travelling by tram.'

'Only when ma and I go to the circus in Christchurch,' Jimmy said in a boastful rush. 'Do you ever go to the circus?'

'I? No, I'm always so sorry for animals in cages, you see. The monkeys especially — they're too like humans, poor beasts. Far too similar,' she smiled.

'I like lions and tigers best,' Jimmy said.

Rose Garnett bit her lip. 'No,' she shuddered, 'no.' And after a pause she opened the front of her coat, showing the tailored lapel of her jacket and a sprig of flowers pinned between the buttons. 'Look, Walter, I discovered a couple of violets under the laurestinus in the garden. It's so late for them, a wonder they've survived the cold.' She fingered the flowers streaked with frost-burn, then drew in her breath. Restively, nervously, her glance fled up and down the lamp-lit road. 'Well now,' she announced, 'I'm going home. Will you chaperone me, Walter? Or are you and Jimmy off to the South Pole on that bicycle?'

'Like Captain Scott,' Jimmy took her up. 'Only he had sledges and dogs . . . huskies.'

'Is the South Pole all explored?' Walter asked Miss Rose.

'Oh, I daresay you'd find a new bit, if you looked,' her gloves waved airily. 'Some little island like a wedding cake. What a pity we can't all set off together some morning, just the three of us.'

The two boys laughed, uncertain whether she could mean it. There was another pause, longer. Then Jimmy wheeled his bicycle into the roadway beside the tram-lines. 'I'll scoot home to ma,' he called, his foot on the pedal. His hurried good nights floated back to them as he dived off, whistling, into the dusk.

'He hasn't got a lamp,' Walter explained, 'so he can't be out late because of the police.'

'I see.' With a small ironical smile she began to stroll beside him. 'What a very dark boy he's become . . . Is he your pal or chum or whatever you call it?'

'Yes,' said Walter. They walked on. 'Why?' he asked.

'Oh, only at your age . . . the attachments of the heart,' she faltered, then pulled on her gloves, shivering. 'But it's all a drift, a dream without passion . . . a thistledown,' she smiled.

Walter looked about him, at the tram-lines, the telegraph poles, the bungalows awake with lights glimpsed between paling fences and hedges of dusty macrocarpa beside the road. He was proud to be walking with Miss Rose. At the same time, because he travelled this road every day in the tram, he wished for something more exciting, special to the occasion and to her.

'We could walk along the beach,' he suggested. 'We could pass the Cave Rock.'

'No,' she said quickly. 'Not the beach.' She looked down at her long skirt. 'Not tonight.'

'The sand wouldn't dirty your shoes.'

'It isn't that. But there's always a wind from the sea — it might be chilly.'

'Don't you like the Cave Rock?'

'Oh, yes, but there are places . . . I remember it well — '

Two elderly women carrying small straw baskets passed them on the footpath. Surprised, the two smiled at Walter's companion, hesitated, then walked on, their faces conferring under large hats.

'The Miss Andersons,' Miss Rose murmured to Walter. 'Friends of mother's who know everything and everybody.' She uttered her trembling uncertain laugh. 'Don't ever live in a township, Walter. It's poison.'

He had followed his own thoughts. 'I met Mr. Macaulay on the beach,' he said now.

'You met . . . ? When?' She slowed her step.

He could not remember exactly. 'A month ago. The day he and Mrs. Hilda came to tea.'

'And how do you get on with — with Geoffrey?'

The Christian name disturbed him. 'He bought me some liquorice straps.'

'I see.' Miss Rose chuckled. 'That's a recommendation I must remember.' The lit windows of a passing tram flickered over her pale face. 'And what did you find to talk about, you and Geoffrey?'

Again he couldn't remember. 'He said you'd been — you'd nursed his mother.'

'I did, yes.' She jerked up her chin, then lowered it to sniff the violets inside her coat. 'She died of pneumonia, poor woman, though I did my best for weeks to save her.'

'What's pneumonia?'

'Something old people can die of.'

'Is it fun being a nurse?'

'I'd hardly call it fun,' she deliberated. 'Far from it, often. It depends on your . . . well, your temperament.' She glanced down at him beside her, at the red peak of his cap. 'I can see that you're rather like me, Walter — we're both wanderers between the stubble and the sown.'

'Is that poetry?'

'Well — it might mean we're both rather on our own, as persons, mightn't it?' And she continued abruptly: 'Do you get on well with my sister Muriel at home?'

'Yes.'

'And my father doesn't bully you, either in school or out?' She spoke lightly.

'He can be cross sometimes.' Walter was uncertain of his ground. 'If I don't do my French — '

'Shall I tell you something? My father's a disappointed man, very. He meant to found a big public school, like the English Etons and Harrows, here in New Zealand, but it never happened, somehow. Not enough money or prestige — or both, I don't know — and too big a family round his neck: Mark and Hilda and Muriel and I. The first school he opened, in Riccarton, was burnt, burnt to the ground; he lost everything. And now it's only this little preparatory place you go to in St. Mary's Street — he's left with that, and his pride. I love him for his pride.' Her voice suddenly quivered. 'I don't know why I tell you all this, except that you must never despise him — or indeed despise any of us, or anybody.'

'I don't,' he said, puzzled by her tone.

'Not me, even. Not even a single unhappy person.'

They reached the side-road leading to the Garnetts' gate. In the distance, under a lamp standard, two boys Walter did not know were kicking a football, their voices echoing in the frost of the twilight.

'Give me your hand, Walter, till we get in.'

He felt her gloved hand grope for his fingers while his boots crunched over the cinders of the kitchen path. 'Tell me some more about Jimmy Nelson,' she suggested easily. 'Your dark little friend with the bicycle. Tell me something to make me laugh.'

'He put coal on his face to look like a Maori chief.'

'I'm not surprised, though perhaps Mrs. Nelson might . . .'
She swung up his hand and inspected it suddenly in the starlight.
'I thought so — you've got chilblains.'

'I catch them on the tram.'

'You must let me massage them for you. We can't have you
with broken hands.' Her voice had become professional, taut.

'They don't itch much. Only sometimes in bed.'

'Muriel must let us have a bowl of really hot water. I'm
surprised she hasn't done something already . . .' She halted,
still holding his hand, and glanced up at the light of the kitchen
window and at the back door in the yard. 'Come,' she said
suddenly, with a kind of revulsion, 'let's use the front entrance,
for once.' She drew him along the side of the house, trembling
with her odd nervous soft laughter. 'It's the front door for us,
Walter. We'll be the bold ones, the irregulars, the crackers of
convention. We'll show them.'

CHAPTER XI

THE tram, sweeping round a curve of the road below the hills, met the wind from the sea, a shrieking wind that pierced the crevices of the windows and floors and exploded in dust and crumpled tickets under the seats. The passengers turned up their coat collars, shivered, braced themselves against the coldest month of the winter. A gleam of snow from the mountain ranges inland lay on the frozen dome of the sky, reflecting its paleness upon the mud-flats and sand-bars of the estuary.

'The war in South Africa was something different, an imperialist scrap,' Geoffrey Macaulay asserted to his father-in-law beside him. 'A threat of war in Europe's a much more serious affair.'

The lilt of his voice rose above the wind and reached Walter in his seat at the rear of the tram. Tonight there had been no trailer attached to the main vehicle: he had been obliged to squeeze himself in behind the front car passengers and only just to the rear of Mr. Garnett and the young architect. The two men did not usually travel to Sumner on the same tram: Mr. Macaulay often made the journey in his own car, later in the evening.

'A serious affair,' he repeated, drawing his neck into the collar of his tweed overcoat and stuffing the evening paper he had been reading into his pocket. 'I wouldn't be surprised if the Kaiser's behind it, as usual, sir.'

'I doubt if the Germans, troublesome as they are, would bother to murder an Archduke in Serbia,' Mr. Garnett mildly objected. 'The Kaiser, after all, may be assumed to be a gentleman.'

'I wouldn't assume it. I don't trust the man.' Geoffrey

Macaulay laughed. 'Ah, but we know so little, out here,' he went on, smoothing his moustache. 'And I should say that most people in this country are as ignorant as I am. How many of us know what England's commitments are, for instance?'

'England's commitments, Geoffrey, are to preserve a balance of power in Europe. It's been her policy for decades ... But a general war of nations is unthinkable, barbaric.' The old man straightened his drooping shoulders. 'Wars are interruptions to the progress of civilization — a fact I am always trying to point out in my teaching of history at school. In any case, I see no reason whatsoever — and discounting the news in your evening paper — why England or the Empire should be involved in a war at present. Any quarrel Austria may provoke upon her minions is her own local affair entirely.'

The younger man looked out to sea: he was never, it was plain, quite at home with his father-in-law, an older generation from an older land: both of them talked to pass the time, for a family link. They had little in common. And with a sense of relief, looking from the tram window, he saw the causeway leading to Sumner ahead of them.

'I came home a wee bit earlier today,' he remarked, super-fluously. 'Hilda didn't seem herself this morning when I left.'

The old man said warmly: 'I'm glad Hilda's to have this child, Geoffrey.'

'The child ... aye, yes ... there's that.' He took off his cap, brushed a hand over the crisp bright hair on his forehead and replaced the cap thoughtfully. 'Yes,' he said again.

In the pause, Mr. Garnett turned to glance behind him at the slatted seats. 'Is that pupil of mine on the tram?' he muttered. 'Young Blakiston?'

'He's there all right.' The other, too, looked round and grinned at Walter. 'Do you want him?'

'No, no. But Muriel said the boy had a cold this morning. I was to see that he wore his scarf ... I'd forgotten.'

Walter had wrapped the knitted scarf round his mouth: he

was engaged in exploring the damp wool with the tip of his tongue, between dry lips. His cold had come upon him the day before, with a soreness in the roof of his throat, uncomfortable. Now, his hands hidden under the satchel on his knees, he was pierced by sharp pins of fever. His eyes ached. Of the two men's conversation during the tram ride from Christchurch only a few sentences, almost unintelligible to him, had reached his ears. An archduke had been killed somewhere in Serbia (a country with small reddish stamps not easily swoppable); that was all of importance. He was glad when the tram had neared Sumner and he could see the black pyramid of the Cave Rock against the whipped-up surf of the bay. A storm-cone flew from the mast at the summit of the Rock. And now the tram ran smoothly between the first houses, the shops and bungalows, the lights of the township. Ten minutes later he had reached the Garnetts' back door and, wiping the drips from his sore nose, was in the presence of Miss Muriel.

'Let me look at you.' She unwound the scarf from his neck, turning his face to the lamp. 'Yes, you do look a bit seedy. You'd better sit here in the kitchen tonight, it's warmer. Hang up your coat now.'

Obediently he hung up his coat. The door from the yard creaked open.

'Are you frozen, father?' Miss Muriel took the old man's umbrella. 'Shall we have snow?'

'It's in the wind. The ranges inland are white enough.' He shook himself, settling his stout body into an indoor shape. 'Geoffrey was on the tram,' he remarked. 'Hilda hasn't been too well, I gather.'

'Her heart perhaps. Was Geoff well himself?'

'A trifle jumpy, I thought. We talked about this murder in Serbia a few days ago.' He took an evening paper from his dispatch case and dabbed at the black headlines with a finger.

'Archdukes are murdered every day,' she said and put the paper aside. 'They probably deserve it.'

'I hope not, Muriel, I hope not.' He ambled towards the door to the dining-room. 'Mother in good spirits?'

'She's been having a serious talk with Rose, father.'

'Why serious?'

'Oh,' she shrugged, 'you know how moody and difficult Rose can be. Only that.'

'You children must be happy . . . Has Rose been up to visit Hilda?'

'Not yet.' Miss Muriel fingered the mole above her lip, unhappily. 'She won't go. I'm worried about her, father. . . .'

After dinner Walter sat himself in the warmth of the range, the exercise-books of his homework open before him on the kitchen table. His head felt as though it had been blown up with a bicycle-pump. His nose had begun to run continuously: his sopped handkerchief was so far beyond absorption that presently he let the drops fall unchecked to the oilcloth of the table, idly pushing them into a pool with the point of his pencil. The twang of the piano reached him from the front of the house — from the room nobody sat in but which was called the drawing-room. Miss Rose had not shown herself at dinner, had not been mentioned. He pushed aside the exercise-books, unstrapped his satchel, and taking out his *History of England* opened it at the grubby page marked for preparation.

'The Vikings, intrepid marauders, now commenced regular raids upon the open coasts to the east . . .' he read, and read again. He knew neither the meaning of the words 'intrepid marauders' nor how to pronounce them. His mind wandered, his nose dripped, arrowy shivers ran up and down his back and loins. 'The Vikings, intrepid marauders,' he tried again, without caring. Did those Vikings, in their damp open boats, never catch cold? He thrust the *History* away, turned elsewhere for comfort.

'Are you all right, Walter?' Miss Muriel bustled in upon him. 'Are you working, dear?'

'Yes.' He would have liked to have joined Miss Rose at the

piano. 'I can't do my homework,' he said miserably. 'Can I play with my stamps?'

'Well,' she was doubtful, 'yes, I think you might as you're off colour.' She brushed back his forelock and left him.

His stamp collection was kept in the special drawer allotted to him in the dresser for his books and Meccano. Now he spread the album open before him, first wiping the oilcloth with his sleeve to avoid staining the green cover. The picture-stamps were his favourites and to these he turned at once: the giraffes of Nyasaland, the orang-utans and toucans of Borneo, the volcanoes of the mid-American republics. As though by the leaps and levitations of dreams they carried him into a region of his own atmosphere, his own choice, where the colours were almost the four primaries — sun-yellow, sea-green, black, amethyst. But his favourite of all — and he flicked over the pages, seeking it — came not from abroad but from his own country: the picture of a sapphire-coloured lake, Lake Wakatipu in the south, a lake fringed with shrubs and fronds of native bush and with snow-pointed mountains beyond, across the water. He could lose himself in this scene, as, seated at the kitchen table, he indeed lost himself now. The mysterious lake was before him, the water lapped the shore, the mountains cut the sky, the snow was cool to the hand . . . cool to the hot fever of his eyes and body. His eyelids drooped, he leant forward over the table, his fingers loosened and quivered.

'Time you went to bed, Walter.' It was not Miss Muriel's voice, as he had expected, but the lighter, gayer tones of Miss Rose. 'You're drowsy.' She came from behind him, laid a hand on his forehead. 'Yes, I think I'll take your temperature.'

'It's only my cold,' he sniffed.

'Wait, I'll fetch a thermometer.' He heard her run upstairs, pause in her room. Two minutes later the glass tube poked at the flesh under his tongue.

'Keep still,' she said. 'Don't wriggle and don't bite.' She

watched the kitchen clock. 'Now,' she whispered at last and with the thermometer pinched elegantly between finger and thumb bent her head sideways under the lamp.

'What does it say?'

'It says that boys with a little fever put their stamps away and go straight to bed.'

'Why,' he asked, closing the drawer of the dresser on the album, 'why, if lakes are blue, is there a colour called Crimson Lake?'

She laughed. 'I've no notion, Walter. Come, I'll tell Muriel I'm going to put you to bed. You're my patient.' She shepherded him into the dark hall, then ran ahead to fetch a lamp from her room while he mounted the stairs.

'Is there going to be a war?' he sniffled as she undressed him. 'Is there, Miss Rose?'

'A war? Where?'

The sheets made him shiver uncontrollably. 'I heard Mr. Macaulay talking on the tram.' His teeth chattered. 'On the way home,' he added.

She folded away his clothes, then absently turned down the wick of the lamp. 'I can't imagine what Geoffrey knows about wars . . . Was he alone on the tram?'

'Except for Mr. Garnett . . .' Walter pulled his knees up to his chin. 'If there's a war — ' he pursued.

'Wars don't happen now.'

'No, but if there is one, I've designed a submarine,' he reflected aloud. 'The top's made of mica so the men can see through it. I've made a drawing.'

'Did Geoffrey — Mr. Macaulay — did he ask after me, Walter? Ask if I was at home?'

'No. I've drawn a lighthouse too, with a sort of magnetic telescope in the top, for seeing ships below the horizon.'

Her pale oval face stared at the lamp. 'You're dreaming,' she said quietly and rubbed her forehead as though in pain. 'I'll leave you now, Walter.'

'Don't go.' He longed for her to stay with him till he slept. 'Stay with me.'

'Well . . .' She sat down on the bed. 'A moment then. What is it, or are you missing your mother?' She bent forward and almost touched his cheek with her lips. 'Or was there something you really wanted to tell me? A message from . . . anyone — '

'Message?'

'It doesn't matter. It's nothing. Only an answer to a note.' She brushed the words aside in agitation, as soon as they had been uttered. 'Well, what shall we talk about?'

'Did you ever collect stamps when you were young?'

'I'm not so ancient now,' she laughed. 'No, not stamps. But Hilda and I, when we were at school, used to cut pictures out of English papers and paste them in a book. I can't imagine why . . .' She gazed at the white tulip-shade of the lamp. 'We both had a passion for pictures of young officers — Scottish mostly — in the Army and Navy. Oh, it was silly, so fatuous. Then one day Hilda hid the collection and I've never seen it since . . . Hilda and I are twins — did you know that? Not identical twins; the other. For that reason I suppose there's something in us feels drawn to the same sort of people.'

There were footsteps on the stairs. 'Are you up here, Rose?'

'I'm here, Muriel. Getting this boy settled.' She went out to the landing. 'What is it?' Walter heard her ask coldly.

'Will he be all right in the night? Comfortable?'

'If he wants anything he can tap on my wall. I'll hear him, I sleep lightly.'

Walter awoke once in the night. The lamp had gone from the table: a wedge of moonlight lay along the window-sill beneath the blind. Through the wall he could hear sounds that, in his fever, he at first thought were subdued bursts of laughter. But it was a sound of sobs, bitter and stifled, that came to merge into his confused dreams of the shore and the mountains, the lapping waves, of a lake with sapphire water.

CHAPTER XII

'Rose and I don't think you should go to school for a day or so, Walter,' Miss Muriel said to him in the morning. 'I've spoken to father and he'll mark you absent. Do you see, dear?'

'Yes,' he mumbled over his breakfast. His head felt no less thick and bursting than it had the night before: the bacon in his mouth tasted like wool. He glanced at Miss Rose. 'I needn't stay in bed, need I?'

'No,' said Rose. 'If you wrap up you can sit on the veranda or walk in the garden.' She took a slice of toast from the rack. 'It won't hurt you to be idle for once.' But her eyes ceased laughing and flickered towards her sister. 'That's of course if Muriel agrees.'

'He's your patient, Rose. I won't interfere.'

'You weren't interfering.' Miss Rose crumbled the dry toast on her plate. 'I didn't imply that for a moment. Though of course interfering is an art you're familiar with, as we know.'

'Must you say that again?'

'Yes.' She rubbed her forehead. 'I must say it again. I never forget it.' Her lips trembled. 'However — '

The sisters were silent. Behind them old Mr. Garnett ambled in from the hall, his gold watch open in his hand, his overcoat drooping from his shoulders. He had finished his breakfast before Walter's late arrival from upstairs.

'Have you got your umbrella, father?' Miss Muriel sprang up. 'And a clean handkerchief?'

'I have, my dear. The old ship's ready to sail.'

She kissed him. 'I'll get mother up when I've lit the fire. And I'll look after Walter.'

'Where's Rose? I must say goodbye to Rose.'

'Here, father.' Miss Rose's smooth arms went round his neck. 'Now don't get chilled on the tram.' She patted his waistcoat, straightening the buttons. 'Too many puddings.'

'Too many years,' he murmured and was gone, his boots crunching over the cinders of the yard.

'I hate the school,' Miss Rose said suddenly and passionately. She wiped her eyes and sat down again. 'I hate it.'

'He'd be lost without it. It's his life.'

'He's over sixty; well over . . . I was shocked to see him so old, when I came home. Though mother had aged more perhaps.'

'I don't notice it,' Miss Muriel said, 'seeing them all the time. They always seem the same to me.'

The other did not reply. Presently she left the dining-room; her footsteps rang light and quick on the stairs.

Walter finished his breakfast. 'I heard Miss Rose crying in the night,' he said suddenly, blowing his nose. 'At least I think I did.'

Miss Muriel did not look at him. 'You had a little temperature,' she said evenly, as though in explanation.

He waited a moment, regretting that he had spoken. 'Is that silver stuff in the thermometer poisonous?'

'I've never tasted it, Walter. It might be.' She took his plate from before him. 'I think you'd better run up now and tidy your room.'

He took himself slowly upstairs, counting the treads. In his room cold air blew through the open window, the blind flapped. Frost had laid an edge of icing on the veranda roof below and had whitened the lawn and the hedge beyond. He folded up his pyjamas.

'Walter,' Miss Rose's voice called along the landing. 'Come in here a moment.'

'Yes?' he said at the door of her room.

'Talk to me. Cheer me up.'

With a duster in her hand she stood by the brass bedrail, her supple waist bent above her long skirt, her cheeks almost as pale as the frost outside. 'I'm feeling lonely,' she said. 'And I always hate the mornings, the horrible beginning of the day.'

He looked from her face to the dressing-table. A silver-backed brush, a small scent bottle with a glass stopper, a scatter of hair-pins, a pair of china candlesticks with ivy-leaf scallops. 'Do the people you nurse give you things?' he asked. 'Presents?'

'Often. One farmer's wife even gave me a pet lamb, once. But I had to leave that behind: lambs grow into sheep.' She smiled and picked up the bottle of scent from the table. 'The people I've just come from in Timaru gave me this.'

'It's strong. Is it magnolias?'

'Lily of the valley.' She sniffed the stopper. 'Expensive rather than good. Too lemony.'

'I can't smell because of my cold.'

'Poor Walter.'

'Mrs. Nelson,' he told her presently, 'said she knew the people in Timaru — the ones you've just been with — the Fitches.'

'Yes ... oddly enough they told me about her when they heard I came from Sumner. They remembered her.' She shook the duster from the window. 'She used to work in the house there ... a maid or a cook, I've forgotten. But that was ages ago. She married a shearer or a rouseabout on the station. It caused rather a stir.'

'Would that man — the shearer — would he be Jimmy's father?' he asked.

She glanced at herself in the glass of the dressing-table, touching the boned collar of her blouse. 'I expect Mrs. Nelson would know the answer to that,' she said lightly. 'Ask her some day, I'm sure she'd tell you.' And she caught sight of his face in the glass, watching her. 'Your nose looks red, Walter. Is it very sore?'

'Only when I blow it hard.'

'Wait — ' she opened a drawer ' — I'll put a dash of lanoline on it for you.'

The whitish ointment was cool on his upper lip, his nostrils.

95

'Lanoline comes from sheep's wool,' she said. 'Did you know that?'

'What sort of sheep?'

'I don't know, Mr. Farmer's-Son.' She held up the handglass in front of his face. 'There, see yourself with a sticky nose! Has your mother ever told you you have a nice nose and may be a handsome man?'

Walter turned away, embarrassed. He was not interested in his appearance. 'Why did you get ratty with Miss Muriel at breakfast?' he inquired.

'Ah, these questions . . .' She became suddenly serious, her petulant upper lip tightened. 'Muriel and I have an old score to settle,' she said abruptly. 'Nothing you'd understand.'

'Is it about Mr. Macaulay?'

'I said you wouldn't understand, Walter.'

Later in the morning he took himself out to the veranda, unfolded the frame of a deck chair and sat muffled up in his coat, his Meccano on a wicker table at his side. The sun, low in the sky, shone warmly on his chilblained hands; the rough grass of the lawn sparkled with frost. A few bare twisted twigs of honeysuckle hung below the iron roof of the veranda. Presently he bent above the cogs, the wheels, the flanges of his Meccano and began fitting them into a pattern, the shape of a small crane, following the instructions in the book. From inside the dining-room came the scrape of a broom, then the emerging voices of a quarrel already begun:

'Why should I admit it?'

'Only the fact that we're sisters — or have you again conveniently overlooked that tie?'

'If he chose Hilda, I couldn't stop him, Rose. I couldn't *kill* him, could I.'

'It might have been better for him — for both of us — if you had.'

'Oh, Rose. . . .'

'I'll never forgive you, Muriel. Never.'

96

There was a long pause. Chairs were lifted across the room, the broom knocked on the skirting. Walter fitted a cog to a spindle, in silence.

'If you came home simply to accuse me —'

'You should accuse yourself: every day. I don't blame Geoffrey so much. But you, yes — every time.'

'Don't talk like that, Rose. Don't, please.'

'How can I help it? It was you who interfered.'

'Even if I did, I can't bear being hated for it. The way you look at me — no — Hilda had some blame, after all.'

'Hilda didn't show those letters. And you know it.'

'But, Rose, for you to go on in this hysterical state —'

'I loved him! I love him now! *Love* him — do you understand? Those letters meant nothing — simply the infatuation of a crippled kid I'd helped. If you'd had any real true feeling for me — for Geoffrey — you wouldn't have —'

'Rose, listen. I won't have you shouting at me —'

'You stole those letters from my room — you gave them to him —'

'Very well, I admit it. But not to spite you, Rose, not really.'

'Why then? Why?'

Walter sneezed: a wheel rolled from his Meccano to the boards of the veranda. The door behind him was abruptly pulled to. He heard no more.

The air was too cold for him to sit still. Presently he got up, blew on his fingers, jumbled the pieces of his Meccano together and restively wandered away from the veranda, over the lawn. At the very far end of the garden, shadowed by the boughs of a pine tree, stood a wooden shed with a blistered tin roof. Until this moment he had never properly explored its musty dark interior, its cluttered treasure of abandoned hen-coops, spades, rakes, battens of rotting timber, piles of broken flower pots, shards of ancient ironwork. Now, peering in from the doorway, he saw that beyond the silent company of these relics, propped in a further corner but accessible, stood a curiously curved frame: a contraption: a vehicle more fantastic than any contrived from his Meccano. It was, he told himself with amazement, a bicycle. But what a bicycle! Stranger almost than Mr. Garnett's tricycle. The enormous high front wheel was partnered at the back by a second no larger than a saucer: the seat was perched aloft like the blackened skull of a bird: the narrow tyres had perished into grey threads: the spokes were thickened, confused with spiders' webs. The whole aspect of the thing was that of a skeleton from some former age, settling into oblivion here in the shed. Walter edged himself towards it, he touched it, he pulled it a little away from the wall. The major wheel, the front one, was as high as his own head. Only a tiny step, a vestige of rusted steel, sprouted from the backbone of the frame and led to the insecurity of the seat. He raised his arm and fingered the straight cross-bar of the handle, the spokes, the tyres.

But to ride such a bicycle — how was it done? It would be as difficult as riding a hoop. Even Jimmy Nelson, that expert on bicycles, might be baffled. Could they, between them, steal this odd relic one evening, rather than Mr. Garnett's tricycle, and make experiments? And might not he, Walter, find himself a hero in Jimmy's eyes simply because of his access to this find? With his nose dripping to the floor of the shed, Walter pondered.

'Walter, where are you? Do you want a cup of milk, Walter?' Miss Muriel's voice sought for him across the lawn. 'Coo-ee!'

'I'm coming,' he called, and thrust the bicycle back against the wall. 'Just coming.'

He left the shed. Across the grass of the lawn the weatherboards of the house seemed to vibrate in the pinkish winter sunlight. The gables poked forward under the frosted iron slopes of the roof, their paint peeling. Beyond the house rose the familiar hills of volcanic rock, their scars and outcrops healed over with tussock, with gorse, with tawny grass, below a sky as hard as an enamel lid.

'Where have you been, dear? I called you twice.'

He took the cup of milk between his hands. 'I wasn't far.' And he asked about the bicycle in the shed.

'That old penny-farthing!' She pushed back the wings of her hair. 'Good Heavens, that was father's bone-shaker before I was born,' she laughed.

'Penny-farthing,' he repeated. The name delighted him.

'It came out with him from England in the sailing ship.'

'Could I ride it?'

'I wouldn't, no. It's dangerous. In fact,' she said with a mild strictness, 'I forbid you.' She took the empty cup from him. 'Why don't you find a book to read, if you're bored with yourself?'

'I'm not,' he said, offended, and turned as Miss Rose came into the kitchen. She wore her coat and feathered hat.

'I'm going out, Muriel,' she said quietly.

'Why don't you stay and talk to mother?'

'I can't. I must get out.'

'You can't go walking about by yourself, Rose.'

'Why not?' She turned fiercely on her sister. 'Why ever not? I'm not a child, like Walter here.'

'I'll come with you, Miss Rose,' he offered.

She refused. 'You stay at home and keep warm.'

'Rose — ' Miss Muriel followed her to the door. 'Rose,' she implored, 'can't I do something for you? Anything?'

'Nothing, thank you.' Her voice trembled into an airy laugh. 'There's no need to play the good Samaritan, I assure you. I'm quite proficient at saving myself. Only leave me alone.'

'I'm sorry about our quarrel this morning.'

Rose shook her head, sudden tears glistened in her eyes. 'No,' she murmured, 'oh, no . . .' She turned away, clutched at her gloves and was gone.

Walter took himself back to the veranda. The Meccano still lay on the table: he finished making the crane, then dismantled it, carefully fitting the plates and wheels into their green-lined

99

box, the nuts into their mica lid. And presently, at a loss, he fetched one of his books from the dresser-drawer in the kitchen: he would lose himself in a world more real than that of the Garnetts'. The sun had grown warmer under the veranda roof. He opened the book at the place he had marked two days before.

Everyone on the island was up and about early next morning, he read. *There was little for breakfast but biscuits and strips of salted beef, washed down with coco-nut milk drunk straight from the nuts themselves, into which Bernard and his father had driven the point of a stick sharpened with the knife belonging to the Scotch bo'sun. The sun cast the shadows of the palms on the sand, for already the fiery orb was some way above the horizon of the clear heavens of this latitude. The combers from the ocean thundered on the coral reefs surrounding the lagoon. As the marooned family and the survivors of the crew of the* Jolly Mary *sat in a rough circle, partaking of their frugal repast with the relish born of relief that they at least had escaped the dire fate of their vessel, a bird uttered a strange chuckling whistle from one of the palms overhead.*

'Is it not wonderful, Bernard,' said Mr. Branksome, 'that birds should find their way across the uncharted waste of seas to this island?'

'It is wonderful indeed, father,' the youth replied as he ate his biscuit in the shade. 'I suppose it would be Providence, would it not?'

Mr. Branksome was pleased with his son's sober turn of mind in their predicament. 'The bird is healthy and cheerful,' he said, 'wherever its home may be and wherever the eye of God may rest upon it.' He lifted his own eyes to those of his wife, who sat beside the breakfast spread on the sands. 'We too, my love, shall find a way, aided by Him, to exist on this deserted island.'

'I have seen some turtles, sir,' now interposed the bo'sun. 'I have heard it said that fine soup may be made from such animals. They may support us.'

'Yes, Angus,' said Mr. Branksome, 'turtles may certainly be caught and may yield us some sustenance.'

'I too have seen the turtles,' piped little Tom, from his mother's side, 'and Angus showed me where they have laid their eggs in the

sand. We saw them early today before the rest of you had awakened.'

'Turtles and coco-nut milk,' exclaimed Mrs. Branksome with pleasure. 'I am sure we shall manage for a time upon such ample fare.' She looked with the gratitude of the destitute upon the bo'sun's rough features. 'I do not like inoffensive animals to be slaughtered,' she said, 'but if the turtles are to be our only meat — '

'I shall see to it, ma'am,' replied the Scotsman. 'Depend upon me. If Master Bernard there will assist my plans.'

'May Tom accompany us, father?' asked Bernard. 'It will not be a difficult expedition.'

'And I will keep very quiet,' cried little Tom. 'I will not shout to frighten the turtles,' he promised Mr. Branksome as the latter threw a questioning glance towards his wife.

'Very well, Tom,' Mr. Branksome said, 'you may go with Angus and Bernard. The rest of the crew will no doubt aid me in building a tent against the sun, while you are away.'

'We will, sir,' and a chorus of 'Aye, aye' came from the ragged men seated on the sand around the Branksome family.

'Good fellows,' said Mr. Branksome, 'I can see that in no time at all we shall be as comfortable here as in our own dear homes across the sea.' Wiping a tear from his eyes, for he was a man of sudden senti-ment, he handed back the knife he had borrowed from the bo'sun. 'Go, do your work on the turtles,' he instructed the man.

'I will, sir,' promised the faithful Scot, rising —

Walter looked up from the book. Somebody, not from the island, had come round the end of the house and was approaching the veranda: a woman in a grey coat and a hat with a feather.

'It's too chilly for you out here,' Miss Rose said. 'Muriel ought to have called you indoors. What are you reading?'

In a dream of the island, he handed her the book. 'It's a stunner,' he said. 'They're going to eat turtles' eggs.'

'Rather they than I.' Her cheeks were flushed, a restless fever seemed to sharpen the soft angles of her body. 'Oh,' she sighed beside him, 'I've been for such a long walk, Walter. Simply miles. And right to the tiptop of the Cave Rock.'

'They're going to dig the turtles out of the sand,' he told her, 'and slice them up.'

'Ah, that's cruel.' She seized one of his hands between her gloves. 'I've done nothing about these chilblains of yours. Come in with me now.'

'The island was in the tropics, Miss Rose,' he said, following her.

'And did the inhabitants have chilblains?'

'No,' he said solemnly.

And while she kneaded his fingers in the bowl of steaming water he went on: 'There's a Scotsman with them — the bo'sun called Angus.'

'Is he a kind Scotsman?'

'He's called helpful in the book.'

'Well, that's something . . . The Scotsmen I know are apt to be cruel.' Her hands clenched his in the water. 'Am I hurting you?'

'Yes,' he winced.

'I didn't mean to.' She drew in her breath. 'Do you always get so engrossed in the people in books; the characters?'

'Yes,' he said, and sneezed over the basin.

'And their actions — what they do?'

'These people,' he said and was once more upon the island, 'are named Branksome. They drink out of coco-nuts, and Mr. Angus —'

'Yes,' she broke in, 'tell me about him. Tell me about that damnable Scot — tell me the worst.'

CHAPTER XIII

'Ten days away from school,' said Mrs. Nelson, 'that's quite a holiday. Let's have a look at you.' With an ample warm caress of her hand she turned his face towards the window of her kitchen. 'No pimples, anyway. And a chin as smooth as the back of an apple.'

'I came to see Jimmy,' said Walter, evasively.

She tapped on the window. 'Jimmy,' her voice yelled across the yard and the clothes-lines. 'Come in here. Hurry, it's Walter.'

A muffled whistle came from behind the pine tree against the back fence.

'He'll be on the privy,' Mrs. Nelson told Walter. 'It's his day . . . Syrup of figs . . .' She gave such a large heave of laughter that Walter drew back. 'It's in the family,' she said and, subsiding into anxiety, opened the door into the yard. 'Are you wearing your coat, Jimmy?' she bawled.

'Yes, ma.'

'Well, keep yourself covered.' She shut the door. 'I have to keep an eye on him, Walter,' she confided. 'He'd go stark naked, bottom and all, if he had his way. No more shame than a cannibal.' She patted her thick hair. 'Don't run away . . . Come into the front room for a change.'

He followed her along the central passage of the bungalow.

'Nothing grand,' she said, opening a varnished door, 'but as comfortable as the Garnetts', I daresay. Don't skid on the lino with your boots.' She urged him into the little parlour. 'Too dark,' she clucked, pulling up the blind. 'Let there be light.'

Walter looked about him shyly.

'Why, you're blushing,' she teased. 'Was it because I said something out of that old Bible?'

He fought back. 'It's only my cold, still.'

'Never mind; you're better.' She opened an inch of window. 'Give you some air, anyway. We've all got to breathe.'

The room was full of a stuffy green light from the garden. Bamboo furniture stood rigidly on the polished floor. In the mirror above the mantelshelf a pair of flamingoes stalked across a swamp, among flower-topped reeds. There were reeds again on the tiles of the grate, behind a copper vase holding plumes of yellow-grey toi-toi. The clock had only one hand, pointing to twelve.

'Quite a boudoir, isn't it?' Mrs. Nelson creaked her weight on to the bamboo couch, drawing the boy down beside her. 'Don't you like being cuddled?' she asked presently.

'No,' he said, in doubt. 'Not much, really.'

'You're a bit young yet.' But her brown, clean-scented forearm remained round his shoulder. 'Jimmy likes it all right, but he's a trifle older. He's a sensual young devil, or will be.' She drew in a deep amused breath. 'Now, loosen your collar, Walter, and tell me news of the Garnetts. I saw Rose out walking one day . . . one morning it was . . . the wind blowing her hat on the beach. How is she?'

'All right.' Walter stared at the flamingoes in the mirror. 'Are they painted behind or in front?'

'Those birds? In front. Is Rose happy?'

After a moment of reluctance he said: 'I think she cries sometimes. Not often.'

'Ah.' Mrs. Nelson gave such an emphatic nod that the couch shook. 'The poor creature . . . Never tamper with a woman's heart — it's all some of us have, Walter.'

'I haven't tampered with it.'

'Oh, not you. Somebody else, I meant.' She paused, found a cigarette under her apron and lit it. 'I suppose she'll know by this time that Hilda's carrying this kid. He can't leave her now.'

'What kid?' he asked.

'Well, if you've seen her, it's plain enough. Furs, lace, long coats — you can't hide everything, though it's early enough yet.'

'Miss Rose?'

'Glory, no! Geoff Macaulay's wife.' She puffed laughter and smoke towards the clock. 'You boys from the country want your eyes skinned . . . You ought to've seen me before Jimmy was born — as big as a traction-engine, Walter.' And she leant down to take off one of her shoes. 'Corns,' she complained, rubbing her foot. 'I slice them off and they come back on me as regular as Monday's wash.'

'But if Mrs. Hilda — ' he began, vaguely disturbed.

Jimmy's round face, with its walnut eyes, appeared in the doorway. He greeted Walter. 'Can I have something to eat now, ma? I've done.'

'Food! In one end and out the other.' She poked her foot into the discarded shoe and heaved herself up. 'The dignity of the human race, I don't think,' she grumbled, shepherding the two boys into the kitchen. 'You can both of you have a buttered scone.'

Walter watched her fetch a knife and spread the thick yellow butter. 'Some people I read about eat turtles,' he remarked.

'Turtles?' Jimmy came alive at once. 'How did they cook them? On stones?'

'Dunno, but they made soup. It was on a desert island, see.'

'Gosh, why couldn't we go there?'

Walter had another surprise in reserve. 'I've found a bicycle in the Garnetts' shed,' he told Jimmy as they ate the scones. 'A high one, rusty. A penny-farthing.'

Jimmy was mystified. 'Do you mean it cost that?'

Walter explained. 'But it's too tall to ride, I think.'

'I'll ride it. You bet I will.' Jimmy leant to Walter's ear. 'Bags I try first. We'll run it out one evening.'

'Don't you kids go breaking your necks,' Mrs. Nelson warned. 'You leave that old bike where it belongs. Do you hear, Jimmy?'

'Yes, ma.'

'And don't yes-ma me so glib. I know you! Lies and larks, with a face that wouldn't melt a candle. Don't you encourage him, Walter.'

Walter attempted a wink at Jimmy. 'No, Mrs. Nelson.'

'I saw you wink, too. I'm surprised at you, a well brought-up boy.' She ate a scone herself, meditatively turned towards the stove, while silence fell upon the conspirators.

'Come and see the rabbits,' suggested Jimmy. He screwed up his face and put out his tongue at his mother's back.

'Is she angry?' Walter asked in the yard.

'She's just off her dot. She's always going for me.'

The yard was dark; the rabbits made thumping sounds from the back of the hutches.

'They've heard us,' Jimmy nudged Walter. 'That's their danger-signal . . . How many wheels has this bike you found?'

'A big and a small.'

'We'll take it out in the road. Some night. What say?'

They began whispering together in the yard. The first stars came out above them, in the black winter sky.

'Some night when Mr. Garnett's gone out to his choir-practice,' they agreed. 'We'll fix it.'

'Walter,' called Mrs. Nelson at last from the back door, 'you ought to go home now, if you've had a cold. And, Jimmy, you've your homework to settle to.'

'Bloody sums,' Jimmy grumbled. 'I used to look up the answers at the end,' he told Walter, 'till Mr. Bush stuck the pages with stamp paper.' And he began a war dance in the yard, swinging his arms. 'If I had an axe I'd bust him in the belly. I'd cut him up like a Maori and cook his ribs.'

'Enough of that,' said Mrs. Nelson. 'Come along indoors.' She glanced at the stars, shivering. 'Miss Rose'll be coming out to search for you, Walter . . . Does she go out at nights?'

'No,' he answered uncertainly, 'but I go to bed early.'

'You haven't heard her leave the house?'

'I can hear the piano through the floor,' he said, 'if she's in.'

They were back in the warm kitchen. 'She hasn't written any letters for you to deliver?' Mrs. Nelson asked, casual but insistent, searching for her cigarettes. 'Nothing like that?'

He shook his head innocently. 'No.'

'I was up at Mrs. Hilda's on Monday, collecting the wash,' she ruminated. 'Rose hadn't been near them, she said, not since she got home. Keeps away, poor girl. Not that I've any time for Hilda Macaulay, mind you; serve her right even now if Rose put her nose out of joint with that husband. Sneering superior creature, she can be — Hilda.'

'Can I take Walter home on my bike, ma?' Jimmy interrupted. 'I've got my lamp now.'

'Just along the road and back then. No tricks, either.' She helped Walter on with his coat. 'Give my love to Rose, Walter,' she said at the door. 'Tell her I wish her good luck.'

'I F I'd been born a man, Walter,' Miss Rose said reflectively, 'I'd have wanted to be a sailor. Something of that sort, I fancy.' She scuffed at the snow on the sand with the point of her shoe. 'I'd have been like that old Flying Dutchman, never able to rest. I'd have sailed on for ever.'

'Who was the Flying Dutchman?'

'Only a legend really. The wanderer, the unsatisfied, the man with a cleft in his heart.' She stared out to sea and a little laugh flew from her lips, deprecating her outburst. 'But, for women, it's so much a matter of chance — they can't *act* — no, it isn't fair. It's a nasty sly dig from fate, or nature. And how it riles me, sometimes!'

She interrupted their walk along the beach to seat herself upon one of the tide-smoothed boulders of basalt at the foot of the Cave Rock. The sun was low in the afternoon sky; the air calm with a premature spring softness despite the wafers of snow lying on the sand sheltered by the huge bastion of the Rock. The tide was coming in; the crests of the breakers on the shore broke in lines as white as the crusts of snow on the dunes stretching in a long crescent towards Scarborough Hill, at the misty distant end of the beach. A little snow lay, too, on the esplanade bordering this flank of the town; on the promenade curving past the boarding-houses and shops towards the pier and the sands approaching the Cave Rock itself.

'Yes, I should certainly have been a sailor,' Miss Rose repeated, smiling. 'And I've have hated the land — anything that confined me.' She flicked at the barnacles on the rock with her gloves, holding a small fur muff, like a pet animal, on her lap. 'Even love,' she said faintly, in abstraction. 'Certainly love.' And she signed for Walter to sit beside her.

He did not want to sit. 'I think I'll look for shells,' he told her. 'Can I?'

'Yes, look for shells then. We used to find a special kind here, as children — a coral-pink kind, a sort of scallop like a — ' she scooped a little shape on the air with her thumb and forefinger ' — like a petal, a peony petal. This used to be a hunting-ground for them, for Hilda and me. A meeting place, too.' She broke off. 'Do you know the shells I mean?'

He knew them well. To find a whole shell, undamaged, the frail scallop unchipped by the rocks, was a triumph. Now he wandered away in a half-circle about her, his eyes bent to scan the flat pale floors of sand between the boulders. Miss Rose turned to watch him in his search, her hat shielding her eyes from the dropping sun, her lips thoughtfully pursed. The bulk of the Rock towered above them — the crags of volcanic upthrust, with the broken cavern pierced through it by the sea's action or by a flaw in the basalt itself.

'If you'd been a sailor,' he called presently, without looking up, 'which countries would you have gone to most?' And, as she did not reply, he repeated above the murmur of the sea: 'Which countries, Miss Rose?'

Surprised at her silence he lifted his head. Somebody, a man in a cap and a brown motoring-coat, had come across the beach from the promenade, his footsteps unheard on the sand. She had risen, she had uprightly taken his offered handclasp.

'You,' Walter heard her exclaim. 'You, at last.'

'Still faithful to our old meeting place, Rose,' said Geoffrey Macaulay. 'Not forgotten, I see.'

'No. If you put it like that.' She turned her face away and in some confusion indicated Walter. 'But this time I'm not exactly alone.'

'So you walk with him now?'

'I — ' She made a gesture for the boy to continue his search for shells. 'I didn't expect to see you here, Geoffrey,' she resumed. 'Not today, at any rate.'

'I saw you from the road.' His cap nodded towards the white car he had left on the esplanade across the sand. 'On my way home.'

'I wrote to you, Geoffrey. Weeks ago.'

'Aye. I had the letter, at the office.' He paused, he seemed to struggle with a physical force stronger than his will to speak. 'It wasn't easy to answer, Rose, or easy to see you again. That's the truth, whatever you're thinking.'

'You thought I'd be so bitter with you? So . . . vengeful?'

'I wasn't certain. I'm not so sure now.'

'I had reason, you know, to be both bitter and disgusted.'

'Aye.' He stared at her, taking in her hat, the curve of her cheek. 'But I'd rather you didn't talk like that, Rose.'

'Yes,' she said and fumbled with the catch of her glove. 'I did so much want to see you again,' she said quietly, withdrawn. 'So very much. Do you understand that — understand me?'

'You're not changed, Rosie. Now I've seen you — '

'Shh!' she said, more lightly. She glanced towards Walter, then resumed: 'How are you, Geoffrey? Tell me true, tell me now?' She studied his face, looking directly at him for the first time. 'I want to know.'

He turned the question aside. 'Ah, Rose . . . Why haven't you been up to see us — to see Hilda?'

'Has she complained?'

'Complained, no.'

'I wanted to come up. But no — ' she shook her head violently ' — no, it wouldn't have helped. Not in any way.'

He glanced round, at the beach empty save for Walter. 'We can't talk here, Rose. Not like this.'

'I think it's safest. Don't go for a moment.'

'I'm not. I was only thinking of you.'

She nodded. 'That was kind. But I'll stay; I've walked and sat here so often. Even the sea-gulls are used to seeing me!'

'You'll have heard Hilda's to have a child?'

'Mother saw fit to tell me.' She laughed suddenly, even mockingly. 'The fruit of lawful union.'

'Rose — '

'No, don't mind me, I say things. Over-excited.'

'Muriel told Hilda that you — well, you'd been what she called neurasthenic.'

'A chronic condition. Drugs prescribed — '

'Rosie, listen — ' He drew off one of his gloves and made as though to soothe her with physical action. 'I've hated myself —'

'No, don't touch me. And don't try to say anything. Perhaps there's nothing to say — except what I wrote in my letter.'

He dropped his hand, turning aside with a blunt, almost plebeian gesture. 'You always had the last word, if I remember.'

'Not always. Your memory deceives you, my darling.'

'I remember enough. You haven't a notion, Rose.'

'Haven't I? I wonder.'

'You've been in my mind. We don't meet as strangers.'

'Beyond the gates of dream — ' she mocked.

'My life isn't quite as contented as you fancy, Rose.'

They stood apart, staring at the sea and the thin crusts of snow on the beach, then began to walk a few paces, to and fro between the rocks near Walter, disregarding him completely.

'And mine — my life?' she reminded him suddenly. 'Do you ever think of that or what's become of me?'

'My God, a man can't be blamed for everything.' He spoke harshly, dropping the usual lilt of his voice, speaking as though with the full force of his powerful body. 'Not everything.'

'A man can be blamed for yielding to half-truths, jumping to conclusions. Those letters — '

'Muriel misled me. That's possible,' he allowed, halting to face her. 'But Hilda — '

'Oh, Hilda dazzled you. She was beautiful — still is, no doubt.'

'She's very like you. Your twin — '

'The flesh but not the spirit. Poor Geoff, you were always a little stupid perhaps. Emotionally stupid. Weak. Blind.'

'Is that how you thought of me always?'

'No,' she said, stricken, crumpling. 'No. I loved you, I didn't judge you. I can't judge you properly now — not when I'm really beside you like this.'

'Ah,' he said and was silent among the shadows of the rocks, pushing at the ridges of snow with his boot. 'Now I at least know.' And he lowered his voice. 'Now I know.' He put out his bare hand and grasped her wrist. 'Rose —'

She drew back, looking past him at Walter. 'No,' she said in panic. 'Not now. I must go home.' She glanced wildly at the sky, the shadows on the sand. 'It's getting late —'

'I'll write to you, Rose.' Blood rushed into the fresh raw colour of his cheeks. 'Though how we —'

'Walter,' she interrupted, calling. 'Have you found your shells?'

He approached, shyly. 'There's too much snow, I can't see them.' All the same, he splayed open his hand to show her, on the palm, one of the coral-red scallops, unbroken, each flange perfect. 'You keep it, Miss Rose. It's a present.'

She took the wet shell on her black glove, turned it delicately this way and that, her chin lowered, then slipped it into the darkness of her muff. 'Thank you, Walter. I'll make a brooch of it. A souvenir. Now take my arm and squire me home,' she smiled.

Geoffrey Macaulay nodded to Walter. 'Look after her, Walter. Keep her safe.'

They walked, the three of them, a few paces over the sand towards the esplanade and the motor deserted on the road.

'Had you been in town, Geoffrey?' Miss Rose said in a cool ordinary voice. 'I thought it was a holiday —'

'Yes.' And as though shaking himself, returning to the actual moment and the day, he drew from the deep pocket of his overcoat a newspaper which he now placed, rolled, between her hands.

'This afternoon's. A special edition, I suppose. You'll see it there, Rose.'

She unfolded the paper, stumbling a little on the sands. 'What does it mean?' And she murmured aloud from the thick black print: 'At midnight last night ... in London ...'

'Midnight would be midday here.'

'Oh, no,' she said in disbelief. 'It can't be true.'

He shrugged. 'I thought Germany would back out, back down, get out of Belgium.'

She almost thrust the paper into his hands. 'It's not true, Geoffrey, not sane. It can't be. Not when we ... us,' she added helplessly. 'Not today,' she said.

'It may not mean much, Rose. Over soon —'

'But how can men be such fools?' She twisted her glove against her muff. 'If women —'

They had halted beside the car. Walter looked from one face to the other, uncertainly. 'Is it the Kaiser?' he asked Mr. Macaulay.

'Partly the Kaiser —' and he turned to Miss Rose, folding the paper again into his pocket. 'I could have told you earlier.'

'I'm glad you didn't. Thank you.' She smoothed her muff. 'Walter and I'll go on now, Geoffrey. We'll leave you.'

'I can drive you.'

'No.' She shook the loose sand from the hem of her skirt, then met his eyes steadily. 'Better not,' she said, and lightly, almost playfully touched his hand. 'Better not.'

'Then I'll —'

'That's understood.' And quickly she had drawn Walter with her away from the car, across the promenade, into the town. Her fingers clutched his arm above the elbow.

'You're shaking,' he told her presently. 'Did you know?'

'Didn't you realize that grown-up people could tremble?'

'Because of a war?' He kicked at the path as they walked beside the tram-lines. 'Could the Kaiser send a submarine and blow up Sumner?'

She held him back a pace. 'Will you do something for me, Walter?'

'Not tell about the war?'

'Not, rather, tell my sister — anyone — that we met somebody on the beach. Will you promise me that?'

'Yes,' he said.

'And if you overheard anything — '

'I won't tell. I won't, Miss Rose.'

To his surprise he saw her twist aside and dab at her eyes. 'Oh,' she shuddered, with tears. 'I was so unkind to him, so cheap. And he's so much gentler than I'd — ' she broke off.

He waited while she controlled herself. 'I won't tell,' he repeated. 'I wouldn't ever.'

'I doubt if you understand . . . but it doesn't matter.'

They walked on.

'If the Germans did send a submarine,' he said at last. 'We could hide in the Cave Rock.'

'Yes,' she said, laughing with a kind of mild hysteria. 'We could do that — Mr. Macaulay and you and I. Three in a cave.' And her voice flew out airily, in a sudden happiness. 'The world abandoned, the world left to its own horrid devices — how wonderful!' She grasped his elbow again, squeezing it. 'Oh, Walter, I don't know what I'm saying!' she cried. 'It isn't true.'

Together they went up the cinder path and let themselves into the kitchen.

'I thought you were both lost,' Miss Muriel greeted them absently. She wiped her fingers on a cloth, then hung a couple of tea-cups on the hooks above the sink. 'It's after five.'

Rose took off her gloves. 'Is father home?'

'No, but Hilda's here. Talking to mother.'

'Hilda?' Rose stood still in the doorway. 'Has she seen Geoffrey?'

'She came for tea. Why?'

Unanswering, followed by Walter, Miss Rose walked through to the dining-room. Old Mrs. Garnett sat straight in her winged chair: Hilda Macaulay crouched on a low stool by the fire, her skirts spread about her, one hand shielding her cheeks from the heat. Her thick auburn hair drooped, a little lopsidedly, over her brow. She got up with a lazy stretch and sway of her body and threw out her hands to her sister.

'Rosie, my pet.' She kissed the cold cheek. 'Don't look so cantankerous. I only dropped in because I was bored with myself on the hill and wanting some news.' She held her sister at arm's length, critically taking in her dress. 'A new costume?'

'No,' said Rose, escaping, taking off her hat, 'old.'

'I haven't seen it before. I'm told all the new fashions in the English papers have narrower skirts, tight below the knee.'

'Yes. So I've heard.'

'You girls and your clothes,' Mrs. Garnett said from her chair. 'Nothing else to think about.' And, to Walter: 'Shut the door, boy, it's draughty.'

'You're thinner, Rose,' said Hilda Macaulay. She touched her own plump cheeks, then indicated her sister's. 'Drawn,' she said.

With a dry smile Rose said: 'I hoped it suited me, Hilda.'

'It makes you look frightfully interesting, of course.'

The other gave an offhand shrug, hung her coat over a chair and glanced at the clock. 'I suppose we've come in too late for tea.'

Hilda too inspected the clock. 'I must go,' she said. 'Geoff will be home and grumbling if I'm out. He took the motor up to town today —'

'He shouldn't grumble,' Mrs. Garnett broke in. 'He's nothin' to grumble about.'

'Geoff?' Hilda uttered a cry of incredulous amusement. 'You don't know him, mother! All the cares of the world rest on that man's head. Heaven forgive the effects of a Scottish upbringing — I'd rather let any child of mine run wild, even if it meant his growing into a rake, a wife beater and worse.' She stretched her arms above her head and yawned. 'Your fire's made me sleepy, mother. And my leg's all pins and needles.' She limped to the table. 'You're looking very solemn, Walter. Would you care to rub a lady's leg for her?'

'If you like,' he said, advancing.

'Mother'd be shocked to the heart.' Mrs. Hilda giggled. 'Putting ideas into your head at your age.' She brushed him aside, lightly. 'One day, perhaps.'

'You said something about having called here for news, Hilda,' Miss Rose interrupted. 'What news did you expect?'

Hilda waggled her foot. 'Oh, nothing much. Only Geoff's been on about a war in Europe — at least he tells *me* that's what he has on his mind . . . I know nothing: I never even open a paper except for the social titbits.' Her face, guileless, turned towards her sister. 'Is there a war, Rose? Ought I to know? Geoff gets in such a paddy if I'm stupid.'

'I don't know myself,' Rose said slowly, without a glance at Walter. She bent over her mother and touched the frame of her spectacles. 'Your specs are slipping down your nose, my dear.'

'The rivet's loose.'

Behind them Hilda began to arrange her hat. 'War or no war,' she said over her shoulder, 'I wish hats would get smaller: I'm tired of these cartwheels. And sleeves — I've never been so sick of long sleeves in my life.' She ran a *papier poudré* over her cheeks in the glass. 'I'm as red as a poppy. I don't know how you keep so beautifully pale, Rose.'

Mrs. Garnett said: 'Are you intendin' to walk home by your-self, Hilda?'

'I was, mother . . . It's away and up the hill for me.'

'You, boy,' the old woman nodded at Walter, 'go with her as far as her gate. It won't hurt you.'

'He might even stay to supper,' Hilda Macaulay laughed, 'if he ventured to take me to my door.' And she gave him a wink through her veil. 'What do you say to that, Walter Blakiston whose mother was a Grace? Would you come?'

He looked at Miss Rose for direction. 'Can I, Miss Rose?'

'He can wrap up,' Mrs. Garnett interrupted. 'Tell Miss Muriel you'll be out for the meal, boy. Don't stand there: do what you're asked.'

'Yes,' he said, hurrying for his coat, his scarf. Five minutes later he was in the road with Hilda Macaulay.

'Let's run a bit,' she said. 'Let's run for a lark.' Scarborough Hill rose above them, high under the risen moon, lights twinkling from the scattered houses. The road, before beginning the steep ascent from the township, flanked the rocky base of the hill at this end of the beach. 'I used always to run up this hill, as a child, Walter. Run down it too. I loved to run.'

But after a few yards she stopped beside him, panting. 'No, I oughtn't to tire myself.' Contorted, she bent forward in the moonlight, one hand pressed to the lace of her dress, the other supporting herself against the rocks at the side of the road. 'It's my heart,' she gasped presently, 'my silly old pump . . . Oh, how I hate getting older. I'd much rather die young.'

'If you'd take my arm,' he suggested.

'Dear young Walter — so polite,' she teased, and lifted herself with a sigh. 'Yes, help me up to the house. Help me up to that Calvinist of a Geoffrey.'

CHAPTER XV

'Do you see that fume on the sky? No, more to the left.' Mr. Macaulay stood beside Walter in the plate-glass windows of the house on the hill. 'That's Christchurch — the lights make a glow,' he explained in his soft accented voice. 'And further, much further — note that line like a white comb? That'll be the moon on the mountains yonder, at the far back of the plains.'

The boy lost himself in the huge dark view across the bay below them. He nodded, pleased, excited. He liked being in the Macaulays' house; he liked the long living-room, the fire-place of reddish uncut blocks, the green chair covers, the pots of late chrysanthemums, the lamps with candle-white shades: every thing different, richer, than at the Garnetts'. The Macaulays' house nestled into the side of Scarborough Hill; a sort of open cage, facing the curve and sweep of the coast to the west and north. Until this evening he had never been in the house at night. And tonight Hilda Macaulay — Mrs. Hilda — had given him sausages for supper: sausages, fruit salad and a cup of cocoa. Now he stood at the window with Mr. Macaulay. A rattle of plates came from the kitchen beyond the living-room: Mrs. Hilda had insisted that she wash up the dishes while her husband talked to the guest.

'By the way, Walter,' said Geoffrey Macaulay. They had finished with the view for the moment. 'By the way, I wouldn't mention to my wife that Rose was on the beach, earlier.' He examined the stem of the pipe in his hand. 'I gather Rose is supposed to be looking after her mother at home.' His blunt face and brown eyes inspected the boy suddenly. 'Do you understand?'

'Yes.' Walter stared back at him, innocently. 'Miss Rose told me, too.'

His eyebrows went up. 'Ah . . . good lad.' And he went back to the vast view of the bay and the night. 'Aye,' he resumed, 'we see most of Canterbury from here. Quite a stretch.' He brooded, a match hovering over the bowl of his pipe. 'Hilda,' he called, not raising his voice and not looking towards the door in to the kitchen, 'Hilda.'

'She can't hear you,' Walter said after a pause. 'Shall I call her?'

'No — I was only . . .' He left the remark in the air. 'No matter. She's busy.' He leant against the window, bracing his wide shoulders into a kind of shrug. 'Hilda,' he called again, this time more loudly.

'In a moment. Just coming.'

She came in, her skirt rustling over the rugs on the floor. 'Ugh,' she shivered, 'I'm frozen. Draw the curtains, dear, will you? Unless Walter wants to look out.'

'I've been showing him the view. A few thousand square miles of an Empire at war.' He left the curtains undrawn. 'At least I suppose that's where we stand.'

His wife held her hands spread to the fire. 'Costello,' she said after a moment, turning the wedding-ring on her finger. 'Costello's the name I was trying to think of at supper. I knew it was Irish.'

'You didn't mention any name.' He stiffened.

'No, but it was running in my head. The name of that young man, the cripple Rose nursed for a time.' She glanced at him, taking in his embarrassment. 'I don't suppose you've forgotten.'

'What made you think of him?'

'Oh, seeing Rose today. And then your talking of Germany invading Belgium. That Costello boy had a Belgian mother — Belgian or French, I've forgotten.'

'I don't know how you bother over such things, Hilda.'

'What things? Families? It's just a diversion of mine — quite harmless, I'd have thought. It doesn't harm you, does it? My diversion?'

'Not in the least.'

'Well then . . . The Costello's boy's dead now, anyway.' She tilted her shoe towards the fire. 'It's curious: Rose's patients, if they happen to be men, inevitably seem to lay their hearts at her feet. And the more helpless — the more desperate, they. They make her offers. Oh, not that Rose herself has told me about it — but she did tell Muriel, once or twice.'

'I'd rather you didn't talk about Rose, Hilda.'

She looked at him, astounded. 'Good Heavens, why not?'

He said stiffly: 'I'd prefer you not to.'

'The trouble with you, darling, is that your sense of humour's stunted. You've got this permanent black monkey on your back, as though it were my fault.'

'At least you might keep quiet before Walter.' He nodded towards the boy.

'Oh, I daresay Walter hears everything! Everything! Little walls have big ears.' She drew him to her side, laughing, rubbing his chilblained hands. 'All right, we'll talk of something else. What do you think about this war, Walter, and the Germans?'

He said after a moment: 'Will they fight with aeroplanes?'

'Ask Geoff. I'm only an ignorant woman.'

Her husband said nothing.

'A whole zoo full of black monkeys,' she commented and thrust the heavy hair back from her forehead. 'Really, I ought to have married an old man like father — somebody at peace with all fleshly demons.' And she twisted her head as her husband strode towards the door to the terrace. 'Where are you off, darling?'

'I'm not sure if I locked the car away.' The door clanged behind him.

Hilda Macaulay frowned. 'Oh, dear,' she said. She yawned and, leaving Walter, rummaged in the drawer of a bureau by the fireplace. 'Never mind, we can at least eat a chocolate.' She offered him a white box with a spray of roses across the cardboard lid. 'Only from the grocer's, but not so bad. Take one. Take two.'

'Thank you, Mrs. Macaulay.'

With the strong-tasting chocolate in his mouth he pointed past her at a black and yellow metal horn that sprang, like the erect calyx of a lily, from the top of a box in the corner. 'Is that your gramophone?'

'Yes. Wait, I'll play you a record.'

The needle ground over the revolving disc under her hand. Presently a tinny coughing jig of sound scratched across the air of the room.

'A waltz,' she told him. 'A waltz called The Blue Danube. Do you approve of my gramophone, Walter?'

'It sounds as if it had a sore throat,' he said and peered into the metal horn. The noise, so close to his ears, was very loud and he drew back.

'Come. I'll teach you to dance.' She lifted her arms, then dropped them to her sides. 'No, I mustn't,' she said. 'The doctor said I mustn't. I must be staid and behave myself.'

The glass door from the terrace shuddered open, then banged shut. 'Better turn that thing off, Hilda,' said Mr. Macaulay and nodded at the gramophone.

'Turn it off? Why?'

He clicked the lever himself. The waltz died in a long wail. 'I could hear it down the hill,' he said in the silence. 'If you want people to think we're friends of the Kaiser — '

'Well honestly!' She sat down by the fire, throwing out her hands. 'You amaze me. I only wanted Walter to hear a waltz. The fact that the music might be German or Viennese . . .' She sighed. 'All right, my dear. Though I think you've taken rather a peculiar revenge on me for talking about Rose as I did.'

'Rose?'

'Yes, oh yes. I can read you like a book, Geoffrey — a book full of very peculiar things. My poor gramophone has nothing to do with it. *Or* the war that seems to affect you so much.' She glanced at him. 'You'd better take yourself off to bed now and lay your black monkey on the pillow — a separate pillow, too, for once, please.'

'I'm sorry, Hilda.'

She let this pass. 'You're simply not fit to talk to tonight. And Walter must go home, anyway. Go on, Walter, get your coat.'

His boots slipped on the shingle of the road as he ran down the long hill. Across the town below the street-lamps winked in bright lines like necklaces stretched taut between the sleeping houses, the gardens, the dark fences. He hurried indoors.

'Late hours,' Miss Muriel clicked her tongue. She lit his candle for him then turned down his bed. 'What have you been up to all the evening? Talking?'

He could not remember. 'Mrs. Hilda played the gramophone,' he told her drowsily as he undressed. 'A waltz.'

'Such amusements. We'll have you too tired for school in the morning.'

CHAPTER XVI

A<small>MEN</small>.' Mr. Garnett placed the prayer-book inside his desk on the platform, stroked his beard and presently studied the faces before him. He had something of importance to say.

'As you will all of you be aware,' he began, 'the mother-country and her Empire are at war with Germany.' His eyes swept past them to the windows at the back of the room. 'Fortunately none of you boys is old enough to be called upon to fight. Indeed, the war may be short and over by Christmas. But meanwhile you will all of you remember that no war must be used as an excuse for slackening in your work, your lessons.' His fingers roamed across his waistcoat, seeking the comfort of his gold watch chain. 'It has occurred to me,' he continued, 'that in a time of strain physical fitness is important. I am therefore arranging that you will all attend a drill-class in the playground. This will be on Thursdays, under an instructor from the Barracks. Only those boys who are ill or who bring a note from a doctor will be excused . . .' He paused, he seemed to ponder, then glanced along the platform towards the seated Miss Threplow. 'Now I think we might begin work for the day.'

Presently Walter received a note from Marriner: a screw of paper pushed along the floor to his feet: 'Got any German stamps for swops?'

'No,' he wrote back.

The hour for English History began. 'What was Danegeld?' Mr. Garnett questioned Overton in the fourth row.

'It was so they wouldn't land, sir.'

' "It was so they wouldn't land",' repeated the master in a distant unearthly tone. 'What was *it*? Who were *they*? And where and why should they *land*? Don't hurry.' His gaze lifted itself to the wooden ceiling, roved the walls. 'History, after all, is a slow process. I can wait.'

The hour passed no less slowly than history. Miss Threplow took over the class.

'Today I want you all to draw a tree for me,' she instructed them. 'A bare tree. Willow, chestnut, poplar — any kind you like, from memory. Draw it in pencil, then let me see it before you colour it with your crayons.' She blew on her hands. 'And remember, boys, no lines drawn with a ruler, please.'

Walter drew a Lombardy poplar, the branches splaying from the trunk like the tines of a fork, with small dots to suggest the fallen leaves on the ground. As the tree looked incomplete he sketched a ridge of mountain behind it, added a horizon of water, even a star.

'Ye-es,' said Miss Threplow, narrowing her eyes over the page of his drawing-book, 'but I didn't say a dead tree, only a bare one.'

'I didn't mean it to look dead.' He pointed to the dots. 'It's autumn, you see.'

'And what are those lines behind, those squiggles?'

'It's country. A river bed or a lake.'

She laughed. 'Well, it shows you have imagination at least. All right, you can colour it now. But mind, not too bright.'

He made the poplar brown and orange, the mountain blue, the lake bluer. The crayons skidded over the surface of the paper. The picture changed, became alive. He was in it himself. Finally — a finishing touch like a signature — he drew a small bicycle in a corner of the page: a penny-farthing.

'I drew a gooseberry bush,' said Marriner as they crouched over lunch in their overcoats, against the wall of the church. 'Then I put some fruit on it, but the fruit looked like apples so I had to start again. I told Miss Threplow it was a fig tree.'

'I drew a lake,' said Walter, 'like the one on the stamp. And a bicycle.'

'Liar. Bet you make things up.'

'Bet I don't.'

Frost rimmed the roof of the bicycle shed and sparkled on the pebbles and flints of the playground. Hard crusts of snow still lay against the buttresses of the church, in the bleak late winter light.

'If ten horses each draw a wagon of coal weighing half a ton . . .' Mr. Garnett dictated during the afternoon lesson in Arthmetic. His lowered head and beard mourned for a moment over the absurdity of horses, wagons and coal. 'It is not sufficient,' he presently wrote in neat capitals on the blackboard, 'simply to look up the Answers.'

The brief light of the afternoon faded to grey. At his desk Walter picked at the purplish craters of his disappearing chilblains: he felt as indifferent to wagons and coal as did the old man himself. Moreover he was hungry: Miss Muriel's lunch had been sparser than usual. Some diversion was needed.

He thrust an arm into the air. 'Please sir, may I leave the room?'

Mr. Garnett inclined his head. 'Two minutes, Blakiston. No more.'

Fresh black tar gleamed on the wall of the brick lavatory. 'Lamb of God I don't think!' somebody — perhaps, Walter thought, a member of the choir who sang in the church on Sundays — had scribbled in pencil along one of the water-pipes. The trough below was thick with saffron suds, sluggish and half-frozen. Overhead starlings chattered, nibbling at the air on the church roof: at night they roosted under the stone eaves between the buttresses.

'Starlings have fleas,' he told himself, buttoning his trousers. He watched the birds for the remainder of his two minutes, wondering if they were as hungry as himself, then ran back to the schoolroom. The electric lights under their white hat-like shades had been switched on in his absence: the air of the room felt less solid, less stuffy. The gold nib of Mr. Garnett's pen moved over an open exercise-book. Walter slid into the seat of his desk.

125

'Two minutes, Blakiston, is not five.'

'No, sir.'

The old man replaced the cap of his pen. 'For homework tonight,' he addressed the class, 'you will solve — I use the word in optimism — solve problems seven and eight on page twenty-one of Nesfield. Is that clear?'

'Please, sir.' A hand was raised behind Walter.

'Yes, Bascomb?'

'Won't you tell us about the war, sir? Would the Kaiser come to New Zealand?'

The master took out his watch, sprung the lid with his thumbnail, frowned at the dial, and said in so milky a tone that the class fidgeted: 'No, Bascomb, the Kaiser is most unlikely to visit us. This is a European, not a colonial war.' He brooded. 'All safety, however, is relative: even the immunity of our planet the earth from the hazards of cosmic space. More I cannot say ... New Zealand, I imagine, will be no sphere of rapine for either the Uhlans of Prussia or for that very unserene highness Herr Wilhelm Hohenzollern himself.' He replaced his watch, patted his waistcoat and glanced along the platform at the cool face of Miss Threplow. 'And now,' he pronounced, rising, 'I think you may all disperse for the day. The shades of evening fall upon us.'

'What did he mean?' Marriner asked Walter. 'The old cock's barmy.' They were on the way to the tram. 'My mother says the Kaiser has a withered arm,' he rambled on. 'You can see it in photos. He keeps it in his sleeve like this — ' he stuffed his own arm stiffly into his mackintosh '— and his wife has to cut up his meat for him at dinner time.'

'How does he ride a horse then?'

'It's trained, see, so it doesn't buck him off.'

They paused at the bridge over the river, their satchels resting on the parapet, and spat into the greenish water, watching the spittle twirl, dissolve, drift under the arch below. 'If you spit in a river,' Marriner said, 'it raises the level of the sea.'

Walter did not believe him. 'How much?'

'You couldn't measure it, man. Nobody could measure it.'

Walter looked down at the water. And for a minute he again wanted to tell Marriner about the dog he had seen drowned. But once more the moment passed. 'Come on,' he said impatiently. 'Let's go.'

They pulled down their caps and sauntered towards the Square. Bicycle bells rang in the cold streets.

'I've heard a gramophone,' Walter told his friend. 'It was a stunner. You've no idea . . .' But the gramophone raised other, more difficult questions: a drop found its way to the larger sea. 'Why can't somebody — a man, I mean — why can't he marry two women at the same time?' he brought out.

'The police wouldn't let him.'

'No, but if he did . . . It wouldn't hurt anyone, would it?'

'The police'd put him in the lock-up,' Marriner insisted. 'It's in the Prayer Book, you mustn't. The cops would shove handcuffs on him in church.'

'Would they put handcuffs on the women too?'

Marriner wasn't sure: they might. And now they joked about handcuffs, pistols and revolvers. Marriner had been taken to a moving-picture, one evening last holidays, in which cowboys had shot at a cattle rustler. 'They hit him in the pants and a lot of dusty stuff flew out, but he wasn't killed. Only sort of stunned.'

'How much does it cost to go to the pictures?'

'I didn't pay. Mum took me after my birthday. I saw another picture too — I didn't like that though: it stopped in the middle when a girl called Pauline was tied to a tram-line . . . Some pictures have love in them all the time. But you needn't look at those, they're barmy.'

'When books have love in them I don't read that part. Stories about exploring are best. Or pirates and shipwrecks.'

'Robinson Crusoe was a good one but too long.'

'Singleton the Searcher too. I liked that. It's in *Chums*. . . . Jungles.'

'Jungles,' Marriner nodded. The word was immense.

They reached the Square. Walter counted the money in his purse, then bought threepenn'orth of caramels from the shop opposite the Post Office. He held out the open bag to Marriner.

'Have one?'

'Gosh, thanks.' With the sweet in his mouth Marriner pointed to a newspaper placard. 'Germans near L — ,' he read out, then spelt the word Liége. 'Leege,' he said slowly.

'Uhlans I expect. They're on horses, with lances.'

'My uncle who lives with us says he's going to enlist. I hope he does, then I can have his room.'

'How old's your uncle?'

'Dunno, man. About twenty, but he's got a moustache.'

'Couldn't we enlist too,' Walter suggested. 'I mean we could go as drummer boys or something.'

'No more school,' Marriner whooped. 'We'd sail off together and biff the Germans on the boko.'

The idea was wonderful. It expanded into a re-planning of their entire lives, then as suddenly drooped, faded.

'Have another caramel?'

They dodged across the Square between the bicycles. Beyond the cathedral flags flew from a building hung with bright windows: a newspaper office lit for the night.

'The Union Jack, the French and the Russian.' Walter detailed the flags one by one for Marriner.

'It's the Allies, see?'

The New Zealand ensign was there too: the four stars of the Southern Cross on a navy blue background. Sombrely it streamed against the flying sky, apart from the rest, as though special to the two boys.

'It ought to have a kiwi on it —' Walter began.

But Marriner had caught sight of his tram, the tram for New Brighton. With a wave of his hand to Walter he scuttled away across the Square, his satchel bobbing on his back, his thin legs twinkling.

'See you tomorrow,' Walter called after him. 'See you in the morning.'

He waved until Marriner was out of sight, until Marriner's tram had gone whining round the curved rails of the Square and the red rear light of the trailer had disappeared between the buildings.

CHAPTER XVII

AWAY from the gas-lamp on the corner the road was almost dark, silent save for the distant murmur of the sea. The two boys, Walter and Jimmy Nelson, edged the rattling bicycle through the Garnetts' front gate, one on either side of the high rusty wheel, on to the gravel of the footpath. As quiet and stealthy as cats they had dragged the machine from its shed at the end of the garden — Jimmy's bicycle-lamp, detached for the occasion, had given wavering light to the work — and had lifted it across the lawn at the side of the house and thence to the gate on the road.

'It's heavier than a ton,' Walter panted.

'Gee, but she needs some oil,' Jimmy said.

They leant the penny-farthing against the palings of the fence: it was bigger than either of them, a kind of stubborn clattering monster they had themselves created and must now tame or abandon. Drops of sweat ran down the ribs beneath their shirts; their hands were sticky with excitement. Now they stood like exhausted hunters and examined the prey.

'I like the small wheel best,' said Walter. 'It's a calf and the big one's the cow.'

Jimmy had no time for such fancies. The smaller wheel, he had discovered by kicking it, had an odd wobble. The whole bicycle, in fact, was rickety and gave out ancient wiry sounds of complaint when attacked. It was also very dusty.

'Let's take her up the road.' Jimmy glanced back at the Garnetts' house. 'What did you tell your Miss Muriel?'

'I said I was going out to post a letter for Miss Rose.'

They hauled the bicycle along the road, the wheels bumping over the gravel. To keep the machine upright was more tricky than they'd imagined: the larger wheel swivelled from side to side, the smaller kept bouncing into the air behind.

'Ma thinks I'm doing errands,' Jimmy said. 'She's ironing.' His small dark face was almost lost in the dusk. 'It's wash day,' he added.

They halted the penny-farthing in the shadow of some fir trees overhanging the footpath. Walter wiped his face. So far he had been driven forward, propelled almost, by the force of Jimmy's enthusiasm. Now he looked at the bicycle with some doubt.

'What do we do now?'

The other was scornful. 'I thought you wanted a bike to ride.'

'Yes, but . . .' The awkward moment passed.

The two of them again inspected the bicycle. It waited, stubborn, unconquered, a spider without sense, utterly dumb. The fir trees stared blankly down upon it, expectant. The time for action, for assault, had arrived.

'You try first,' said Jimmy.

'I thought you wanted to go first.'

'No, you go. I'll help you up.' Jimmy's breath blew a white mist on the air. 'Wait,' he whispered, retreating against the fence, 'somebody's coming along.'

A man approached with stumping steps along the footpath. He passed the boys, paused, shook his head, then gaped back at the penny-farthing.

'Christ,' he muttered beneath the peak of his cap. 'Kids been robbing a bloody museum.' He hiccoughed away down the road.

'Dirty Mr. Dakers,' Jimmy remarked. 'Drinks like a fish. His daughter lives next door to ma and me.'

They tackled the bicycle afresh. 'If we lean it against the fence first,' Walter directed, 'then I can climb up.'

'I'll shove when you're ready.'

Walter planted the toe of his boot on the tiny step and gave himself a helpful spring upwards. The bicycle, however, had ideas of its own: it wobbled, tipped forward, lunged sideways.

Walter's foot slipped before he could reach the seat. His knees, at the third try, hit the gravel under the fir trees, his cap fell off.

'I can't,' he said.

'Have another go. I'll hold her.'

Again Walter reached up to the crumbling leather saddle, grasped it and made a spring towards the pedals on the hub. This time his legs fell on either side of the frame, the iron smacking against his tenderest parts. He slipped to the ground, bending himself double in pain.

'Caught you in the pills,' grinned Jimmy and as a revenge on the penny-farthing kicked savagely at the shrivelled tyres. 'Gee, she's a stumer all right.'

The pain thawed through Walter's groin and passed away. 'You try now,' he said, holding his crotch. 'You try, Jimmy.'

'Watch me!' Jimmy made a dashing jump for the saddle — so dashing that the whole frame, upending over the high wheel, flung him forward in a half-circle to the ground. The smaller wheel spun in the air; the penny-farthing crashed sideways to bump and clatter against the fence.

Jimmy picked himself up. 'Gosh,' he snorted, 'what did I do?' He dusted the gravel from his shirt. 'She's a bloody buckjumper.'

Both boys sat down to rest on the gutter-edge of the road. Momentarily defeated, they contemplated the fallen bicycle, their enemy. A gust of wind waved the fir branches overhead: the houses along the road slept behind empty verandas.

'I know,' said Walter, reviving '— what say I climb up the fence and lower myself on the saddle? You hold up the bike.'

Jimmy agreed. He pushed the penny-farthing into position, crouching below the big wheel, breathing heavily. 'Now,' he cried.

Walter found himself with the saddle between his thighs, his boot toes on the pedals. The ground seemed a long way beneath him; the air felt thin, alpine.

'Right,' he called down to Jimmy. 'Shove and let go.'

With enormous energy, Jimmy shoved, and let go. Walter

pressed on the pedals. And with a prolonged squeal, almost a snore, of rusty bearings the machine clanked forward up the path.

'Got her,' Jimmy shouted alongside. 'Got her!' They reached the street-lamp up the road. 'Go it, Walt! Pedal!'

But now a second bicycle — or rather, as Walter saw, a tricycle — had wavered to a halt in the roadway. A known voice addressed them across the winter dusk.

'A singular sight,' said Mr. Garnett, dismounting as Walter crashed to the gravel. 'I wasn't aware that more than one penny-farthing existed in this township. Not after all these years at any rate.'

Walter disentangled his legs. 'It's yours, sir — this one.'

'Extraordinary.' The old man's tone was brooding, far from hostile. 'Extraordinary ... And who's this with you?' He peered at Jimmy. 'This companion in crime?'

'It's me, Mr. Garnett.' Jimmy showed his white teeth.

'*Me?* Oh, Mrs. Nelson's son. Yes, I see.' He straightened his hat before contemplating the bicycle prone on its side. 'And this relic is mine, is it? Stolen — or more directly, pinched — from my shed by you, Blakiston, of all boys.'

Walter stood accused, without words.

'Though you were not riding it very well, as far as I noticed,' the master continued. 'Not as it should be ridden.' Stiffly he righted the machine and regarded the rust, the dust, the perished seat. 'Not as I used to ride it,' he meditated aloud: 'by no means. Are you hurt, Blakiston?' Walter had withdrawn himself towards the fence. 'Are you damaged?'

'No, Mr. Garnett.'

'We couldn't get on to the saddle properly,' explained Jimmy with confidence.

'No. It was never easy.'

The old man turned down the collar of his overcoat. His beard quivered a little: to Walter he appeared to be listening to the far murmur of the sea from the beach.

'It was never easy. Simple skill is the result of art not force. Hold the bicycle up, both of you.'

The boys obeyed, eagerly. Perhaps — and more than faintly dawned the hope — they were not to be punished. They held the penny-farthing as though by the bridle, a captive horse.

'Yes,' said Mr. Garnett with solemn approval. 'Now, you see — and pay attention, both of you — the important thing was always to get away to a flying or a moving start. A push and then a jump. But you boys are both too small,' he remarked and peered up and down the road in thought. 'Dangerous,' he murmured, 'very dangerous. Wheel it along under the trees. Gently now, gently . . .' He followed them beneath the fir trees. 'Young thieves and hooligans,' he muttered in their wake.

In the shadow of the firs his thick figure cast a shade along the fence. And now it was Jimmy Nelson who spoke.

'If you'd show us, Mr. Garnett,' he said with a respect Walter had never heard in his voice, 'if you'd show us, then we'd know another time. See?'

Again the old man glanced slyly up and down the road. 'Once only,' he said and passing his gloves to Walter seized the handle-bars. 'Once and no more. In all that matters I am, and regretfully I admit it, no longer of an age for such nonsense.' All the same, and with an agility that amazed the two boys, he gave a thrust to the bicycle and a kind of bear-like lunge upward to the saddle. A moment more and he was astride, high and solid, the wheels creaking forward below him over the gravel footpath. Walter and Jimmy ran behind.

'It's like the circus!' Jimmy's voice was jubilant, ecstatic. 'It's like the clowns.' And, beside himself with delight, he threw up his arms. 'Wa-wa-wa,' his war-whoop challenged the night.

The war cry might have been a sign: a crackling and snapping of spokes, a sound like that of a decrepit harp in collapse, came from the penny-farthing. Mr. Garnett careened sideways in a confusion of darkness and old iron. The ride finished abruptly.

'I was afraid so.' The old man picked himself up with

difficulty. 'I was very much afraid so.' He looked down at the ruined bicycle, adjusted his hat, his trousers. 'Not to mention the loss of my self-respect before a concourse of whooping gutter-snipes.'

Walter touched the bicycle with his boot. 'Shall I pick it up now, sir?'

'You will not only pick it up, Blakiston, but you will carry it back to the shed whence you stole it.' He turned to Jimmy Nelson. 'Furthermore, if I have any inkling from your mother — '

'I won't tell her. Ma won't know.'

'I'm glad to hear ma won't know, as you put it. Ma knows too much, without the delectable news that I have been riding on the footpath without a light, after dark.' He beckoned to Walter. 'And now fetch my tricycle. It's time I arrived home from the relative innocence of choir practice.'

Half an hour later Walter entered the kitchen.

'You've been out a long time.' Miss Muriel lifted her brow suspiciously. 'Father told me he'd met you in the road and asked you to put his tricycle away. Is that true?'

'Yes.' He did not look at her.

'You seem to have got yourself very dusty.'

'It's the shed,' he explained. 'Cobwebs.'

'The cobwebs have spread to your knees.' She brushed a hand down his clothes. 'Goodness alone knows what your mamma'll think of your wardrobe when you arrive home for the holidays.'

'I'm going to gran's,' he reminded her.

'Your grandmother then. She'll think we make you work in a flour mill . . . You'd better slip off to bed now, anyway. Say good night in the dining-room first. Father's resting.'

Mr. Garnett sat alone in a chair before the fire, his hands planted on his knees, his beard sunk on his chest, as though hibernating. Walter mumbled his good night.

'Good night, Blakiston.' His eyes opened, faintly he smiled. 'You did what I asked, I trust?'

'Yes, Mr. Garnett. I put away your trike.'

' "Trike".' The old man winced. 'Terrible,' he murmured and closed his eyes. 'A country of barbarians and illiterates. "Trike", indeed!' But he glanced sharply at Walter. 'You will forget about this evening, of course.'

'Yes, Mr. Garnett. And thank you for — '

'Nothing at all.' He waved the boy airily away.

CHAPTER XVIII

'WHY are some of the notes black?'
'They're the sharps and flats,' Miss Rose explained to him. 'But you'd have to start at the beginning if you really wanted to learn music.' She slid from the piano stool, stretched her arms, yawned and pushed aside the curtains from the windows of the room called the drawing-room. 'It's time I became Nurse Garnett again, Walter,' she said happily. 'Time I took myself off to another patient.'

'Will you go soon?'

'In a few days perhaps. Before the end of your term.' She laughed. 'The old urge is on me again. How long is it before you go to your grandmother's?'

'Three weeks,' he said. 'Three weeks and two days.' He looked at the sheet of music spread open on the rack of the piano. ' "Shepherds' Dance",' he read aloud, idly. 'Why's it called that? The shepherds at home don't dance.'

'They did in England once, I suppose, in the old days.'

'And why's it by Edward German? If he's German he must be an enemy.'

'German's a surname too, you know, or can be. Some English names don't always sound English.'

'Like Costello,' he said. 'Only that's Irish.'

She stared at him. 'Where did you hear that? . . . No, don't tell me. I don't want to know.'

The name had slipped out. Now he touched the keyboard of the cottage piano. 'The black notes,' he said, 'ought to sound sadder than the others. Shouldn't they?'

'Not always.' She chuckled. And she took his hand and splayed the fingers over a chord. 'That's the dominant of C major,' she told him. 'Your chilblains are almost healed.'

'You play well. I listen when I'm in bed.' He withdrew his fingers. 'I've heard you singing too.'

'Shall I sing for you now? Shall I?'

'Yes,' he said.

She played a simple spread chord, lifted her chin and sang in a soft soprano towards him:

> Yestreen the Queen had four Maries,
> The night she'll hae but three;
> There was Marie Seaton, and Marie Beaton,
> And Marie Carmichael, and me.

'There,' she laughed, 'that's a Scottish song, and a very touching one too.'

'What happened to the other Marie?' he asked.

'Oh, she, poor girl, she was going to die. But we mustn't think of her. Not when we're happy.' She stroked the neck of the white woollen jacket she was wearing. 'Have you finished your homework, Walter?'

'No.' He had left his books on the kitchen table and had been drawn by the sound of the piano to join her. 'Why do you always sit in here?' he asked.

Her eyes travelled round the dark small room. 'My retreat,' she said, dismissing it. 'Nobody else uses it now Hilda's — ' she stopped, then continued: 'Even father's given up holding his choir-singing in such an ice-chest.' She nodded towards what seemed a large box of pale wood between the fireplace and the window. 'Do you know what that is?'

'Mr. Garnett's organ.'

'Well,' and she threw back her head, laughing,' it's his harmonium, anyway.' And presently she drew him towards her again, straightening his tie. 'How was school today? Awful? Unbearable? Boring?'

'We had drill.' But he did not want to talk about school. 'Mr. Macaulay was on the tram, coming home.'

Her alert eyes searched his face. 'You didn't tell me.'

'I talked to him,' he said after a moment.

'What was he wearing, Walter?'

'A cap and a — you know — a mackintosh.'

She bent forward intently. 'No gloves? Wash-leather gloves — did you notice? Tell me that particularly.'

He couldn't remember. 'No,' he told her.

'The coward,' she laughed. 'He won't wear them.' She shut down the lid of the piano while a flustered colour came into her cheeks. 'Never mind . . . Tell me what you think of him, Walter.'

His mind went slowly over the image of the young man in the tram: the fresh reddish skin, the crisp sandy-gold hair, the moustache, the muscular blunt shoulders and hands.

'Tell me how he strikes you, Walter,' Miss Rose repeated and pulled him round forcibly to face her. 'You who're too young to hate or love. Has he changed lately? Does he look different?'

'I like him,' he told her truthfully.

'Everyone likes him,' she laughed and stroked the wool of her jacket. 'There've been times when I've wanted to torture him, tear him apart, break him, kill him — all for that power or attraction he doesn't realize.' She got up, flinging her voice out lightly. 'And yet, and yet . . . Happiness, great happiness, is all a part of those uncertain thoughts one can't help.' She paced across the room and back, her skirt brushing the carpet, her lips biting the back of her hand. 'I suppose,' she said presently, 'it was Muriel who told you the name Patrick Costello, Walter?'

'No,' he answered. 'Mrs. Hilda said his mother was a Belgian and the war — '

'Hilda? I see.' She hesitated. 'But the Costello boy was only a child, a youth,' she murmured as though to herself. 'He'd lost his legs in a farm accident: he was dying. I nursed him, I had to pretend to comfort him, mother him, love him. I couldn't refuse to go to him — I couldn't abandon him as a patient, even with Geoffrey to keep me away. I'd have been inhuman to do that; callous.' She sank down on the piano stool. 'If only I'd known — ' She lifted the lid of the keyboard and banged her fist on the notes, angrily.

'Are you upstairs, Walter?' Miss Muriel's voice called from the passage beyond the door.

'I'm here,' he said.

She came in. 'This boy ought to be doing his homework, Rose.'

Miss Rose got up impatiently. 'Take him,' she said in a hard voice that cut like a whip at her sister. 'But don't talk to me about interference — '

Walter followed Miss Muriel to the kitchen. He opened his books and began his homework, without concentration.

'What's wash-leather?' he asked presently.

She stood with bent head, staring at the shelf of the dresser. 'Wash-leather? It's stuff like . . . stuff like a cloth used for cleaning windows.'

'Is it white?'

'Yellow, rather.' And now he could hear the tears in her voice. He had never seen her cry before and was astonished. He sought for words.

'Why is she always angry with you?' he asked at last.

The expected rebuke did not come. Instead, the tears burst into sobs: her shoulders trembled, hunched forward over the dresser, wisps of hair shook on her neck, sighs like moans choked her throat. Not for several minutes did she speak.

'I did something I shouldn't have done,' she managed between indrawn breaths. 'It was wicked — I don't know now why I did it — I wasn't myself.' And suddenly she seemed to relax, to unburden a solitude she could not bear. 'I showed some letters written to Rose — I showed them to the man who seemed to want to marry her, Walter. She'd left the letters upstairs, in a hat-box on top of the cupboard in her room. I stole them, I knew they were there, I made Geoffrey read them. I thought she was deceiving him — playing with him. It made me angry.'

She broke into tears again, then wiped her cheeks. 'It was Geoffrey I thought of all the time. I wanted him to be happy, to marry somebody he ... I thought he was a fine man, the finest I'd ever met. I wanted to help him — as though he were my brother, somebody very dear to me who mustn't be injured or trifled with.' She was silent for a long time, her fingers straying over the mole on her lip, her sobs fading into broken sighs. 'You see now what I've done to Rose, Walter — why she's angry with me,' she whispered at last. 'But nobody — nobody sees what I've done to myself: the pain I've brought on my own heart. I did something unforgivable ... not Christian. I've prayed so often, but the relief doesn't come, and there didn't seem anybody I could tell my sin to. We're all so alone in distress, all of us.'

She glanced at him with reddened eyes and distorted mouth. 'And now I've told you, a child,' she whispered. 'Why did I do that?'

He had no explanation. He looked down at his books, biting the end of a pencil, embarrassed. The kitchen clock ticked above the stove, then struck eight in the silence.

'When I've finished my homework can I read one of my books?' he asked at length.

'I must go and bathe my eyes,' she said after a moment. 'Yes, read one of your books.' She touched him on the head, lingeringly, affectionately, then left him under the lamp.

Half an hour later he fetched a red-covered book from the drawer in the dresser, pulled the lamp an inch closer to his elbow and plunged into the world of his own choosing, the infinitely desirable world of adventure.

A hundred torches — nay, more — flickered between the palm trees on the beach ahead. The breeze, laden with a perfume of wood-smoke and of the blossoms of the tropical forest, sighed in the rigging below the schooner's furled sails. On the deck, just abaft the main cabin-housing, Tom crouched beside Chinese Jack: the latter with his bare

feet planted on the warm timbers, a fearsome knife a-dangle from his
belt. The two faced the shore.

'*Will they have seen us already?*' *the lad whispered.*

'*Plenty eyes, plenty see,*' *snarled the Chinee, his left hand gripping
his young companion's shoulder in a hard grasp.* '*Keepee down under
gunwale.*'

*His warning was necessary, for at that moment an arrow, flaming
at the shaft, whizzed past their ears. Tom ducked.* '*They've
spotted us,*' *he cried.*

'*Very powerful mens.*' *The Chinee did not move a muscle.*
'*Muchee clever mens.*'

'*But they're only pigmies,*' *Tom objected.*

'*No pigmy. Big mens.*'

*And suddenly, as though at the very words, a howl from a thousand
hostile throats burst from the forest, echoing over the schooner as she
drifted on her silent course nearer the shore. The howl was —*

'It's ten to nine, Walter. You must go to bed.'

He did not glance up, even listen.

'Walter!'

'Five more minutes, Miss Muriel.'

'No, dear. Go now.' She bent over and looked at the book
under his hand. 'Who's this Tom in the story?' she asked.

'He's been stolen by a press-gang,' he told her out of his
trance. 'He hasn't got a mother or father, only a grandmother.'

CHAPTER XIX

'ANYONE with a name like Von Kluck,' cried Marriner in the playground, 'ought to make a noise like a broody hen.'

The name of the German general was a joke that had already run through the school. The boys could not believe it: Von Kluck must be a nickname, an invention of the Allies (the word Entente had been dropped as not pronounceable), a piece of humour from a comic paper. They could not credit Mr. Garnett's assurance that the name was true — that the general's armies had overrun the forces of Belgium and that the war was the more serious in consequence. Much more serious indeed.

'A broody hen or an ostrich,' Walter agreed now with Marriner.

'Ostriches don't cluck.'

'They lay big enough eggs to cluck. Bigger than a kiwi's — twice as big.'

They sat over their sandwiches between the buttresses of the church. 'Gosh,' Marriner ruminated, 'I bet it hurts to lay eggs like that.'

The speculation widened, became more richly silly.

'Wonder what sort of eggs Von Kluck lays. Bet I know.'

'Cannon balls. . . .'

'The news is grave, boys,' Mr. Garnett announced, the following morning after prayers. 'The beautiful country of France is once more in history the victim of an invader's ravishment —' a glance along the platform at Miss Threplow '— of ravin, I should say perhaps.'

A map of Europe hung unfurled beside the blackboard, pricked with small flags. Daily, Mr. Garnett regarded it with distaste. 'The greatest musicians have all been Germans,' he said sadly as the flags crept towards Paris and the term drew to its end. 'And Von Kluck, I daresay, is not a gentleman.'

But Von Kluck, nevertheless, was still the joke, the password, hitched to everything. Somebody declared that the Forsaken Merman's name must have been Von Kluck: somebody else — Bascomb — had an old-fashioned bicycle with fiercely upturned handle-bars like the Kaiser's moustaches — this was called Von Kluck's Bike. In Mr. Garnett's absence a picture of the bicycle was drawn — by Marriner — on the blackboard, with the description scrawled below. At the last moment the Prussian general's name was imperfectly rubbed out and the master's own name chalked in its place: Mr. Garnett's Bike. This, for Walter, had consequences not foreseen.

The caricature was discovered by the old man himself, returning to the alarmed class. He regarded it distantly: the war, the discord, was much in his mind already, without this impertinence.

'Is this your handiwork, Blakiston?'

It was not Walter's. But the assumption was plain: Walter had remembered the adventure of the penny-farthing: he had hinted at it surreptitiously, disloyally, in the picture.

'No, sir.'

'Are you certain?'

'Yes, Mr. Garnett.' Walter thought the accusation unfair: he had not sneaked. 'I didn't do it.'

'Very singular. Your drawing-book, I've heard, has bicycles in it. In any case, it will not perhaps do you great harm to act as a scapegoat.' The master rubbed out the drawing then dusted the chalk from his fingers. 'You will remain behind for half an hour after school this evening.'

Marriner's hand went up. 'I did it, sir.' His small skull-like face trembled with dismay.

'You and Blakiston, Marriner, can arrive at the truth of that, between you, later.' The old man's voice was grieved, preoccupied. The afternoon class began: the Vikings again raided Britain.

Walter remained behind at four o'clock. Fifty times he wrote childish words across a sheet of foolscap: 'I must not draw on the blackboard.'

Marriner was waiting for him outside the gate of the playground, his satchel hunched on his back. He burst out at once, contrite:

'Sorry, man. Gosh, you can have half my lunch tomorrow. I'll bring you some squashed-fly biscuits.'

In a renewed blaze of friendship they sauntered towards the Square and the trams.

'But why did the old cock pick on you?' Marriner asked as they paused on the bridge and as usual spat into the water. 'You didn't do it.'

But Mr. Garnett's fall from .majesty on the penny-farthing was a secret, even now not to be told. Walter was silent.

'Von Kluck'd have shot him,' Marriner cried. 'I bet he would. It wasn't fair.'

They reached the Square. The evening lamps were lit: office windows, one by one, went dark for the night. Before the sweet shop shut its glass door Marriner bought two chocolate bars. He gave one bar to Walter.

'Mine's peppermint. What's yours?'

'Sort of coco-nut, I think. It crumbles.'

Idly they munched the chocolate, their eyes on the passers-by, their legs dawdling round the Square. The hands of the Post Office clock drooped to half past five.

'If you send me a postcard in the holidays,' Marriner began, 'I'll send you one — '

But it was at that moment that Walter saw Miss Rose. It was a moment he was to remember. She was, he saw, hurrying ahead of them, her slim body bent forward, a bunch of imitation violets on her dress, a black fur cape over her shoulders, one hand lifting her skirt an inch above the asphalt of the footpath. For a second she hovered under the veranda of a draper's shop, threw a glance to right and left, then slipped beyond into the shadows of the building itself, where an alley, a lane, led out of the Square. And hidden in the shadow a man waited to greet her; a man in a cap and mackintosh, with pale hands that Walter saw were not hands but yellowish-white gloves. Their faces touched. He took her arm, their bodies appeared to sway together, to merge into one person. A moment later they were engulfed by the shadows between the buildings. They vanished along the alley.

The glimpse, the sudden view of the meeting, had been so unexpected that Walter stood still on the footpath. He knew only that the woman had been Rose Garnett and the man, as unmistakably, Mr. Macaulay. For a second, gulping down his chocolate, he gazed after them, forgetting Marriner beside him. But Marriner had followed his eyes.

'Who was that? Did you know her, man?'

He did not speak the name. 'She lives at the Garnetts',' he said instead. Miss Rose, however, had not lived at the Garnetts' since at least a week earlier. She had not said goodbye to Walter but had left during his day's absence at school. Miss Muriel had delivered no message from her: her sister, she said simply, had gone back to her nursing, to a patient in Rangiora. Walter had kept quiet. Miss Rose had been kind to him and he'd wanted to say goodbye before the holidays. He'd missed her.

'Wait for me.' He threw the words at Marriner and deserted him on the footpath. He would catch up with Miss Rose. And between the buildings, into the alleyway, he raced after her. On either side were cement walls, advertisements, shut doors, darkened windows. His running steps echoed under him. The far end of the alley opened into a street beyond the Square, with bicycles hurrying under the lights. Walter halted on the corner, lost for direction. Then, two hundred yards to the right, he had a glimpse — no more — of Miss Rose's hat, her bent head, the back of Mr. Macaulay's overcoat. Shielding their faces, the pair were again turning a corner. Walter followed. The street they had taken was called, he knew, Manchester Street: it led southwards, in the direction of the railway lines. At this time of the evening people were returning home: the footpaths were impeded: Walter was not tall enough to see clearly between the shoppers, the walkers, the women with baskets. He had one last view of Miss Rose, her raised hand namelessly concealing her face, before both she and Mr. Macaulay disappeared. He had lost them.

He ran to where he had last seen the tops of their heads. A paper placard flapped from a wall, bicycles were propped against the entrance to a house with peeling gilt letters above the doorway, a dog lay curled on the mat of a shop. Dust blew along the gutters. He was alone, wondering why he had come so far, vaguely alarmed by the dog's one watchful eye. His mouth felt dry, his heart thumped in his chest.

He found his way back to the Square and the trams. Marriner had gone; had not waited. The Post Office clock struck six. The usual tram for Sumner had left twelve minutes earlier.

'I've kept your dinner for you,' Miss Muriel upbraided him when he finally let himself into the kitchen. She wore an unfamiliar red dress. 'However, I was late myself — I went up to Hilda's for tea. On the hill. So I suppose you're forgiven.'

'I missed the tram.'

She took his satchel from him. 'Father said he'd kept you in after school,' she remarked with amusement. And she called through the doorway to the dining-room: 'Walter's home, father. Don't worry.'

'Was he worried?' Walter hung up his coat.

'Oh, considerably. He thought you'd run away — to one of those islands you're always reading about.' She took his dinner from the oven. 'What made you miss the tram?'

He watched her, then turned away, the dog's one open eye upon him still. 'I forgot to look at the time,' he excused himself, and shivered.

Part Two

HOLIDAY

CHAPTER I

'Now you're here, Walter,' said Mrs. Grace, 'you must forget school; you must be your natural self. And you must *eat* — you're dreadfully thin.' Herself, the grandmother was a large woman: only her feet, in neat black shoes, were elegantly small, and she had tiny plump hands. 'Don't those Garnett people feed you properly? Have they a cook?'

'Miss Muriel's the cook. She's the eldest daughter.'

'I see. I get her muddled up with the others.'

'She's the one who has cold baths. Miss Rose has hot ones, and Mrs. Hilda's married.'

The grandmother considered this slowly, creases of laughter appearing round her eyes. 'You must tell me more about them. Meanwhile, they sound at least a clean family, I'm glad to hear. That's something. Though I'm not at all sure you ought to live in such a grown-up household — not at your age.' She shook her head, sighing with a reserve of tenderness. 'However, it was your parents' idea, not mine. All very difficult to understand . . . Is there a Garnett son?'

'I haven't met him yet,' Walter explained. 'He's a lighthouse keeper, I think.'

'What a most curious profession.' Mrs. Grace brooded. 'Like a hermit's. And have you no friends of your own in Sumner?'

'One. Jimmy Nelson. I like him a lot.'

'Is he a gentleman, this Jimmy?'

Walter had no idea: the question took him by surprise. 'He's got a bicycle,' he told her seriously. 'And his mother's a washer-woman.'

Mrs. Grace straightened a knife on the tea table, then lost herself in contemplation of the hills beyond the dining-room windows. The house was set high to one side of the valley; the veranda faced a lawn and a long slope broken with poplars. Across the valley were the hills, with blue ranges of mountain behind them to the west. In the bottom of the valley ran a creek, between limestone boulders. The air was clear and very sharp.

'What kind of jam do you like best, boy?' Mrs. Grace considered him again after a minute. 'Raspberry? Plum? Or just plain golden goosegog? You must tell me which one you prefer.'

He took a moment to decide. 'Goosegog.'

'Then goosegog it shall be. I made all the jam myself last year — cupboards full of it. Your grandfather doesn't care for jam, unfortunately.' She rose, turning the wedding ring on her finger. 'And now, if you've eaten enough, come along and see him. He's had sciatica lately, poor man. It makes him tetchy but you mustn't mind that. He's anxious to see you again.'

In his room along the veranda Walter's grandfather sat in a high-flanked chair, a green plaid rug across his knees, his hands folded on a crumpled newspaper.

'Here's Walter, Edward. Sayers brought him up from the station before tea.'

The fine thin nose and deep-set amethyst eyes turned towards the boy. 'He's grown,' said the powerful voice. 'More like his mother too, I'm glad to note. Are you married yet, Walter?'

'Don't tease him, Edward.'

'It's a simple question, after all.' The tuft of beard on the grandfather's chin wagged a little, in silent laughter. 'Do you *want* to be married, Walter?'

Walter bent to stroke a white cat that had appeared, purring, from beneath Mr. Grace's chair. 'Doesn't it cost a lot?' he asked, embarrassed.

'*Cost?* Give him sixpence,' Mr. Grace waved at his wife. 'Give him sixpence, Rachel. That'll change his mind for him. *Costs* too much, indeed — I never heard such sophistry.' But his eyes crinkled at Walter. 'Between ourselves,' he said, 'you're only too damned right, my boy. Did you learn that in class?

Is that what they teach now in the preparatory schools of these benighted islands?'

Walter did not reply. The white cat arched her back under his hand, gaping her mouth in a soundless mew.

'You're to pay no attention to your grandfather, Walter,' Mrs. Grace directed. 'If he's not teasing he's swearing.' And she settled the cushions behind her husband's shoulders. 'I don't know which is the worse — an old person in pain or a young person in love.'

'A fussy woman's a sight worse than either.' The grandfather snorted; his fingers scratched at the paper on his lap; he settled himself against the cushions with an invalid's distaste. 'I'll tell you what I'd do if I had my way,' he confided to Walter. 'I'd join the cavalry and be off — ' his thumb tapped the newspaper ' — be off to fight these Uhlans in France. I'd leave your grandmother to run the station here by herself. That'd teach her I'm not so useless as she makes out!'

Walter took his grandmother's part. 'I'd come and help her,' he said. 'Gran'd take me, wouldn't you, gran? I could ride with the shepherds — '

Mrs. Grace shook the question off lightly. She turned towards the door. 'I've given you the little bedroom at the head of the stairs, Walter. I know that used to be your favourite. You could carry up your luggage now.'

After dinner that night he helped her to unpack his clothes. 'I told your mother I'd look at your things.' She splayed a pair of his stockings over her fingers. 'Does Miss What's-her-name do your darning for you?'

'Mostly.'

'She seems a good-hearted creature, I must say: an admirable foster-mother . . .' And later she watched him as he undressed by the light of a candle on the dressing-table. 'Why, your shoulder blades stick out like flags.' He felt the cool gold of her rings on his flesh. 'How strange young boys are — like little skinny kittens.' She kissed him on the nape. 'And they need so much affection; so much . . . Did you mind coming to stay with your old gran?'

'I wanted to.'

She turned down the stiff linen sheets of the bed and shook out his pyjamas. Everything she did was precise, calm, even beautiful: he was surrounded, protected, by her tenderness: and she had always loved him.

'Your mother hasn't been well, you know,' she told him. 'Her letters to me and your grandfather have worried us a good deal, these past months.'

He caught his breath. 'Is she really ill?'

'Well,' the grandmother considered. 'No. But perhaps we'd better not talk about it. Not now, before you sleep.'

'She won't die?' He stared at her, alarmed, full of pangs, suddenly homesick.

'Oh, dear no. Nothing like that . . . Women are not as strong as men, you know. Not always.' She snuffed the wick of the candle reflectively. 'I don't mean physical strength. It's more a question of resilience, fortitude. Men are tougher.'

Disconcerted, thinking of his mother, he rubbed the palm of his hand over his chest. 'I'm tough too.'

'Not very tough.' She smiled. 'At any rate, while you're here with us I don't want you to go worrying your head over your mother. She has a good doctor, an English doctor; and I expect you'll see her at Christmas. Meanwhile, you must make the most of your holiday, as boys do — you can fish and ride and picnic as much as you want. And you must eat . . . Now I'll turn my back and you can put on your pyjamas. Or don't you mind me seeing you?'

'I don't mind.' His nakedness did not trouble him. 'Can I read before I go to sleep, gran?'

'For a little then. I see you've brought a book with you.'

He showed her the illustrations. 'Can you read what's written underneath?'

Mrs. Grace held the book away from her under the candle,

154

murmuring with her lips. 'Pirates, sea-dogs,' she remarked. 'Very fierce, by the look.'

In the morning he awoke early, hearing the first thrushes and bell-birds singing behind the house as he pulled on his clothes and hurried down the steep stairs. Nobody was about. The pendulum of the clock in the hall wagged slowly behind glass. Outside, on the veranda, his grandfather's cat crouched in the sunlight, her white paws soaked with dew: she stared, round-eyed, at the boy as he plunged his fingers into the warm fur of her breast. The lawn sloping away from the house was frosted blue in the shadow of the poplars. Listening, Walter could hear the creek among the stones at the bottom of the valley, half a mile away across the paddocks. On the further slope beyond the creek a flock of sheep was grazing among the yellowish tussocks of the foothills, their backs grey in the sun. The grass of the paddocks sparkled. Walter drew in a long breath: this up-country world of his grandparents' farm was to be for three weeks his, without reservation: its freedom was huge, its possibilities endless.

'A day to be young,' exclaimed Mrs. Grace at breakfast. 'Bliss was it in that dawn to be alive,' she observed to the silver sugar bowl on the table.

'Your grandmother,' Mr. Grace turned to Walter, 'has a head for poetry, I'm afraid. The result of winning a prize at — wherever she absorbed her education.' Shakily he sat at the top of the table, a silk scarf tucked into the neck of his dressing-gown, his back to the portrait of a cavalier in wig and armoured breastplate on the wall. 'Does this Mr. Garnett teach you poetry at school? Shakespeare? All that stuff?'

'Miss Threplow teaches us — ' he began.

'You're fond of Shakespeare yourself, Edward,' Mrs. Grace objected.

'What was that, my dear?'

'Fond of Shakespeare. "To be or not to be" — I've heard you bring that out often enough on occasion.'

'And why not indeed? A sheep-farmer, God knows, isn't necessarily blind to the riddle of existence.' He helped himself to butter. 'I am philosophical, however, rather than poetical: always have been. Poetry evades the issue.' And he winked aside at Walter. 'Your grandmother's a woman — has to be put in her place from time to time. And the older she gets the less she listens.'

'We learnt about the Forsaken Merman last term,' Walter informed them presently.

The grandmother shook her head. 'That poor Merman — crazed for love. Oh, I used to cry for him, thinking life so short, Walter.' She contemplated the view, the sunlight across the veranda. 'Though I suppose human passion — '

'Human passion,' her husband broke in, 'if you must talk of it at breakfast, Rachel, is always ridiculous: ridiculous at least to those beyond it or those not yet old enough to feel its sting — to the ancient and the naive. That means to me and you, Walter, Heaven help us. I won't include your grandmother this morning as she's on her best behaviour.'

'Leave Walter alone, Edward.'

But Walter had not been listening: there was too much else for attention. Below the table he had felt the fur of the white cat brush against his bare shins. 'Does Tab ever catch fish in the creek?' he asked his grandfather.

'Tab? No, she's scared of the sheep coming down to drink. But she does wander off into the hills occasionally, I've noticed: some sort of tryst with Nature, no doubt.' He touched the cat gingerly with his slipper. 'Once she was even found in Geraldine — that's twenty miles off. We had to send a shepherd to fetch her.' He hauled the cat into his lap. 'I prefer dogs,' he grunted after a moment. 'Less subject to the caprices of the female heart.'

Breakfast finished; the morning expanded.

'Gran — ' Walter went through the house calling for her ' — where are you?'

He found her upstairs counting blankets from the linen-cupboard, singing a hymn to herself. 'I'm here, boy.'

'Can I go fishing?'

'The rods are in the smoke-room. Worms in the garden. Try the earth behind the pigsties for the fattest. Take a tin.'

The stones and limestone boulders of the creek were yellow and red with lichen in the sunlight. The water came crackling down from the hills at the head of the valley and fell to a hush in the shallows beyond the paddocks, under a few stunted willows and bushes of gorse and broom. Walter baited the small hook then let it trail downstream from a cascade among the stones. From time to time he could see the trout in the water: the larger fish, most of them, moved away and past the hook, warily. Only a few of the smaller, as the morning advanced, took the worm and came flicking, jerking, on to the tussocks of the bank, frantic in the frightening air. Walter disentangled them from the hook and threaded their gills with a sprig of broom. Dying, they lay among the stones, with dry grass-blades stuck to the rainbow spots of the flanks, the silver-grey bellies, the olive and blue sheen along the back. He crouched over them, watching the ebb of their mysterious lives. He was completely happy, the heat of the spring sun falling on his head and neck.

He fished until midday, moving upstream with the bamboo rod and the worm tin, then hurried back with his catches across the shallow warm paddocks of the valley to the white house among the poplars.

'Your grandfather put the first trout into that creek thirty years ago,' Mrs. Grace told him, inspecting the fish.

'Thirty *years?*' Walter stared. The time seemed infinite.

'At any rate when your mother was a baby here, I remember. We showed her the young fry in their pail after their trip from the coast. That was not long after we'd arrived from England, Walter: in the early days.'

He dangled the trout above the polished floor of the hall.

'Take them out to Annie in the kitchen,' said the grandmother. 'They're pretty but the poor beasts have an appallingly fishy smell.' She put her handkerchief to her nose.

In the late afternoon he fetched his book from upstairs and, tired, lay reading on the veranda. Behind him old Mr. Grace, a captive in his chair, sat by the window, an open ledger spread on his knees.

'If you want to be a farmer, boy,' he remarked presently, 'don't neglect your multiplication tables. Not even Harrow and Oxford ever taught me the mystery of eight times seven. Your grandmother's always had to work out my men's wages for me every month, I regret to say.'

The pirates had no arithmetic either. Walter glanced up. 'What?'

'And no gentleman says *what* in that tone to his grandfather.' Mr. Grace frowned down at the white cat curled beside his feet. 'A decline in the English tradition, Tab,' he continued, touching her warm fur with his slipper. 'Cats and men — we're transplanted gentry and we keep to our standards, you and I. We preserve our manners, we don't forget the old country and — speaking for myself, Tab, though alas not for you — we do not couple with lesser breeds outside the law.'

The white cat turned over on her back. She did not purr.

'Did you listen, boy?' the grandfather asked Walter.

He had returned to the pirates in their cave. 'Yes,' he said. 'I heard every word.'

'I'm delighted to hear that. Nobody else seems to listen to me. Even your grandmother's ceased to pay me that compliment.'

'Walter,' Mrs. Grace called from along the veranda, 'your tea's ready, child, if you'd come.'

Beside his plate he discovered a glass jar with a paper top. Orange-green seeds sprinkled the jam behind the glass.

'Goosegog,' said the grandmother and took up the tea-pot. 'I hadn't forgotten, you see.'

CHAPTER II

'YOUR mother sends you her love, Walter.' Mrs. Grace folded the letter from her daughter and tucked it thoughtfully into the belt of her white dress. 'Have you written to her?'

'Yes.' He had told his mother, he explained, about his fishing, his riding, his collection of fossil shells found in the limestone gullies — 'everything,' he finished. 'Is she better?'

'Much better, though not sleeping well yet, she says.' Mrs. Grace looked along the table at her husband. 'Did you hear that, Edward? Caroline is much better, much improved.'

'I am not yet deaf, Rachel.'

'No, my dear, but you seldom attend.' She twisted a diamond and sapphire ring on her finger. 'So now,' she continued to Walter, 'now you know your mother's better, you won't mind going back to school, or not so much.'

It was the last full day of the holidays. He nodded, drooping for a moment: the wrench away from his grandparents would be hard, desperate, it would make him homesick again. His stomach fluttered uncomfortably.

The grandmother too was moved: she returned to consolation. 'You'll have the summer ahead of you,' she brought out, studying his face. 'You've managed to get yourself sunburnt already,' she added. 'As brown as a young Maori.'

He revived. 'I wouldn't mind being a Maori,' he said and lost himself in the provident dream. 'A Maori chief, with tui's feathers.' And he remembered Jimmy and Mrs. Nelson. 'Would you like to have married a Maori, gran?'

'I?' She fluttered a tidying hand over her hair, considering. 'Unfortunately,' she laughed, 'as it happens, I never had the chance, Walter.'

'No, but say you *had*?' He plunged into the game. 'Would you — would mum have been a half-caste if — '

'Your grandmother,' Mr. Grace interrupted, affronted, 'happened to have become my wife, Walter, before she ever saw such a species as the Maori.' He frowned at the boy in mock horror. 'Before she ever set foot in these islands,' he amended, 'or clapped eyes on their native fauna . . . Don't put ideas into her head: she's susceptible.'

'Rubbish, Edward. Pooh to you. And stop talking for effect.' Mrs. Grace bit her lip, the smooth skin about her eyes crinkled in thought. 'As a Maori's wife,' she resumed, undeterred, 'I'd rather have fancied myself in a flax and raupo skirt, you know . . . with a greenstone earring or two. I've always had a craving for those more barbaric kinds of jewellery, if I must admit it.'

'The inherent immorality of women,' the grandfather remarked to the ceiling. 'Not to mention that intermarriage between diverse stocks is a mistake, for which the wife usually pays.'

'You make cross-breeds of your sheep, surely.'

'That, my dear, is a very different matter. Animals have no codes as we understand them, thank God — they're simply fertile or infertile.'

The argument continued over Walter's head. 'What else did mum say in her letter?' he asked his grandmother when silence had fallen on the meal.

'I think she mentions that your last term's report had reached her.'

His entrails fluttered again. 'Was she pleased?'

'Fairly pleased, boy, I think. The drawing-mistress had said pleasant things about you.'

'May I see the letter, gran?'

'No, child, I don't think that's advisable.'

'Why not?'

'Your mother'll explain when she sees you.' Mrs. Grace glanced at her husband. 'Don't you think that's best, Edward?'

'I do, Rachel, I do.'

After breakfast Walter wandered about the house. Outside, a thin misty rain blew across the hills: the pleated blue of the mountains was dimmed by a bloom like that on a grape. The crackle and plunge of the creek in the valley sounded far away, the other side of the spring mist. Nearer, the poplars stood green and still across the lawn, sentinels about the house and veranda. Walter, standing at the window, set himself to watch one of the shepherds on horseback rounding up sheep among the tussocks: the shepherd's dogs ran among the grey flock; a faint whistle pierced the rain. Already homesick in advance for the life on the station, the life in his grandparents' house, he sought out his grandmother, scuffling his boots along the polished floor of the hall. He would at least make sure of future holidays.

'I can come back, can't I, gran?'

'Always, boy. As long as ever we live, your grandfather and I.'

'Always,' he repeated idly. 'How long does "ever" last? A million years?'

'We none of us know, Walter. It's one of the mysteries. You must ask the Almighty.'

'He wouldn't tell me, anyway.'

'He might. You believe in Him, don't you?'

'Yes,' he said doubtfully. 'I do, but —'

'But what?' She began to run a duster along the drawing-room mantelpiece. 'But what?'

He did not answer. The Almighty was mixed up with Scripture, with a white beard like Mr. Garnett's, with Sunday school and with a picture of the Israelites crossing the Red Sea in the Line-upon-line his mother had given him. If you sinned, God had his ways of revenge. He was terrible. For no particular reason Walter's thoughts went back to his mother. He asked Mrs. Grace:

'Did mum want to leave here when she got married?'

'She wanted to go and live with your father, naturally,

Walter.' She smiled, disentangling the duster from a long silver chain she wore over her dress. 'She was in love with him, madly in love — couldn't live without him — threatened to run away, I remember. She was only nineteen then, you see: just a young girl and not very sophisticated.'

Walter considered the image of his mother he carried in his mind and memory: the face, smiling, had an air of distance and dreams; the fair hair was up-piled; the soft shoulders opened bare as he had seen them at her dressing-table in the mornings. But his mother 'in love', 'madly in love' . . . like a stranger of whom he could ask nothing . . . caught, like Miss Rose, in some unaccountable turmoil of the senses! He did not believe it: his mother was different, serener, mistress of herself.

'Marry she would, and marry she did,' Mrs. Grace continued. 'And, after all, one didn't blame her — your father was the handsomest young farmer in Canterbury, or one of them. The best looking, if not the gayest,' she added with a teasing reserve. 'Also of course he had other advantages — an English background, money, a station of his own. All eminently suitable. Edward and I could only approve when it came to the point, lonely though your mother left us here when she departed.' She paused, blew her nose. 'All the same, your father can be a very difficult man, Walter, as you know. He has a temper, a temperament as they say nowadays; fixed ideas of his own. As a matter of fact,' she went on, pursing her lips at the taste of truth, 'your grandfather and I have sometimes thought him inexplicable . . . Other people's motives, however, are not always easy to understand. Don't you find that?'

The question, like so many others, was beyond him. To escape it he found himself bending to touch the tiles of the drawing-room grate: behind the glaze were pictures of melon-like fruits bowered in some kind of tropical extravagant leaves. He knelt before them on the hearth-rug.

'They're breadfruit,' he told Mrs. Grace.

'I've no notion, dear. Perhaps.'

'You could live on them if you were cast on a desert island.'

'I'd rather not be cast on a desert island, Walter.' She shook the duster from the window on to the terrace. 'This place here was enough of a desert when we arrived from England — enough of a desert to last me a lifetime.' The memory disquieted her. 'Your grandfather and I lived in a tent until this house was built . . . We hung our hats on the floor, and the wekas pecked our toes if we put them out of bed.'

'Yes, tell me . . .' He loved hearing the story, as he had heard it often before. His grandparents had been pioneers.

'I must go up and pack your clothes,' she interrupted herself at last, 'if you're really off tomorrow.'

But the packing was postponed until the evening, when they went through his clothes together, with the shadow of school and parting approaching them both.

'These Garnetts,' Mrs. Grace reminded him, 'even now you've told me so little about them, Walter.'

'There's nothing to tell,' he said stubbornly.

'Nothing? There's always something about people. . . .'

He did not answer but sought in his mind and heart for some topic to take the Garnetts' place. 'I saw a dog run over by the tram,' he said at last. 'The driver . . . he threw it over the bridge afterwards and it drowned. It was alive before he threw it.'

To his astonishment he saw tears in her eyes as she fumbled with his packing. 'You're crying,' he accused her.

'Only —' she dabbed at her cheeks ' — only because you're going away, Walter. We shall miss you here, so much. You've been like a son, for us.'

'I'll come back.'

'You'll be different. You'll grow up.'

And presently she kissed him good night. 'The gig'll be round in time for the train after breakfast, child. Sayers'll drive you to the station.' She blew out the candle. 'No reading tonight. Sleep well now.'

He slept fitfully, with disturbed dreams of the dog in the water.

'A present,' said his grandfather at breakfast. The sovereign gleamed in Walter's hand. 'Not to be blowed all at once, is it, Tab,' he murmured aside to the white cat. 'Except perhaps on a hair-cut.'

'My own present's packed in your luggage, dear,' Mrs. Grace told him. She was again on the verge of sobs. 'Under your stockings.'

'Is it goosegog jam?'

The gig wheels crackled over the gravel before the house. A moment more and he was perched on the warm leather cushions of the seat, beside the young shepherd.

'Not goosegog jam,' called Mrs. Grace above her tears. With one hand she held the white cat closely against her breast, with the other she waved him goodbye, sadly, lingeringly, the early sunlight catching her forehead through the trellis of the veranda.

Part Three

IN THE WATER

CHAPTER I

'Jimmy's got a shift this term — he's in a higher class.' Mrs Nelson patted her son's shoulder. 'Aren't you, Jimmy? They've given you a shove up for good behaviour to the girls.'

'You don't know anything about it,' Jimmy said rudely.

'You told me so yourself . . . And don't fly off the handle like that at your mother. Understand?'

'Yes, ma.'

She threw up the lower half of the kitchen window, leaned across the sill and cast a weather eye over the lines of wet sheets and towels that flapped in the sunshine of the yard. 'I'm sure Walter never says the cheeky things to his mother that you say to me,' she remarked over her shoulder. 'I'm sure he has more respect, as a well brought-up kid.'

Walter fidgeted, looking at Jimmy. They had made plans to slip away for an exploring expedition on the pier. 'Can we go for a walk, Mrs. Nelson, Jimmy and me?'

'By yourselves? How about taking me for a walk too? I need a walk, Lord knows, after scrubbing dirty clothes all day.'

Jimmy screwed up his face darkly at Walter, disapproving. 'You can come with us,' he said to his mother, 'if you promise to walk behind.'

'I'll do no such thing!' Her ample body swayed over to the table, cigarette ash scattering a grey rain down her apron. 'You'll walk with me or not at all, James Nelson.' She pulled out a kitchen chair and planted herself heavily, facing them. 'Besides,' she said, 'I want to hear Walter's news. We haven't seen him for a month. How's school, Walter?'

'It's just the same.'

'And the Garnetts?'

Jimmy swung his arms, bored. 'I'm going out to feed the rabbits, ma, if you're going to talk.'

'Go then. Those rabbits,' she sniffed; 'a damn nuisance. I won't keep Walter long.'

Jimmy departed, slamming the door. There was a silence in the warm kitchen, where Walter stood with his back to the dresser, his cap rolled in his fingers. He felt cornered.

'How did you get along with your granma?' Mrs. Nelson asked him presently. 'All right?'

He told her. The sense of constraint was eased: he lived his holiday over again, its cherished moments. 'One of the shepherds took me out riding . . . he showed me a cave in the hills, with maidenhair ferns in it . . . I had jam to eat every tea-time.'

'Here,' said Mrs. Nelson, heaving herself up, 'have a slice of cake now.' She produced a seed-cake from a tin. 'Have two slices.' She pushed the yellow wads of cake into his hand. 'Fatten you up. . . .'

And now her comfortable voice had returned to the Garnetts. 'What's become of Miss Rose?' she asked easily, puffing at her cigarette.

'I haven't seen her — not this term,' he murmured. 'She's still away.'

'Ah, this nursing . . . When did you see her last?'

Walter looked down at his boots, his mind still lulled by thoughts of his holiday, his teeth biting into the cake. 'Just before I went away,' he said. And suddenly the words slipped out: 'I saw her in the Square while I was waiting for the tram.'

'You saw Miss Rose in the Square?'

'Well, it was just off the Square?'

The soft brown bulk of her face swayed towards him through the smoke of her cigarette. 'I wonder now,' she said slowly, 'if she was alone.'

'No. I ran after them —' he stopped, feeling the handle of the dresser drawer bite hard between his shoulders . . . 'I mean they —'

'Don't be shy, son.' She came across and cuddled his head against her with an impulsive warmth that stilled his caution. 'Was it a man she was with? Did they go off together?'

'No . . . Yes,' he said reluctantly.

'It wouldn't by any chance be a chap who lives in Sumner, I suppose, would it?'

His cheeks burnt; he looked down again at his boots, silent.

'All right,' she said. 'I guessed it, anyway. Geoff Macaulay.' She nodded. 'I won't tell anyone you gave the game away, Walter. I won't tell anyone you told me.'

'I didn't tell you.' He snatched himself away from her, confused by a mind acuter than his own. 'I didn't catch them up,' he floundered, 'they went too fast.' Her cigarette made him cough; crumbs spattered from his mouth to the floor.

'Where did they go?' she pursued. 'Was it to a hotel, a boarding-house?'

'I don't know . . . I didn't tell you, Mrs. Nelson!'

'No — you didn't tell me.' And she added, more softly: 'Good gracious, what does it matter if you did? What are you getting into such a stew about?'

He couldn't explain. He hardly knew what he had told her or if his words had had any real meaning. All the same, a sharp shame pricked his soul: he had betrayed Miss Rose. But how or why or to what end?

'I didn't tell you, Mrs. Nelson,' he repeated stubbornly, pathetically. 'I didn't.'

She strolled away from him, relighting her cigarette.

'Well,' she said to the window-sill, a snatch of laughter, like a triumph, pursing her lips, 'I always did like Rose more than that snob of a Hilda.' Her eyes swept over the lines of washing in the yard. 'Rose has a way with her.' And she chuckled to herself. 'So she's got him at last,' she reflected aloud. 'She's got him back.' She turned, her hands on her hips.

Walter stared at her cigarette. Innocence spoke for him: 'Will Mr. Macaulay marry her now?'

'Because they — ?' And a wave of amusement took her. 'It won't work out like that, sonny. Hilda's got this kid coming. She's the wife.'

'But if . . .' he floundered afresh. The whole thing — Miss Rose, Mrs. Hilda, even Miss Muriel — seemed to him as strange, as involved, as a language of which he did not know the grammar. 'I don't know,' he said, crumbling the cake in his hand.

'Why should you?' She chuckled again. 'You can't know everything.'

He stood before her, embarrassed, longing desperately to escape from her, from the kitchen itself. 'Can Jimmy and I go for a walk now, Mrs. Nelson?'

But Jimmy was already at the door, his brown eyes blinking at Walter. 'Got something to show you, Walt.' And he drew Walter into the yard, by the elbow. 'Come where ma can't see us.'

A crack in the paling fence showed them a few square yards of the section next door. On the sandy grass, close against the fence, a small girl stood holding a half-naked doll in her bare arms.

'It's Ivy Dakers,' Jimmy whispered. 'Hullo, Ive.'

The girl stared back at them angrily, fixedly. 'I'm not to talk to you,' said her high thin voice.

'Who says?'

The girl frowned at the doll, slowly twisting its neck. 'I'm not going to say a single word.' Her lank blonde plaits shone on her shoulders in the sun. 'Not to you, anyway.'

'Who says?'

'Your rabbits smell,' said the girl, 'and you smell too.'

'Gosh, nothing to you!' Jimmy spat through the crack in the palings. 'You pong like rotten fish.'

'Don't be rude,' said Ivy Dakers. 'You're the rudest boy in Sumner. Easily.'

'Who says?'

The girl turned her back on them. 'Everyone.' She stalked

away with stiff knees towards her own back door. 'Your Daddy's a Maori too,' she flung in retreat.

Jimmy kicked the palings. 'Yours is a dirty German,' he bawled after her. 'Hun! Stinking German! Boozing old German!'

The girl reached her door. 'I said I wasn't talking to you and I'm not.' She disappeared.

'What did you have to show me?' Walter asked.

'Her. She's always putting her snotty nose through our fence.'

'Is her father a German?'

'I only said that to get her rat up. Gosh, she's awful.' Jimmy gave a hitch to his trousers as they left the fence. 'Do you ever get a hard on you?' he asked Walter, below his breath.

Walter did not know what a hard meant, and was afraid to show his ignorance before Jimmy. 'Where?' he said.

'In your pants. I do, when girls say rude things.'

Behind them Mrs. Nelson came solidly out of the kitchen, a clothes basket balanced against her hip. She lowered the props supporting the clothes lines and began to gather dry sheets into the basket, large damp patches showing beneath the arms of her dress. In the lowering light of the sun she squinted towards the two boys in the yard.

'How was your girl, Jimmy? How was Ivy?' she teased, smiling at Walter. 'I saw you at the fence again.'

'I hate her, ma!' Her son began dancing round the yard, swinging his arms, kicking at tufts of grass. 'I hate her — I wouldn't touch her with a clothes prop!'

'You'll marry her one day. You'll see.'

Jimmy opened his mouth as though to be sick into the basket, his mauve-pink tongue lolling. 'Ur-r-r,' he groaned.

'You'll see. Ivy's after you — too right she is. — Unless she's got her eye on Walter now she's seen him. You'd better mind your p's and q's, both of you.'

'We'll sail away,' Jimmy cried, recovering. 'We'll sail away to the South Seas where she won't get us. Won't we, Walt? A million miles.'

'That'll do you a fat lot of good.' Mrs. Nelson held a clothes-peg between her lips as she swept the sheets into the basket. 'Ivy'll be after you,' she mumbled to the boys. 'She'll teach you about girls who never let men go! You wait!'

'She said my pa was a Maori, ma,' Jimmy cried.

'Oh she did, did she?' Her voice changed as she glared over the fence at the bungalow next door. 'Young slut,' she said, aggrieved. 'I could have her up for defamation or something, saying things like that in public.'

The hot Saturday afternoon began to wilt between the hills. A horse and cart rattled down the road in front of the Nelsons' garden through a blue light that was already scented with smoke from evening chimneys. Mrs. Nelson wiped her hands on her apron.

'You two kids carry in this basket for me,' she directed, 'if it won't strain your lordships' strength.'

'Is it your washing, Mrs. Nelson?' Walter asked. He and Jimmy seized the wicker handles. 'All of it?'

'Some from the Andersons and some from the Macaulays.'

'From Mrs. Hilda's?'

She nodded, throwing open the back door for them to enter. 'I'm late this week, one thing and another. If I iron all day to-morrow I'll take it up to her Monday or Tuesday.'

'Do you see her — Mrs. Hilda — when you go to her house?'

'Well, someone's got to pay me.' And with another glance over the fence she shepherded the boys into the kitchen. 'Yes, I see her. I'll see her this week — too right I will. I'll have a little chat with Mrs. Hilda.' She laughed, shrugged, looked round for a cigarette.

Walter gaped at her flushed face: at an expression upon it he had not seen before. Without knowing why, and without a word spoken, he knew that in some way she had already betrayed Miss Rose — betrayed her through him, for ever. He could not speak.

'I've got a splinter in my finger, ma.' Dimly Walter heard Jimmy's cry. 'Ma, I've got a splinter from the basket.'

'All right,' she said calmly, 'you're not dead. Don't howl.' She fetched a needle that had been stuck in a shelf of the dresser. 'If you make a rumpus like that Walter'll think the heavens have fallen.'

'It's hurting, ma.'

'A simple thing like a splinter, good gracious . . . You drown before you leave the bank.' And she twisted his hand towards the light, probing for the splinter, her cigarette wobbling between her lips. 'You wait till I tell that Ivy Dakers,' she chided.

'I hate Ivy.'

'She won't half have a tale about you howling for a splinter.'

'I wasn't howling, ma.' His dark little face fought his mother's.

'And you tell tales yourself. Stinkers, you do.'

'Me?' She flung his hand away. 'Say that again and you get a taste of the slipper, my lad.'

The clock struck seven. A mild panic overcame Walter: the afternoon had flown. His walk with Jimmy was off for the day. Now he would be late for dinner at the Garnetts'. And he flung himself from the house, almost without a word of goodbye to Mrs. Nelson, and raced down the road, his cap swinging in his hand.

'My brother Mark's here, Walter,' Miss Muriel called as he washed his hands in the scullery. 'He arrived this afternoon — on holiday, for a change.' Her voice came light and gay. 'Hurry up, he wants to meet you.' And presently she led him through to the dining-room. 'Mark, this is Walter.'

A thin young man going bald grinned at him from a chair beyond Mr. Garnett. 'How are you, Walter?' said a clear open voice. He pointed at the boy with the stem of a clay pipe. 'All right?'

'Yes.' He shook hands.

'Shut the door, boy, if you're comin' in,' old Mrs. Garnett interrupted. And she went on with a conversation directed at her son: 'That family were always a shiftless lot; never got anywhere. Too little money and too little sense.'

'I suppose so, yes,' said Mark Garnett. 'Poor but dishonest,' he smiled. 'Not even that.'

'One married a carpenter,' the old woman continued. 'At least they said she did. You can't tell today; girls marry whom they please.' She pushed her spectacles up the bridge of her nose. 'And now this war's goin' to loosen standards worse than before. Sure to.'

Her son yawned. 'Quite possibly, mother, quite possibly. I'll take your word for it. Wars are apt to be shakers-up of any civilization. Do you agree, father?'

'Undoubtedly, Mark.' The old man grunted. 'Though they settle so little.'

Walter stood waiting, feeling himself separate, his eyes upon Mark Garnett. At the first chance he would ask Mr. Mark about the lighthouse he had come from. Meanwhile, Mrs. Nelson was almost forgotten: he would not think about her.

CHAPTER II

IDLY, Mark Garnett reached over and picked up the school-book Walter was reading at the dining-room table. 'H'm,' he pronounced after a moment, turning the pages, 'all the old lies and nonsense over again, I see.' He shifted the clay pipe from one side of his mouth to the other, screwing up his eyes with distaste. 'History as a collection of dates and battles! — Not a word about what goes on under the clothes, not a syllable about the mental climate of the times. God, what a swindle it is, to ram all this muck down kids' throats year after year.'

Since his arrival in the house several days before, this was the first time he had spoken alone with Walter. Now he sat on the edge of the table, coolly surveying the boy and his homework. The silver ring he wore on his left hand gleamed like an extra knuckle as he dropped the book on the others at Walter's elbow.

'What else do you read? For pleasure, I mean: not this arbitrary stuff.'

Walter hesitated. 'I read about pirates, sometimes.'

'They've some honest blood in their guts, at any rate. Ever tackled any Dickens?'

He did not know what Dickens was: it might be a kind of game. 'No,' he said.

'I've read the lot myself, over and over. Helps to pass the time at night, when the bogeys prowl. Good lighthouse reading.'

Walter forgot his homework. 'How many wrecks do you get? Many?'

'None, if we can help it! The Straits are pretty safe if the skippers and pilots keep an eye skinned.' He expanded; the fine pale dome of his forehead flushed in the lamplight. 'However, let's talk about you, Walter. I suppose you won't know what I'm getting at if I ask whether you're happy?'

Wondering what he was expected to answer, Walter drew a line with his pencil on the table-top. 'In the holidays, I am,' he said.

'Ponies, guns, fishing-rods . . . H'm.' The other brooded. 'Sending children like you away to school,' he went on with a kind of chill tenderness, 'it's a hellish business really. Nobody learns adult behaviour that way — only fright and furtiveness . . . And as for schoolmasters, I'd cheerfully dump the whole crew in the sea, my revered father included.' A wry smile lit for a second on Walter as the stem of the clay pipe tapped the heap of books at his side. 'My father doesn't seem to have the remotest notion he's educating boys for a colonial life, not an English: for the farm and not the Foreign Office or the Church . . . He even wanted me to be a priest because I hankered after solitude.' His thin face was contorted by a contemptuous inward laugh. 'It wasn't God I was after, I can tell you!'

Walter had his eye on the silver ring: he had never before seen a ring on a man's hand. 'Do you wear your ring when you're at the lighthouse?'

'I do.' Mark Garnett rubbed the flat boss of the ring against his knee. 'I do, Walter,' he said, amused. 'Even in my bunk — a snug little bunk with grey blankets, in a room with curved walls. Would you like that yourself?'

'Yes,' he said, entranced.

'The schoolboy's dream!' You'd hate every bloody moment of it, Walter, believe me. Fellows get the jimjams and go crazy in the loneliness.' He rubbed the ring again, reflecting. 'My wedding-ring — I'm betrothed, Walter — betrothed to iconoclasm, curiosity and the damnation of my too-human nature. The fate of a man with too much control over his own instincts — the victim of an Anglican evangelical upbringing common to my sisters and myself. If I'd been born in England I'd have been a don in some nice cosy university.' He smoothed the hairless crown of his head and again his eyes took in Walter at the table. 'I'm interrupting your homework . . . What do you think about? I remember now — Rose told me when she wrote last term that you were a silent kid, reserved. You sit there like a mouse — a white mouse — and listen to your elders. Or are you silent because you've nobody to talk to in a house of strangers? If so, I don't blame you: I've often felt that way myself.'

'Mark, you ought to let that child get on with his work.' Miss Muriel bustled in from the hall. 'Father'll be home presently.'

Mark Garnett swung his legs from the table. 'Heigh-ho. So much for that. How's mother?'

'I've just put her to bed.' She pulled the curtains across the doors to the veranda, shutting away the twilight. 'She's getting old, you know. She gets in a muddle if I leave her too long.' For a moment she sank into a chair; her lips quivered. 'Oh Mark, I'm so tired,' she whispered. 'So fagged.' Her eyes closed.

'You do too much, old girl. Rose ought to come home and do her whack. She's the nurse — '

'She's on this case at Rangiora.' Miss Muriel opened her eyes quickly. 'At all events, she has her own life, as you know. Separate.'

'It isn't as though she had a husband to look after.'

'No.' She glanced across at Walter under the lamp. 'Would you like to finish your work in the kitchen, Walter?' she said in slack tones, then suddenly raised her head, listening. 'Hilda's voice,' she whispered, alertly surprised, to her brother. 'I heard her call.' She jumped up. 'We're in here, Hilda!'

'Anybody at home?' Hilda Macaulay appeared at the kitchen door, holding her collar under her chin. 'Don't turn me out, my dears. I saw the light in mother's room from the road.'

'Hilda, whatever — ? At this time of the evening — '

'I wondered if Geoff were here. He's not come home.' She paused, her eyes taking in the room. 'No, he's not with you.'

'But he hasn't been here for weeks, Hilda.' Miss Muriel shifted a chair for her sister. 'Certainly not tonight. Did he tell you he might be late?'

'No . . . I don't remember.' Her wild eyes fought them off. 'Well, I don't suppose it matters.' She kissed her brother. 'How are you, Mark my pet? Your head's shinier than ever.'

'I polished it for you, after tea.'

'Silly.'

Miss Muriel stood stiffly regarding her sister. 'Hilda, you oughtn't to be wandering about the township like this — '

'I don't know — ' the other shrugged ' — but I felt I just couldn't stay in that house on the hill a minute longer.' Her head sagged; she sat down, opening her coat. 'Get me a cup of tea, Muriel. I do feel a bit like a duck in a thunderstorm — a little breathless.'

'Of course.' Miss Muriel hurried away. 'Anything.'

'Oh dear, I'm probably making a fuss about nothing.' Mrs. Hilda pressed her gloved hand to her side. 'Geoff's car's probably broken down,' she laughed, 'or the tram's been blown off the rails.' But her eyes, as she looked up at her brother, did not laugh. 'Am I a fool, Mark? Another jealous wife?'

'The first I've heard of it. Jealous of whom?'

'Oh, something humiliating.' She found a handkerchief in her belt and wiped her lips. 'But Geoff's not happy,' she resumed at a tangent. 'He's not been eating or sleeping properly, Mark. And he won't see Dr. Thomson.'

'He could be worrying about you, Hilda.'

'Why? Because of this baby?' She pulled her coat over her lap. 'He'd put a stop to that, I believe, if he could.' She bit her lip. 'No, that's a dreadful thing to have said — a mean beastly thing.'

'Depends how you look at it.'

'Oh you, you're always so detached.'

'All right.' Her brother tapped the pipe against his teeth. 'Is he often so late coming home?'

'Geoff? Sometimes, recently.'

'He's a man, after all — he has his work to do.'

Her laugh flew out. 'Yes, the conscientious young architect — the lad with plans and a place in the world — ' And her glance sought Walter under the lamp, as though only now aware of his presence. 'I thought you'd gone out with Muriel, Walter.'

He looked up. 'I'm reading — '

'I always forget you're in the house at all.' She got up, restlessly smoothing her dress. 'You didn't see my husband on the tram, earlier this afternoon, I suppose? On the way home?'

'No,' he said, staring at her. 'No, Mrs. Hilda.'

Tea-cups rattled in the doorway from the kitchen. 'I've made it weak,' Miss Muriel announced, 'as there isn't much milk. Mark you'd better not have a cup.'

'I'll leave it to you tea-swilling women.'

'Are you feeling better, Hilda? Your colour's come back again.'

'I'm all right, Muriel. Just my heart, for a moment.' She took the cup. 'I'll swill this, as Mark says, then run home. Where's father?'

'Choir.' Miss Muriel turned to Walter. 'You can pack up your books now, dear.'

'Poor father.' Hilda Macaulay put down her tea almost before she had sipped it. 'Still, only the old have any peace, I suppose, in this awful world.' She looked wildly at her reflection in the glass, tilting her hat, pulling at the buttons of her gloves. 'I must go, Muriel. I can't drink my tea. Mark dear, would it be an imposition to ask you to see me home, up the hill?'

'No imposition at all. It's a fine night. Walter might even come with us.'

The boy, piling his books into their satchel, turned his face to Miss Muriel. 'May I?'

'It's so late — '

'Let him come,' said Mark Garnett. 'The air'll give him an appetite for bed.'

'Well, just this once. Take your scarf, Walter.'

In ten minutes he was walking with the brother and sister under the warm stars of the night. Hilda Macaulay leant on her companion's arm as they passed the tram-lines and approached the hill.

'Look, there's the new moon. You must wish, Mark.'

'Another life, then.'

'Hush, you shouldn't tell.' She nudged him affectionately. 'You ought to get married, my dear.'

'I wonder. I don't see it in the cards, somehow.'

'Silly-billy. Deal again.'

Walter walked beside them, silent, not regarded. He too had wished at the new moon: a complicated wish that Mrs. Nelson would not . . . but he couldn't straighten the thought into words. Not at once. The feeling of betrayal, guilt, anxiety came back. He pushed it away and listened to Mrs. Hilda's low flurried voice speaking to her brother.

'You weren't at my wedding, Mark, but I'll tell you something that'll surprise you.' Her tone was charged with emotional pain.

'Revelations?'

'Only in the sense that I've never told anybody else.' She halted for a moment, catching her breath, pressing her side. 'Though, to be truthful, it was before the wedding,' she took up. 'Geoff wrote me a note — more of a letter perhaps — saying he wanted to put off the whole thing. Just like that, at the last moment, two days before! Said he wanted more time, a break. Of course I rushed straight off to see him — I was very certain of myself — and after all a breach of promise is a breach of promise, you can't get away from it. I found him at his office, up to the eyes in black monkey, so to speak . . . I had to talk him round, and I did. Everything was all right again in half an hour.'

'I'd always heard it was Rose he wanted to marry, in the first place.'

'Oh, that. Yes . . . until he fell in love with me. Or rather I think he wavered into love with all three of us, even Muriel, in his own funny way.'

'Muriel?'

'No, perhaps not. Never explicitly. At any rate, he can't do without a woman behind him. That Scottish mum of his — he was devoted to the old creature — he'd never kissed another human soul until he was twenty-four, would you believe it? And she'd dragged him to church — to *kirk*, I suppose she'd call it — twice every blessed Sunday of their lives, until her last illness. So, you see, when she died he was lost, absolutely lonely: no woman to rely on. When Rose brought him home to us we were all women to him, we gave him firm ground again . . . Oh, but he's strange, so dour often, and sometimes such a child you wouldn't believe it.'

'But to get back to Rose — '

She walked on, her arm clutching his. 'You know how Rose can be, Mark. Vague, odd. And Geoff's just as odd — suspicious of being duped, philandered with, *diddled* even. It's the Scot in him, the Calvinist monkey.' She paused. 'At any rate, Rose took herself off and the point came when he wanted me, however it happened. And of course I wanted him . . . Even now, I love him very much, in so many ways, whatever beastly things I say against him to others.'

Her brother sighed. 'If human beings *can* complicate their lives — '

'No, don't preach to me. I can't bear it. Oh, I'd fight for him if I had to. I'd fight . . .' She halted again, breathless, glancing up at the stars, the moon, the bulk of the hill. 'I'm not really scared, Mark. Even with this child to make me look like a mountain I'm still pretty, good-looking, I've got advantages.'

'You're worried, old girl, nevertheless.'

She did not answer but turned her head to search for Walter behind them. 'Some evening, Walter,' said her lightest voice, 'we'll play the gramophone again, and this time we'll really dance. Don't forget. Put it in your diary.' She drew him forward, touching his cheek in the moonlight. 'You're looking dreadfully serious. What is it?'

Under the shadow of the hill, where the cutting of the road began, a man's figure loomed forward to meet them, his face a pale raw smudge against the darker rock.

'Is that you, Hilda? Are you there?'

Hilda Macaulay disengaged herself and ran forward: she threw her arms upon her husband's neck. 'Geoff — oh, darling —'

'I was late. Come home.'

'Yes, of course. I was so anxious — '

'Come now.'

Mark Garnett turned aside to Walter. He nodded and the two of them went back down the road the way they had come. The gritty shingle slipped under their boots.

'Well, Walter, that's that. Our cue for minding our own business.' He halted to put a match to his pipe. 'A fine example — and put this in your diary too — of at least one human dilemma.'

'What's "dilemma"?'

'Mess, generally . . . Ever hear of a little three-letter word — sex?' The match spurted into a glimmer about his chin and mouth. 'It's another way of spelling hell.' They walked on. 'Just let the smell and smoke of it get into a man outside his marriage and he's in trouble, no matter how good his private resolutions. The more strictly he's been brought up the worse the poor devil's likely to fall . . . Broken promises, the wife forsaken, the animal crying in the double bed — none of them'll hold him back. He'll rush to the lust that's in him and that other body he can't get out of his mind. If he's religious, so much the more damnable for himself and everyone concerned — so much the more expense of spirit. And all because a man isn't born complete in his own image — he craves something outside his own flesh . . . Believe me, Walter, sex has never heard the word mercy, and never will.'

The rush of words had gone over Walter like the wind. He was silent. They came to the tram-lines and the lighted road.

'I've over-reached myself perhaps,' said Mark Garnett. 'And the possible infidelity of a brother-in-law isn't . . .' He stopped.

'Besides,' he murmured to himself, 'I'm sorry for Hilda. Confoundedly sorry, if it's true.'

They reached the cinder path leading to the Garnetts' yard. At the last moment Mark Garnett tarried to peer down at Walter in the light from the kitchen window. His face seemed to grow larger, even threatening.

'I'd like to have had a son like you, Walter. Do you understand that — my solitude?' He turned away, abruptly. 'Run in now,' he continued in a louder voice. 'Run in before I betray my soul or before my sister Muriel starts reading any of her private Riot Acts to you for lateness.'

Walter went in. Miss Muriel sat sewing under the dining-room lamp.

'We met Mr. Macaulay on the way,' he told her.

She seemed to catch at words he had not spoken. 'Don't mention to father that my sister Hilda was here, Walter. Don't tell anyone.' She had not raised her head. 'Do you hear?'

CHAPTER III

BOTH Marriner and Walter, squatting among their sandwich papers against the buttresses of the playground, looked
up as Miss Threplow dismounted from her bicycle at the gate.
Seeing them, she smiled, waved a hand. Both boys returned the
smile, watching her wheel the bicycle across the pebbles to the
shed. This morning she wore a light grey dress: the weather was
warmer.

'Her brother's volunteered,' Marriner remarked to Walter.
'He went to the barracks and volunteered.'

'I know.'

'He'll be in the Expeditionary Force.'

'I know.'

In admiration their eyes followed Miss Threplow into the
school corridor.

'Perhaps he'll get the Victoria Cross,' Marriner said. 'Then
she'll bring it and show us.'

'Perhaps he'll capture a thousand Germans in a fort.'

'The Expeditionary Force is in Egypt, man. No Germans there.'

'I know,' said Walter again, abashed.

They returned to the crumbs and crusts of their lunch. Marriner rooted in his brown cardboard box. 'Have half this
squashed-fly? It's the last.'

'Gosh, thanks.'

The day was not only warm but hot. The asphalt by the
church, softened by the heat, was dented with the heel-marks of
those boys who had hung their coats on the ramps of the bicycle
shed and were bouncing a tennis ball against the buttresses. The
tall dusty fir tree pointed, motionless, to the turquoise of the
sky, to the white clouds over the city.

' "Theirs not to reason why, theirs but to run and die",'
Marriner's high voice piped during recitation, in the afternoon.

'*Do* or die,' Miss Threplow corrected. 'You make it sound
as though they were retreating, not charging. Next boy.
Bascomb?'

'I was excused homework, Miss Threplow, please. I brought
a note for Mr. Garnett from my mother.'

'Oh dear. Were you ill?'

'I had a pain.'

'I'm sorry to hear that. The fruit's not very ripe yet, no doubt.
Next. Blakiston?'

Walter started from a dream: he was concealing an adventure-
story beneath the flap of his desk, on his knees. 'Why was it
called the Light Brigade?' he asked, to gain time.

Miss Threplow sighed, smoothing her forehead. 'The opposite
of heavy,' she ventured. 'Anyway, don't bother about that. Go
on, recite me the next verse.'

' "Onward — " ' Walter began.

But a hare had been started among the class. 'Were the horses
light, or the men, Miss Threplow?' Collins interrupted.

'I've really no idea. Tennyson doesn't say. . . .'

The recitation hour trailed away, languidly, the Light Brigade
still in full charge. After school there was cricket on a pitch
beside the oak trees of the Park. Mr. Garnett guarded the pile of
coats and satchels on the grass and watched the game distantly,
his grey hat tilted above his eyes, his short legs stiffly planted, his
umbrella hitched over one elbow. The shrill cries of the players
seemed to bounce back from his solid waistcoat and beard.

'I see no potential W. G. Grace amongst you, unfortunately,'
he remarked after the game, his brood gathered about him.
'Some of you, however, have a wild style of your own. Blakiston, you may make a slow bowler yet. But you — Marriner —
you just do not care, I notice.'

'It's the war, sir. I dreamed about Von Kluck.'

'Very singular, that, as the war news is improving.'

But several mornings later, after prayers, the flags had again to be moved nearer Paris on the map: the Germans were advancing over the country that had once been Gaul. And the first hour of the day was rendered to a more ancient conqueror.

' "Caesar crossed the bridges",' Mr. Garnett wrote on the blackboard, then dusted the chalk from his fingers. 'Can any boy translate that at sight?'

'Is Caesar the same as Kaiser, sir?'

'The words have the same root, Marriner, yes. All the languages of Western Europe have their bases in the concision and sonority of the Roman tongue.' His voice sank into the heat of the room as into a blanket. 'Every word you boys speak has a history half as long as that of the human race.'

'Was Caesar married, sir?'

'His wife, Trent, was named Calpurnia — a woman above suspicion. And now let us return to Caesar crossing his bridge. *Pons* is a word, you'll find, with as many derivations as *trans* itself. . . .'

Under the roof of his desk Walter cautiously opened the book on his knees. He could not wait for Caesar: he had reached that chapter in which a boy named Dick Creherne and his friend and shipmate Mike found themselves on a night expedition. With bent head he plunged in:

The creepers hung in long snaky festoons from the crests of the trees. Occasionally a monkey or other animal uttered a plaintive cry and the sound was taken up by the weird half-human screeches of birds drowsing overhead. In the jungle's shadow the darkness was striped with paler lines and flecks that might, Dick well knew, have been the panoply of a leopard out to kill. And from every side, trees and undergrowth alike, the strange unceasing drone and gurgle of insect life made itself heard like the tuning of some orchestra that never began to play.

'*Have you got your knife?*' *Dick whispered to his companion as they trod the damp leaves underfoot.*

'*Sure, me knife's safe in me hand,*' *Mike whispered back.* '*And it's ready I am for that wicked son of Satan, should he appear. . . .*'

Walter glanced up. Drops of sweat ran down his ribs. Caesar was still upon the bridge.

'The second conjugation, let me point out once more,' Mr. Garnett told the class, 'has not the same accusative as the first.' He frowned at the blackboard. 'Latin case-endings in fact are more rigid than you boys would seem to realize.'

Walter went back to Dick Creherne in the jungle.

To the right, where the valley fell away in cliffs to the river, there came a rustle from among the trees.

'He might be hiding in the caves below,' said Dick.

'Sure, he might,' grimaced Mike, 'and the whole of his black tribe with him. They'll have their sentries on the alert, I'll swear.' His stalwart frame gave an unwonted shudder. 'If me uncle had only a sight of me now,' he hissed.

'We are not cowards,' said our hero. 'We have a sacred trust to undertake revenge. Bear up, Mike, and let the two of us go forward. . . .'

Again Walter glanced up. The class had become silent about him.

'One boy at least,' said Mr. Garnett's voice closely above his head, 'has no interest in Caesar's progress, I see. The blame may be Caesar's or it may be mine; but I suspect neither.' His hand, swooping, lifted the book from Walter's knee. 'I thought better of you, Blakiston.'

Walter sweated, miserably.

'You will oblige me by waiting after school.' The tone was firm but kindly. 'Meanwhile, I shall keep this singular production.' The tale of Dick Creherne vanished into his pocket: the class let out a repressed snigger. 'Now, the rest of you, back to Caesar.'

But at that moment, as though Caesar himself had interrupted from the shades, the door of the class-room rattled, the handle turned. The caretaker of the church buildings, a shirtsleeved man whom Walter had seen only once before, stood offering a folded paper. 'The boy didn't know the way, Mr. Garnett, so I brought it along.'

'Thank you, Hinkson.'

The master fumbled open the yellow paper with a finger. The class waited, silently. Telegrams were unusual, suspicious. It might be the war, Von Kluck, even the Kaiser. The caretaker left.

'Yes,' said Mr. Garnett on an indrawn breath. He sat down at his desk on the platform, folded the telegram into a pocket-book and shook his head. 'Extraordinary.'

'I must leave you for today, boys,' he said humbly. 'I must go home. Miss Threplow will be in charge here.' He groped for his hat and umbrella in the corner behind the blackboard. 'I must take the tram home,' he murmured.

The class watched his back as he spoke to Miss Threplow. They saw her eyes widen, blink in surprise. Then, with umbrella trailing, he was gone.

'My mother got a telegram once,' Marriner said after school. 'When my Auntie May died in Wellington.' And he questioned Walter: 'What were you reading when the old cock copped you in Latin?'

Walter told him. '*Dick in India*, it's called.'

'Gee, you had a lucky escape. Bet you he doesn't remember tomorrow. Bet he doesn't cane you. Bet you get off.'

Walter said nothing. The telegram, the yellow slip of paper, had frightened him more than the threat of the cane in prospect: obscurely he felt himself in some danger he did not understand — some entanglement, some closing-in of events. Sweat soaked his shirt.

'I hope the old bird stays away for ever,' Marriner shouted. 'I hope the school has to go bust.' And he ran off to catch Miss Threplow as she wheeled her bicycle out of the shed.

'Would a German spy send telegrams?' Walter heard him ask. 'Or was it about your brother?'

'Neither, fortunately. Mr. Garnett had some bad news about one of his daughters. We may expect him back tomorrow.'

Walter stood staring at the brown fibre on the trunk of the

tree in the playground. Words came into his mind: 'Please God, let Miss Rose be all right. And if it isn't Miss Rose — '

Cold fear gripped him.

'Coming to the tram?' It was Marriner, beside him, as cheerful as ever. 'Gosh, your eyes look funny. All sort of pushed-in.' He ran ahead of Walter. 'I've heard about old Garnett,' he called back. 'It was only one of his barmy daughters.'

CHAPTER IV

'Is it Miss Rose?' he asked from the kitchen doorway. 'Is it Miss Rose?'

Miss Muriel was alone in the kitchen. She turned towards him as he came slowly in, and from her eyes he knew that she had been crying again as she had cried when she had told him about the letters. 'What makes you think it was Rose?' she said now in a stifled voice.

'Was it, Miss Muriel?'

She opened a drawer of the dresser, took out a clean tea towel, shook it, then moved towards the range. The kitchen smelt of burnt milk. 'Not Rose, Walter,' she said.

'Wasn't Mr. Garnett's telegram —'

'No.' She faced him, the fingers of her left hand exploring the mole above her lip. 'Now look,' she went on as he swung his satchel to the oilcloth of the table, 'look Walter, we're all of us upset and worried. Don't ask questions, please. Hang up your cap and wash your hands.'

The soap slithered away from his hands under the scullery tap. As he retrieved it from the plug he heard somebody come into the kitchen behind him. He listened through the open doorway, softly splashing water against the zinc bowl.

'No message?' The voice was Mark Garnett's — Mr. Mark's. 'I thought the back door —'

'It was only Walter. No message.'

'I wondered . . . I don't know . . . Geoffrey might have sent somebody.'

'He wouldn't now.' Miss Muriel's tone faltered then rallied. 'I'll go up to the house again directly after dinner. He can't be left alone, even with the nurse there and however much he wants to be by himself. It isn't natural or good for him at such a time.'

'I'd go up myself if it didn't seem an intrusion. I hardly know him, you see.' Walter heard the tap of a clay pipe on the window-sill. 'My God, what a thing to happen. Of all the . . . didn't this Dr. Thomson ever warn her?'

'Often. But she always seemed so strong in other ways.'

'No question of losing the child itself, I suppose?'

'The hospital was sure they could save him — sure he'd be all right.'

'This Plunket idea?'

'Not exactly. But they can do such wonders, even with pre-mature births.' And again her voice quavered. 'It's more of Hilda herself I keep thinking, Mark. All the time. It seems such a wicked waste, somehow so purposeless.'

'That, yes, certainly. Though I doubt if life has a purpose, in that sense, except perhaps to reproduce itself. One dies, another's born.'

'I don't believe that. No, I can't, it's not Christian.'

'Neither am I, if it comes to the point . . . How's mother taking it?'

'I've put her to bed. I was heating some milk for her and then — look, such a mess — while I was trying to cook some sort of dinner for father and Walter.' She blew her nose. 'Not that I imagine father has much appetite, but I absolutely must do some-thing to occupy my mind.'

' Meals go on, you know. Even in wrecked ships — '

Walter, having dried his hands, presented himself in the kitchen.

'Mark,' said Miss Muriel, 'get this boy to help you set the table, now.' She wiped her eyes then tucked away the handker-chief. 'I must get mother's tray ready.'

Mark Garnett piloted Walter into the dining-room. 'Come along, young chap. Work to do.'

In the still, late sunlight at the veranda door old Mr. Garnett sat slumped back in a cane chair, his gaze fixed on the grass of the lawn beyond. His son touched him on the shoulder.

'Nothing new, father. Are you all right?'

'Thank you, Mark, yes.' The words came gently from a distance. 'I'm tired, I suppose ... We might have a game of chess later, if —' his head came round, his eyes rested for a long moment on Walter. 'Ah, Blakiston, you're home, I see.' And his puffy hands wavered to one of his sack-like pockets. 'That book you were reading. Take it. Sexton Blake is better.'

'Thanks, Mr. Garnett.'

The schoolmaster's gaze returned to the veranda and the lawn. 'Latin,' he nodded to the evening, 'is a serious subject, worthy of the attention of even a sheep-farmer's son. Don't overlook that.'

'*Vesper adest,*' Mark Garnett murmured. He helped Walter to spread the white cloth on the table. '*Vesper adest.*'

'Yes, Mark, yes.' The old man smiled. 'If I taught you nothing else at least you know your Virgil.'

'Catullus, father.'

'Catullus then.' The cane chair creaked. 'The comfort of the classics. If I could teach that to at least one unformed mind ...' The voice trailed off against the clatter of knives and forks in the room.

'Dinner, father.' Miss Muriel set the roast on the table. 'Could you manage a little?' she asked softly, at his ear.

'No, Muriel. Well, just a bite then.' He let her help him to his feet. 'One must eat, I suppose.'

The meal passed, was endured. Walter ate in silence.

'I'll wash up, old girl,' Mark Garnett said to his sister at the finish, 'if you want to slip away.'

'I must.' She rose, looked at the clock, then fetched her hat from the hall. 'Geoff must have somebody ...'

'He'd better come back here.'

'He won't do that. I've already asked him.' She kissed her father's forehead. 'I'll be back at ten or before, father ... Don't grieve, dear. It's the same for all of us.' She patted him and was gone.

Nobody spoke to Walter. No homework, in Mr. Garnett's

absence from the final hour at school, had been set for that evening. Walter looked at his familiar stamp collection: he flicked open the lid of his box of Meccano and counted the nuts: he read yet another chapter about the pursuit of the rebel chief in the jungle. None of these occupations, however, was satisfying at such a moment. Something had happened, and he was shut out, uncomforted, thrown aside. In silence Mr. Garnett and his son began to play chess on the veranda.

Walter left the house. He had longed throughout the evening to ask one question, and he had not asked it. Now he would go off by himself; he would take himself to the beach or as far as the pier, content with his own company. And idly he touched the telegraph posts as he sauntered up the road towards the dunes: one by one he counted the gate posts with red tops, the houses with verandas, the stones by the footpath. He reached the sands, the open beach.

The tide was out. Black at the far end of the shore the Cave Rock squatted like a castle or a vast chocolate drop: the floors of wet sand before it reflected the lemon tinge of the sky. Walter ran along the beach towards the Rock, kicking at the scatter of kelp with his boots, his hands in his pockets. A hundred yards from the Rock he paused and looked back at the headland of Scarborough Hill: a light showed already in the windows of the Macaulays' bungalow, a still glimmer in this night of early summer. Below, far out at the edge of the tide, a solitary dog gambolled and barked in the shallows. The barking was very clear above the roar of the sea. Walter waited a minute or two, listening, then shivered and hurried on towards the Rock. He sat down to rest against one of the darker boulders, knocking his heels against the sand, panting, watching the lamps start to wink along the esplanade. A lighted tram vanished into the town. Presently he turned again to watch the dog. Its black insect-like form was nearer now in the dusk, far away yet approaching; it seemed to bark a challenge at the sea then hurl itself back in fear. The dog, Walter thought, could be a ghost, frenzied. And, shivering again, he was afraid of those approaching sounds, which seemed to echo in his own troubled mind.

And now another, a different sound caught his ears: a whisper of shoes on the dry sand behind him, a restrained agitated breathing. His nose tingled to a familiar perfume on the air.

'Miss Rose,' he whispered, astonished.

For a second she did not see him: beneath her hat she was intent upon the long headland at the further end of the beach, her gaze searching the lights on the hill.

'Miss Rose!'

Her eyes stabbed towards him. 'What are you doing here, Walter?' She twisted aside as though to stumble away over the sand. 'You mustn't see me — go away! Oh, go away!'

He jumped up, to follow her. 'Are you lost?' was all he could think of to say.

'You mustn't tell anyone you saw me.' She brought out the words tightly, in distress. 'You mustn't, Walter.'

But at once he knew why she had come to the shadow of the Rock. 'Are you looking for Mr. Macaulay?'

'Oh, you wouldn't understand . . . Have you seen him?'

'Somebody's dead or ill,' he said. 'I don't know, Miss Rose.'

'Dead? Ill?' She shivered in her long coat. 'Who told you?'

'They were talking, in the kitchen.'

She launched herself upon him, grabbing at his wrists. 'Walter, tell me! Tell me! I haven't even seen Geoff for two days. Is my sister ill — Hilda, I mean? Is she ill?'

'I don't know. But there's a baby, in a hospital.'

'The baby? But not yet, not already?'

'Mrs. Hilda's baby, I think it is.'

'Oh my God — don't you *know?* Can't you tell me? What did you hear? The baby — '

He looked at the crags of the Rock, the fading sky. 'It was all right, they said. But could Mrs. Hilda have died? Could she die?'

Miss Rose flung away his wrists. Her head, lowered, swung

from side to side. 'Yes, she could die,' she said slowly, almost in a moan. 'Yes, you little fool, she could die. That mightn't be difficult for her.' She was still for a moment, her lips quivering, taking it in. 'Oh dear God, is that what it is? Hilda?' And again her head began its anguished to-and-fro swing. 'Yes, I see now. Some mistake — some accident — without her realizing what she was doing.'

'I don't know anything else, Miss Rose.'

'But you know she's dead? How can you be sure?'

'Mr. Garnett got a telegram and came home.' He waited. 'But why would she die?'

'It might be anything . . . her heart. When I saw her in town she — no, I mustn't think that. It can't be my fault: it couldn't be.'

He could feel her helpless trembling. An odour of sweat and pain, mixed with the lemony perfume he knew, drifted from her body towards him, on the salt air of the evening.

'It can't be my fault — not any more than *his*,' she ran on; 'or we're both equally guilty. Both. And my poor Hilda —'

She sank down on one of the boulders under the Rock. For a moment, exhausted, she had no more to say. Walter stood watching her lowered chin, the soft agitated rise and fall of her dress.

'Shall I take you home now, Miss Rose?'

'What? . . . No, I can't go home, Walter. Not now, anyway, not tonight. They think I'm away —'

'Did you come down by tram, from town I mean?'

She waved the question away as of no significance, then presently answered it: 'The tram? Yes. You see, I hoped to — I was desperate —' She glanced distractedly back at the lighted esplanade and township, then along the beach towards Scar-borough Hill and its few twinkling windows. 'Anything to be near him . . . we haven't been able to live without one another . . . it came to that.' Her voice wavered to a whisper. 'I've been living in a kind of boarding-house, a cheap hotel near the station,

Walter. Not as a guest, and not nursing, but as a sort of . . . it doesn't matter. Only Geoffrey knew until yesterday — or today, I've forgotten which — then Hilda knew. She found out.'

Walter opened his mouth to speak, then closed it in confusion. He too looked along the beach: the dog in the shallows had come closer: now it ran past them, loping away in silence among the rocks towards the outflow of the estuary.

'I'd never known real happiness, ecstasy, before these last months, Walter. Never! I knew it couldn't last but I had to hold it to me, cherish it like a child. And now — this.' Her hands flew out in a gesture. 'This.'

In her dark hat and dress she seemed to him part of the twilight, as obscure as the mystery in which she moved and of which she had spoken. Her pale hands twisted upwards on her knees as she asked, more pensively:

'And my sister Muriel? Her?'

'She's gone up to the house. She went after dinner.'

'To be with him?'

'She said that.'

'Where I ought to be.' Walter heard the bitterness of her laugh. 'Muriel? Well, that's — '

She did not complete the ironic comment but at once sprang up. 'I must go, I must go back to town. I can't see him now. We'd kill one another out of common blame. We're lost, both of us, as surely as if murder and not love had been in our minds.' She began distractedly to walk away over the sand towards the lamps of the esplanade, disregarding Walter's existence behind her.

'I won't tell them I saw you, Miss Rose. I promise.'

If she heard his cry she gave no sign. He watched her slim figure stumble on to the road, her hat hiding her face, her elbows drawn closely into her sides. Presently she disappeared between the houses. He was alone again on the beach under the Rock, a cool night wind blowing in from the sea, a few stars pricking the sky over the hills. The dog, like Miss Rose herself, had vanished. He shuddered, then ran home along the sands.

'Hullo, young fellow.' Mark Garnett sat smoking under the apricot tree in the yard, his bald head faintly lit by the kitchen window. 'You deserted us. Where did you make for?'

'The — I've been along the beach.'

'What song the syrens sang . . . ' Smoke floated into the tree. 'Did anyone speak to you? Were there other lonely souls abroad on a warm night?'

'No.' He thought a moment. 'Only a dog.'

'A pity. Life has no sense of the appropriate.' He yawned. 'Well, I must trot up the hill and collect Muriel.' Stretching, he rose, reflectively knocking out the bowl of his pipe against the wash-house wall. 'The unlovable must succour the unloved,' he observed to the sky.

Walter stood on the step, looking down at the iron scraper, touching it with his boot. 'Is Mrs. Hilda dead?'

'She is.' The young man spoke soberly, distantly. 'My sister's dead, Walter. And as yet only the doctor and blind fate would appear to know the how and why.'

Walter did not take his eyes from the scraper. He could see this death — and Death itself — only as dark sluggish water below the parapet of a bridge, frightening.

CHAPTER V

W ALTER wrote:

Dear Mum: I hope you and Dad are all right, and thanks for your letters. It is very hot here now for two days and school is hotter even with the windows open. I have been read- ing a story where the natives go about without clothes on in some islands so they won't be as hot as we are. There was a white boy in the book too who made a hat out of a parm leaf from a banana parm. It's a stunner. Could you send me a book about islands or a new Chums some time, they have good stories about people I get interested in a lot . . . Gran gave me a book of cowboys with some Indians in which I liked, she put it in my luggage as a present but I have finished it now. Also Dick in India. Or send a book about fish or the Wild Animals of the World. I like all those. The nights are not dark now so I can read them in bed, sometimes I wake up before Miss Muriel's clock goes off which I can hear when she gets up in the mornings. I hope you are better and not ill at all. I have put all your letters under my handkerchiefs in my drawer. I have no cake or chocolate biscuits you sent which I have eaten. The mice hop on top of the tin and smell but can't get in, but Miss Muriel sets traps in the larder. One night she caught two in one trap how I don't know. Her brother from the lighthouse in Foveau Straights is here now still. It is very interesting to talk to him. He says birds get bashed dead against the lamp and the men can see porpoisses round the rocks some times. Once they saw a whale blow up water like steam far away. But I haven't heard much lately as we have had a funeral in the house. This ink has got flies in it because the cork is lost. I have seen a fountained pen in a shop window on the way to school from the square, not very dear. Miss Threplow's brother is in Egipt with the army she says, but our map doesn't go far enough down for Egept. We are learning the Charge of the Light brigade though it is all learnt now. Miss Rose is away. It is hot here but I told you that. I haven't seen Jimmy Nelson lately. I don't know what is happening here. I often think of you and am looking forward to end of term and Chrismas. I don't cry any more, that was only when I came to the first term for the Garnetts. Now I'm only homesick wanting to see you. I must go now, Miss Muriel is making a currie and wants me to go to the store for her for rice. I will post this on the way. My love from   WALTER

'Shall I go now, Miss Muriel?'
She placed the basket on the table beside him. 'Run in and see mother a moment first, Walter,' she said while he licked the envelope and wrote the address. 'She may have a letter to post too. Knock first.'
'Yes.'
'Wait,' she drew him back, nodding towards the envelope in his hand. 'You haven't written anything unkind in your letter?'
'No.' He was uncertain of her meaning.
'It's so easy for the young to hurt. And your mother doesn't know us.'
'Do you want to read my letter?' he asked.
'No, dear. Go now.'
Old Mrs. Garnett sat upright to the far side of the enormous bed; a lace cap drooped over one eye. The brassy bright rails of the bedstead were as high as a fence, top and bottom.
'Oh it's you,' she said. 'Close the door. You're afraid of me, aren't you.'
'No, Mrs. Garnett.'
'Well, you ought to be.' The sunken mouth clamped down on a smile, the eyes wandered to the bedside table. 'Yes, I had a letter to Rose, somewhere ready.' Her hands — as scaly, Walter thought, as a hen's feet — poked among the medicine bottles, searching. 'Here, and don't you go droppin' it in the gutter. It's to my daughter, in Rangiora.'

'But Miss Rose isn't — ' he stopped. That was a secret. 'I won't drop it,' he promised.

The ash-coloured face relaxed. 'A boy with big eyes,' she croaked at him presently, 'shouldn't stare so much. What are you gapin' at?'

He had been gaping at the hollow in the right side of the huge bed, beside the old woman: in that hollow, every night since long before he himself was born, the bulk of his schoolmaster, a leviathan, must have sunk to sleep, the mattress groaning, the bed knobs trembling . . . Behind the bed the wallpaper, faded mostly to a colour like porridge, still showed a faint rash of pink sweet-peas on a trellised background. 'The flowers,' he said, to explain himself.

Mrs. Garnett sniffed. 'They were red when we came here.' And she waved him away, towards the door. 'Do you wash your neck?' she asked of his back.

'Yes, Mrs. Garnett.'

'I doubt it. No boy ever washes if he can go dirty. My son Mark never washed at your age. Girls are better. My daughter Muriel was the cleanest of mine,' she wandered, 'then Rose, then Hilda. But Hilda was so pretty, so takin' . . .' Her voice trailed off into silence, her mouth sunk, her hands scrabbled at the sheet. 'This is a terrible war,' she murmured. 'Englishmen dyin' . . . the finest in the world.'

Walter shut the door and left her.

'A pound of rice,' Miss Muriel reminded him on his way out. 'Quick, before the store shuts.'

Unripe apricots hung on the tree in the yard, under the heavy leaves. He pinched the cheeks of several, hopefully, then ran down the cinder path, the basket bumping on his thighs.

'A pound of rice for Miss Garnett.' He stood panting before the counter. 'Please.'

'Which Miss Garnett?'

'Miss Muriel.'

'Wanting rice all of a sudden,' the man said; 'is she going

200

to a wedding or something? Funerals and weddings . . .' He wiped his face, dropping the packet into the basket. 'A real lady, Miss Muriel, say what you like.'

Walter said nothing.

'What's happened to Miss Rose, the other one?'

'She's away,' he said carefully.

'A peach, she is — moody though, too moody. No use bringing up girls to be English misses, not in this country. Cuts them off.' His pale sweaty face blinked at Walter. 'I was sorry to hear about young Mrs. Macaulay, very sorry. An accident like that, when a woman's alone — '

Walter escaped. At the end of the road he posted his letters, then dawdled along the tram-lines, swinging the basket. A bell shrilled; a bicycle drew level beside him.

'Hey, Walter,' called Jimmy Nelson. 'Kapai,' the voice added. 'Kapai, kapai, kapai, haeremai.'

'What's that?'

'Never hear Maori before?' Jimmy swung himself momentarily to the road. 'My pa's home. He's going to enlist for the war. And gosh, he's a Maori all right — you ought to see him!'

'What's he like?'

'He smokes cigars. Ma got as big a shock as I did when he turned up.' Jimmy sprang back across the bicycle, his boots clattering against the pedals. 'I've got to go buy him some beer now. Come round and see him when you can. He's hot stuff. Gosh.'

The bicycle whirled away. 'Kapai,' Jimmy crowed back. And his war-whoop echoed along the road: 'Wa-wa-wa.'

CHAPTER VI

'COME in, Walter.' Mrs. Nelson opened the back door to him three evenings later. 'A long time since we saw you. Jimmy's somewhere round, in the house.' Her voice rose in a sudden squeal: 'Jimmy! Show yourself.'

'I'm here, ma.' Boots clattered on the linoleum of the front passage. 'Can I have a match?'

'If your pa's given you a cheroot again you get no matches from me, my lad. Stunting your own growth like that.'

'You smoke cigarettes, anyway.'

'I'm big enough. Here's Walter to see you.'

'Hullo, Walt.'

'Hullo, Jimmy.'

A vase of dashed-looking roses sat on the kitchen table. 'We've had a home-coming,' coughed Mrs. Nelson and lit a cigarette from a yellow packet. 'You wouldn't hardly know us, Walter. How do you like my new costume?' She swelled inside a green dress as bright as grass, her throat expanding in waves of flesh over her strong breasts. 'All right for the races, eh?'

Walter agreed, shyly. He thought the dress alarming.

'Improves the architecture, gives me quite a balcony,' she said. 'Glad you like it.'

'It's awful, ma,' said Jimmy. 'It's too tight.'

'Oh, it suits me. Sit down,' she commanded Walter. 'Jimmy, heave your pa's braces off that chair. Make yourself a gent for once and give Walter the throne.'

'Don't be so bossy.'

'Bossy?' She waved a fly from her piled hair. 'You and your cigars at your age, and sucking lollies all night to spoil your nice teeth. Thinking yourself a man already. I know who's bossy, all right.'

Jimmy made a face at Walter. 'Hell,' he said softly, 'plurry hell.'

'I can't manage you since your pa came back.' Mrs. Nelson subsided into a chair. 'I can't and that's the truth . . . Well, let me talk to Walter. You weren't at the funeral, I saw, Walter.'

He stared at her, reluctantly. 'No,' he said. On the day of the funeral he had been sent to school as usual: Miss Threplow had been in charge on the platform.

'I saw the family go past,' Mrs. Nelson nodded, 'up the road here. I was having a sit down on the veranda and I saw them. The old man and the rest — except for Rose.'

Anxiety struggled in Walter. And for the first time he asked a question he did not now expect to be met with silence. 'Did Mrs. Hilda — did she die of anything?'

'You might call it that, Walter, or you mightn't.' She did not look at him. 'Depends on how you see it.'

'I don't know — '

'You might say it was an accident, like the doctor did. Like they said at the inquest too. Women'll do funny things,' she ruminated, 'when they're carrying an unborn kid and they're left to themselves all day. You don't have to tell me *that*. Before young Jimmy there popped into the world I had fancies enough one way and another — saw the Virgin Mary and thought I was due to pop off any moment. Too right, I did. Yes, you might say it was an accident, Walter. They found her on the Scarborough Road, you see. All she could say, poor thing, was that she'd been shifting a bed out of a room — '

She was interrupted. A queer fluting shout arrived from somewhere along the passage towards the front of the house.

'Pa's woken up,' Jimmy told his mother. 'He's heard us.'

'What your pa wants is a drink,' Mrs. Nelson snorted. She shuffled up from her chair, straightening her dress. 'There's beer in that voice if ever I heard it. Come and meet my old man, Walter — come and say hullo to Jimmy's pa, blast him. Jimmy, you stay here.'

Walter trailed behind her large hips towards the front room. Mrs. Nelson paused at the door, stood aside, and pushed him ahead.

'Rahi,' she called, 'this kid's name's Walter. You've heard of him.'

Exposed to Walter's shocked curiosity a youngish Maori with grey-black tumbled hair and with a nose as broad as a penny lay facing him on the sofa, his stockinged feet dangling, enormous, over the bamboo rail. A white shirt was split open down the gleaming sepia-brown of his chest; his trousers were tight clayish-yellow dungarees; a leather belt sagged round his loins. A whiff of tobacco and sweat floated in the room, the windows of which were shut behind the drawn blind.

'Hot day,' the man greeted Walter. 'Plurry hot day.' His startling white teeth bared themselves in a droopy grin. 'Good day to sleep.'

'They won't let you sleep all day in the army,' Mrs. Nelson warned. 'You wait.'

'Plurry hot day now.'

She laughed. 'Of course it's hot if you lie in here.' She snapped up the blind. 'I suppose you want a drink, howling out like that.'

'A drink.' Indolently his tongue tasted his magenta lips. 'Almighty yes, a drink. I could put one down.'

'Booze and snooze, that's you, Rahi — as if I'd forgotten.' She picked up his boots from the floor. 'A fine example for young Jimmy, I must say.'

'A good boy, Jimmy. Got some go. I beat the Germans then I take him down south with me.'

'Gold-dredging's no life for Jimmy,' Mrs. Nelson clucked. 'You do what you like, but leave Jimmy to me. I've fended for him all these years on my own, I have, and I'll do it again.'

'I take him to Otago. I take him. We'll fight the bastards of the world, Jimmy and me — bust everyone!'

'You're too free with your fists. I know you when you're

roused — too right I do. Dangerous, that's you. You'll have the police — '

The Maori, grinning, lazily stretched out a hand and stroked his wife's ample buttocks. 'Come and sleep,' he said. 'Too plurry hot for talk. Come, sleep.'

'I sleep at night.'

The man wriggled his head against the cushions of the sofa. 'Aie, it's good to be home with a wife,' he muttered.

'I'll get you a drink.'

'Almighty yes.' He pulled her back by the skirt. 'I love you pretty much.'

'Get along with you!'

'You don't believe?'

'I've heard that sauce before.' But her voice, as she broke free, was warm, without edge. 'A fat lot of love or maintenance I've had from you, my boy.'

'Love,' he said soothingly, 'buckets of love in Rahi. Plenty cash, too.'

She caressed his damp tangled hair. 'You lump of flesh . . . you great lazy body, you, telling me fibs always. Crawling back to me with lies of love and cash. Getting me to bed with you for nothing but a blasted promise.' She pushed his head aside. 'No, you smooging randy savage!'

'Tell Jimmy bring me a drink, eh?'

'I suppose so.' Mrs. Nelson turned to the silent Walter. 'Come on, we'll leave him. Let him snooze.' She took herself out.

'Hey,' the Maori called Walter back. He stretched down a bare arm and pulled up a brown box from beneath the sofa. 'Hey, a cigar for you, Walter. Make you plurry big fellow. Strong, eh?'

Walter took the short cigar. 'Thanks, Mr. Nelson.'

'Rahi,' the other corrected. 'Not Nelson. That Nelson my wife.' He pointed at Walter's Norfolk jacket. 'Hide cigar quick.'

'Yes, I will.'

'And you be a friend to Jimmy, eh yes. Plurry good friend.'

Mrs. Nelson, bustling back, drew Walter from the hot room into the passage. 'Enough of that.' She shut the door, shaking her head. 'That joker was my mistake all right,' she remarked to the walls.

'I like him,' Walter told her.

'Well, he's *comfortable*, I suppose. I like a real man about, sometimes. And he's not so bad when he isn't drunk.' She straightened a mat on the floor, bending with difficulty in her tight satin dress. 'The wonder is he hasn't crept in here one night and slit my throat, these past years; he wants the kid, you see.'

'But you like him, don't you?'

'Me? He raped me, for a start. Oh, I enjoyed it all right, but it was rape, Walter, call it what you like.' She drew herself up. 'After that it was marriage. I was crazy about him till he left me flat before Jimmy was born.' She breathed heavily, swelling herself out in disdain of the past. 'And now he's volunteered himself for a soldier, like the rolling stone he is. I'd written to him for money and he blows in here, calm as you please, and throws me money on the table as if he'd never been away. Jimmy,' she called ahead as they reached the kitchen, 'take your pa a pint from the box. And see that he doesn't swig it from the bottle, either.'

'Right, ma.'

She drew him to her, kissing him for a moment with a sort of careless pity and warmth as he wriggled away from her, wiping his mouth. 'Go on now,' she said.

Jimmy went off, clutching the beer bottle to his chest. 'I'll hold it up for him,' he called back, and vanished.

Mrs. Nelson poked at the stove, clattered a flat-iron in the fender, then lit herself a cigarette. 'I'd have a drink myself if I was in the weight competition,' she said, smoothing the dress over her hips. And almost at once she seemed to become more sharply aware of the boy standing by the table, Walter himself.

'So you don't know what happened to Hilda Macaulay? They've kept mum about it?'

At that moment he was afraid of her, nipped by a nameless panic: shadows trembled in his mind — a threat, the image of dark water, the bridge, the drowning dog, unimaginable death itself. He thrust the images, the panic, away.

'They haven't told you how it happened?' she insisted.

He shook his head uncertainly, his fingers clutching hard over the cigar in his pocket, another secret. 'I don't want to hear,' he brought out and shrank from her towards the dresser.

'Oh, it wasn't murder — don't worry!' Suddenly she was beside him, patting his hand, immensely sinister and uncomfortable in her self-control. 'She strained her heart, Walter, then got herself into a fright and started a gallop down the hill for the doctor. On her own, you see: lost her head. With a seven-month child kicking inside, that finished her — she fell down by the road, against the rocks. The kid was born all right but not before she was almost a finisher herself: too late anyway for the doctor to do much except try to ease her breathing. She died after they'd carried her back to the house, before they could even get hold of Geoff Macaulay in town . . .' Mrs. Nelson swayed to the window. 'So it was a kind of accident, see, though you might say she'd brought it on herself, Walter.'

Out of his confusion and innocence he had a sight of a sharper, more hidden possibility behind these events. And, haunted, faltering, he began: 'But Miss Rose — you didn't tell Mrs. Hilda that Miss Rose and —'

'I don't know what you mean.'

'I only thought —'

'Then don't think any such thing.' Mrs. Nelson swung round, an alarming pink spreading from her cheeks to the bosom above the bright green dress. 'If people treat me well I treat them well. No insults.'

His heart struggled upwards with relief: perhaps she had not spoken, perhaps his panic was part of a dream from which he was about to wake. 'Yes, Mrs. Nelson,' he said, without directly thinking.

Across the silent room the fire rustled in the stove.

'Well,' she went on presently, as though the battle were finished, not joined, 'that's that, Walter.' She nodded, her colour fading. 'Accidents will happen. And as for Hilda's kid — Rose'll look after him, I shouldn't wonder, when the hospital's got him going properly.'

Jimmy's boots clattered over the linoleum of the passage behind them. 'Pa's drank his beer,' he announced to his mother, entering.

'Come here. Breathe on me . . . Yes, I know who helped him drink it too.'

'I only put my tongue in the bottle, ma. Honest.'

'Quite enough.' Irritably she slapped her son's ear, glaring past him at Walter. 'Now, both of you, get out into the yard and play. You make me jumpy as a cat, with your nonsense. As if I hadn't enough on my hands already with that man in the house.'

'Your dad asked me to look after you,' Walter said to Jimmy. They inspected the rabbits in the yard. 'He told me to keep an eye on you.'

The other did not answer. Bending forward he blew a beery breath at the rabbits behind the wire, then threw a slack arm round Walter's shoulder. 'Pa killed the black one, the doe,' he said, 'and ma made a stew of it with onions. Gosh, it was good too.'

CHAPTER VII

WALTER lay flat on his belly, his stamp album spread open before him on the dry boards of the Garnetts' veranda. He had not long returned from Sunday school at the far end of the township: now it was late afternoon, with a moist summer haze from the sea lying over the valley between the flanks of the hills. A scent of coarse grass floated in waves across the veranda: Mark Garnett, helped by Walter himself, had mown the lawn during the morning. A sabbath sleepiness drooped over the house: from time to time, in the open doorway between the dining-room and the veranda, a curtain shivered in the landward breeze. The house was screening itself from the heat.

The boy turned the stiff pages of the album slowly. Close under his chin the stamps of his collection were counted and touched, one by one — the pictures of Nicaraguan volcanoes, the Sphinx of Egypt, the castles of Herzegovina, the monkeys of the Asian tropics, the crocodiles, the giraffes . . . He held himself back until he came upon the stamp he loved, the picture of the blue lake, Lake Wakatipu. He had only to turn the page now — and, ah, there it was: there lay the sapphire water, the mountains beyond, the darker but still azure-tinted trees of the foreground. Deeply, as into an unexplored beckoning world, he gazed at the oblong of paper that was no longer a stamp but a window, an open arch ahead of him. And presently he was in a canoe upon that lake: the glassy water dropped from the blade of the paddle, the mountains flickered with crystals of snow, birds flashed overhead towards the bush and raupo reeds of the further shore. The adventure could never finish, never have any end. Other boys might join him, the beautiful lake teem with canoes, the air split with shouts of triumph, but he himself would be the leader, the Dick Creherne, the bo'sun, the kidnapped boy on the schooner. The Garnetts, the Nelsons, Sumner itself, were forgotten.

'I can manage perfectly. Good gracious, a baby isn't such a trouble these days.'

'You've enough to do as it is, Muriel.'

The voices drifted from inside the house, beyond the veranda doorway, their tones carrying the echo of the room.

'I can't just plant the child down on you,' Mr. Macaulay was protesting. 'I can't do it, Muriel.'

'But why not — why not?'

'It's my own child, you see.' The Scottish lilt seemed to hesitate, to consider. 'I must be responsible.'

'But Geoffrey, you can't just leave him at home all the time. Not even with a nurse, and not even if I come up the hill every day. It's so inhuman.'

'What you're proposing then is that you should take him in here, bring him up?'

'Of course. Don't be stubborn, Geoffrey, don't. It's so little to ask of me, and Hilda would have agreed, I'm certain.'

Walter closed the pages of the stamp-album, softly. The blue lake became a part of the ordinary afternoon, the sunny veranda. For a moment he picked at the dry boards of the floor with his thumbnail. An ant scurried out, past his elbow, to fall over the edge and struggle among the jungle of new-cut grass blades on the lawn. He watched it, not listening, but hearing again the voices from behind the curtain.

'Don't disappoint me, Geoff, don't argue. You know very well that father and mother would have not the slightest objection to the baby being here, one of us.'

'It isn't that, so much.'

'What then? Are you thinking of Rose?'

'Her, amongst other things. She hasn't written to you?'

'No. Mother's letters, and mine, were returned from Rangiora through the dead-letter office. She was never there. But of course you knew that — you've known all along.'

'Aye, I knew that.'

'You don't really have to explain, you know.'

'God, what a mess it's all been.'

There was a pause.

'And now you're thinking of Rose?' she asked.

'I have to, since you've brought up the child's future. Though I doubt whether Rose'll want the poor little devil . . . I haven't been able to ask her, somehow.'

'Have I any right to ask, as a sister, what you and Rose mean to do, Geoff? Now, I mean?'

'That's largely for Rose to say. She knows what I want. Even if we couldn't live here in Sumner after the marriage — '

'You speak as though you were doubtful.'

'Rose isn't well, Muriel. She hasn't been well, not for months — since this business began between us. She's only been happy at moments — very fugitive ones too.'

'She was in town all the time?'

'In that hotel place, aye . . . though I could see her only rarely.' His voice hesitated. 'You ought to hate the sight of me, Muriel. For Hilda's sake, at all events.'

'I don't hate easily. A Christian, you see, shouldn't. I'm sorry that sounds smug, Geoffrey, but it's true.'

There was another pause. The voices moved in the room.

'I've never behaved well to you, Muriel. Not justly.'

'I accept you as I find you.'

'You do that because you're a good sort. One of the best.'

'A qualification of the lonely, often. I am lonely, Geoff, you know. That's partly why I want to take the child: it would give me an interest.'

'Leaving Rose free?'

'I owe something to Rose. A great deal. A debt.'

'You?'

'Those letters I insisted you read. It was partly the fault of my jealousy — yes, I admit it — that you didn't marry Rose in the first place. Do you understand that? Do you, Geoffrey?'

'It was my weakness — and then Hilda's attractions — rather than any fault of yours.'

'No, I was jealous . . . Let me tell you this, let me. It's weighed on me so much.'

'I don't think you have to tell me — not about the jealousy anyway. I guessed that. Or I've guessed since.'

'It was true. Those letters — I wanted you to turn to me after Rose, but you chose Hilda. I acted from jealousy: it's tormented me and Rose has never forgiven me for it, never.'

A silence. The curtain shivered in the doorway. Then the man's voice continued:

'And now you want to take Hilda's boy, adopt him, so that Rose and I — '

'The boy would be some part of you, at any rate. A consolation. Let me have him, Geoff. It's not just sentimentality, don't think that, and you'll have Rose.'

Walter leant on his elbows. The ant had vanished in the grass: he felt disturbed, vaguely shameful. The voices were not for him, yet he must listen. To distract himself he fumbled in his pocket and from among the pencils, the rolls of string, the lumps of almost fossilized gristle, the cigarette cards and odd screws and tacks, brought out the cigar Mr. Nelson had given him. The tobacco leaves, as he pinched them, faintly crackled; the gold and scarlet band round the waist could be made to slip lightly up and down. Now he rolled the cigar on the boards of the veranda, beside his stamp-album. The cigar, he told himself, was the same shape as a German Zeppelin. And, lifting it, he pushed the brown object to and fro in the air above his head, seeing it flying, soaring above the blue lake of the stamp.

'I haven't seen Rose since Hilda's death, Muriel.'

'She's coming home, this week. Perhaps to live here for a while. We did hear that much from her — or rather, Mark did. He leaves tomorrow, you see.'

'Aye, I know.'

'Both father and mother have been told that Rose has been travelling, down south.'

'I haven't been able to see her. Not yet . . . Am I a murderer, Muriel? I feel like one.'

'Hilda didn't die purposely. She'd never have done that. And the inquest — absolutely certain — heart.'

'Aye.' He waited. 'It's odd, you know, how you comfort me.'

'I've told you, I accept you, Geoffrey.'

'Yes,' said his voice slowly, 'you accept me. You're the only person of whom I feel that at present, the only one. Conscience isn't a joke. Not in me; not even if this passion I had for Rose excused it. Conscience, it's the devil.'

'What Hilda used to call your Scottish black monkey.'

'More than that. All human sin, somehow.' He was quiet for a minute. 'Do you still want to take the boy, Muriel?'

'Certainly. For myself and for Hilda, and for you. Will you ask Rose about it, Geoffrey, directly she comes here, directly you see her?'

The cigar fell from Walter's hands to the floor of the veranda: he had dropped it involuntarily. Now the slight sound of its fall brought Geoffrey Macaulay to the door. Parting the curtain in surprise, his blunt alarmed face and brown eyes took in the eavesdropper on the veranda.

Walter jumped up. Guiltily he snatched at the cigar, his treasure. 'Mr. Macaulay,' he began in contrition as the other turned abruptly indoors. And he ran towards him, proffering the cigar in his hand. 'Mr. Macaulay, you can have this. Please, I don't want it.'

The door was closed in his face, the latch clicked, the curtain was tugged across the glass inside.

CHAPTER VIII

THE drill-instructor stood on his toes. 'Forward, bend,' he shouted across the playground. With a tight crinkle of his eyes, his chin lifted, he surveyed the double rank of boys assembled in front of the church buttresses. 'Bend,' he ordered. 'Don't stoop, bend! And keep your hands on your hips, all of you. Again — bend!'

Thirty heads, the upper parts of thirty small bodies, were lowered in obeisance towards the gravel.

'Right. Up! All together now. You — to the rear there, third boy, dreaming on parade — are you deaf?'

'No, sir,' said Walter, waking.

'Soldiers should listen to the word of command,' the instructor shouted. He was a retired regular, Major Pender, spruce, with a moustache that appeared to drape his upper lip with straw. He carried a small cane tucked beneath his right arm, smartly. 'Right,' he continued. 'Hands to sides, all of you. Down!' He swished the cane, gathering his voice together, watching the rigid faces under the school's red caps. 'Now we'll try marching. A soldier, a British soldier, doesn't walk, he marches. The Empire is his parade ground, he thinks of his king and country.' The words came out in a harsh chant from beneath the moustache: a droplet of spittle caught the afternoon sun on his chin. 'Right. Listen for the command. Left — turn! You, that boy with the crooked tie, don't you know left from right?'

'No, sir, yes, sir.'

'You'll never win a war if you don't. Now, attention — quick *march*!'

Thirty pairs of boots shuffled over the playground towards the iron railings. Major Pender exploded in despair beneath the fir tree.

'Company, halt!' The dust settled. 'Such marching I never seen in all my born days. A girl's school would do better on a picnic. A widows' outing would knock you all sideways. The newest German recruit'd put his head in his knapsack and blub for you . . . Right, we'll try again. By the left, quick *march*!'

Up and down the hot gravel straggled the school. The sky sweltered. Somewhere at the far side of the world, the boys had been told, a fort named Lille (Lilly, to Marriner) had been captured by the Allies. England, furthermore, had declared war upon Turkey. Drill and Major Pender were more than ever a necessary evil. Each morning after prayers Mr. Garnett, grunting, rearranged the little flags on the map: the school plied Miss Threplow for news, any news, about her soldier brother in Egypt. Turkey and Egypt, Mr. Garnett explained with distaste, were both on the Mediterranean, that lizard-shaped sea. A new map was unrolled, stiff with varnish; new flags were cut from cardboard.

'Does Turkish delight come from Turkey, sir?'

'It does, Barrett, it does or did. You boys are all stomach, like boa constrictors.'

The class, postponing arithmetic, shivered with pleasure at the name.

'My mother wears a boa, sir,' Collins remarked.

'Not round the stomach, I trust.'

The class, taken aback, were not sure of the joke.

'Tell us how boa constrictors catch their prey, sir . . . Do they eat sheep, sir? . . . Why are there no snakes in New Zealand, sir?' The questions flowed.

The schoolmaster adjusted the black mourning band on his sleeve, opened his dispatch case and drew out a wad of exercise books. 'I have your Tuesday's homework here, duly corrected,' he remarked, silencing the class. 'Blakiston, distribute these baubles, would you? Quietly, please. Your own homework, I recollect, was abominable. You are not suffering from another cold?'

'No, Mr. Garnett. . . .'

'What sort of sandwiches has she given you?' Marriner asked Walter over their lunch in the playground.

'Sausage.' Walter unrolled the newspaper wrapping. 'Saveloy sausage.'

Marriner's own sandwiches held layers of cold beef. Despite the richness of his lunches he did not get fatter: the bones of his knees showed as pale as egg shells through the rough skin. 'Swop you a beef for a saveloy.'

Walter was not hungry. Not even Turkish delight would have tempted him.

'Gosh,' said Marriner, 'I'd sizzle those Turks up with a bomb. I'd burn their dirty old flag with my magnifying glass.'

Walter threw the crusts of his sandwiches to a pair of sparrows on the asphalt. As he moved, something stiffened the pocket of his jacket. 'Look,' he said.

'Golly, a cigar. Where'd you get it?'

'From a Maori I know.'

'Honest?' Marriner, impressed, snatched the cigar and sniffed it. 'It won't go bang, will it?'

'It says Corona on the band.'

'Dare you to smoke it.'

Walter glanced round the almost deserted playground. A breeze licked the gravel in the heat. 'No,' he said.

'Dare you.'

Walter brooded. 'I'll smoke half if you smoke half. But bags I keep the band.'

Marriner produced a rusty pocket knife and sliced the cigar into two. He also produced his magnifying glass. 'To light it, see? Useful when you're in the desert.'

'Yes.' Walter smiled, drawn into the plan.

'C'mon. Behind the church. Nobody'll cop us.'

They doubled up behind the grey buttresses, the sun hot on their caps in the sheltered corner.

'I'll light my bit first.' The white prism from Marriner's

glass steadied on the cigar top. Five minutes passed. A smoulder stirred in the stub, a fume wandered upwards, a steam, a smoke, an odour.

Marriner sniffed. 'Gosh, man, what a stench.' He poked the unlit end in his mouth, sucked in his cheeks, blew out his chest. A few flakes of grey ash broke from the cigar tip. 'The smoke tastes like liquorice,' he said. 'Now you light yours from mine. Not funk, are you?'

'No.' Walter advanced his own stub, sucking in his cheeks, drawing from the spark Marriner kept alight for him, his nose close against the other's. And presently a hot fume tickled the roof of his mouth, a taste new to him, acrid and scented, invaded his palate. He puffed it out quickly, his tongue tingling. 'It's all right,' he said uncertainly. 'Not bad.'

'It's a stunner, man. Wonderful.'

They lounged back against the sun-hot stones, warily watching one another as they puffed.

'Who's this Maori bloke?' Marriner asked.

'Just somebody.' Walter blinked. 'What's rape? Isn't it that yellow stuff with flowers that sheep eat?'

Marriner had no idea. 'Farming's barmy,' he said.

Again they puffed, at ease against the church. The smoke presently tasted stronger, almost bitter, choking. Beneath Walter's belt something fluttered; his eyes felt hot, his nose dry. Marriner, in his turn, had begun to poke at his own cigar with a black finger-nail: he cleared his throat.

'Say we smoke the rest tomorrow,' he suggested at last. 'Only a Maori'd smoke a whole cigar anyway.'

Walter took a final puff. 'All right.'

'We'll snuff them out and keep them hidden, see?'

The half-cigars were rubbed against the stones, extinguished. Not looking at one another the two boys walked unsteadily back to the playground. Mr. Garnett stood in the sun, the school bell poised in his fist. Marriner drew Walter aside.

'We ought to eat peppermints. My uncle does.'

'You smell me and I'll smell you. In case.'

'Can't smell a thing. Gosh, I'm sweating though.'

The bell tinkled.

At three o'clock Walter had a note from Marriner, pushed along the floor under the desks. 'They'd blow up the Turks all right,' he read.

'Too strong,' he wrote back.

'You look pale, Walter,' said Miss Muriel that evening. 'Are you sickening for something? Tell me.'

'No.' And he added, vaguely: 'We had drill.' His forehead throbbed, his belly fluttered. He had seldom felt so sick in his life.

'Drill ought to make you strong, not weak.' She held his face to the light. 'You must eat a good dinner and you'll feel better.' She gave him a light push towards the dining-room. 'Rose is home again. Run in and say hullo.'

'No. Not now.'

'Why not?'

He escaped to the yard, groped his way to the privy against the fence and, bending over the wooden seat, vomited as though his very entrails wished to leave him. He fumbled for the cigar end in his pocket. That, too, disappeared into the darkness below, leaving only the gold and scarlet band.

'Miss Rose is home,' he told the ring of bright paper. 'Miss Rose,' he repeated in comfort and anxiety.

CHAPTER IX

Two evenings later, when he had come in from the tram journey, Miss Muriel pointed to the kitchen table. 'Another letter from your mother, Walter. Do you want to read it now?'

'Yes.'

'Yes, *please*.' She cleared a place for his satchel on the table. 'Sit down then. I won't interrupt.'

He glanced at the stamp — no new issue — then tore open the azure envelope.

My dearest boy:

I hope you don't feel I've forgotten you. I've thought of you constantly as always, but I've been busy in the house and the days have been so hot that I'm exhausted as soon as I sit down to write in the evening. I loved getting your letter, though your spelling is very odd. I long to see you. Your school-term must be coming to an end, so you'll be already thinking ahead for the Christmas holidays. This time you must come home, really come home at last. You must let me know the train and the date and I can meet you at the station, or dad can. We have a motor car, hold your BREATH, a small Renault now, with a sloping bonnet all painted green, so you can imagine we do not use the old family gig so often, in fact it is stored in the stables. Your father won't let me try to drive the motor, nor do I want to.

All the grass and tussocks on the hills here are scorched by the sun, the garden is dusty and there's not enough water to drown a mouse in. The nor-westers have nearly blown the roof off, a horrid wind at night, though the trees do shelter us a little. I haven't been sleeping well but am much better than I was.

Your father is working far too hard, even with the two shepherds to help him, and a rouseabout for the horses and the milking. The shearing has taken a long time this year, the shearers had a Maori cook who caused trouble outside the shed and was difficult and extravagant with food. One of the shepherds, Malloy, wants to enlist for the war, so we shall let him go as he's a young man, but it worries your father.

I have been helping with Red Cross meetings in the village hall once a week, knitting scarves and rolling bandages to be sent to headquarters in London. The whole Empire must help against these revolting Germans and their beastly Kaiser. Some of us are also collecting clothes for the Belgian refugees who reached England. I have given an old coat of yours, with five brass buttons you had as a little boy, do you remember? Sailor buttons.

I have so much to say to you when you come home after so long. But no more in this letter now. The wind is blowing hard and the windows rattling upstairs. Your father has fallen asleep over his paper, snoring. We look forward to seeing you at Christmas, in fact I would like to keep you home for a year; we may make plans. I can't tell you yet.

Don't be homesick, Walter. Your loving mother says good night to you.

Miss Muriel watched his face across the table. 'I'll write you a letter myself one of these days, Walter, as they seem to make you so happy.' She smiled. 'Does your mother say you're to go home for Christmas?'

'Yes. Gosh, I'm glad.'

'Who taught you to say gosh?'

'It's soppy not to. Everyone does.'

'That doesn't mean you should copy them.' She came close to him; tenderly brushed the fringe of his forelock. 'Well-bred sensitive young boys don't simply do what everyone else does. Remember that.'

He twisted away, folded the letter and stood listening for sounds in the house. 'Where's Miss Rose?' he asked after a silence.

'She went out. Possibly to meet father at the tram later.' Miss Muriel spread a newspaper over the table. 'I must mix a pudding,' she remarked and fetched a bowl from the dresser, 'or you'll all go hungry . . .' She began to hum a tune to herself. 'I'm bringing the baby home next week, Walter. Are you going to loathe having a baby in the house? Will it put your nose out of joint if I mother him instead of you?'

The summer evening called to him through the window. 'Can I go and meet Miss Rose?'

'If you want to. Don't be late.'

He ran down the cinder path to the gate, swinging his arms. He was going home for Christmas: his heart knocked on his ribs with relief, delight, longing. An extraordinary happiness made his head ring light and empty, as though it did not belong to his body but floated like a balloon from his shoulders. In the gardens beside the road tulips and bunched red and striped ranunculus glowed in the hot twilight, behind spriggy hedges of macrocarpa and veronica. A fantail, snapping for gnats with its small beak, flitted across his path, almost brushing his face. He swiped at it with his arm, imitating its chatter, twirling himself round in his ecstasy. Softly, like the run of the blood in his own body and nerves, the sea sounded from beyond the sand-dunes at the end of the road. He had forgotten the bridge, the dog, the water, Mrs. Nelson herself.

At the tram stop there was nobody save a conductor counting tickets. Walter approached his lowered head. At any other time he would have been too shy to question the man.

'Have you seen — ' he started.

The other totted down something with a pencil. 'What d'you want?'

'Has Miss Garnett been here? Miss Rose?'

'Not this trip.' He glanced up, along the hill above the tram terminus. 'Mr. Macaulay came home on the five-forty. I haven't seen any other of the family.'

Walter drew back: he had recognized in this very man the conductor who had advised the driver (so long ago yet seemingly only yesterday) to throw the wounded dog into the waters of the estuary. The man had the same narrow jaw, the same dark-shaved chin.

Walter hurried away. He knew now that he must look for Miss Rose, find her. But where? And would she welcome him? Since she had come home they had hardly spoken: she was, he thought, avoiding him, fighting off the recollection of their last encounter on the beach. She might avoid him still. Her withdrawn, frantic face, as he had seen it in passing, on the stairs or in the hall, haunted him. And he wished now that he had someone to help him, somebody who could talk to him as Mark Garnett had talked, with a flattering hint that they were both adults together. But Mr. Mark, his holiday ended, had returned to the lighthouse in the south, in Foveaux Strait. On his last evening, however, he and Walter had sauntered along the beach, on the pier together. The yeasty rush of the tide ruffling across the bar from the sea had flowed beneath the wooden piles and stanchions below them. The Cave Rock had stood up darkly against the twilight.

'I suppose you want me to send you something from the lighthouse, Walter?'

'Send me some shells, or seagulls' eggs.'

'The corruptible to the incorruptible.' The older man gazed into the water below, reflectively. 'No, I shall send you nothing. I shall simply remember you and leave you with a word of advice: don't be afraid, timid, ever. Speak up for yourself — let humanity have it between the teeth and be damned to them, man and woman alike. Your soul's your own: respect it.'

Later they had strolled back through the lamplit township. 'When I was your age,' said Mark Garnett, 'I used to think this town was the whole world. Even now I'm not so sure it isn't.'

'The whole world?' Walter was doubtful.

The other's voice had taken a slight lift in tone, so that Walter realized the words were a quotation from poetry: ' "Everywhere the world is man and woman, everywhere the old sad sins find room." That's what I mean, Walter. The world's humanity, from China to Peru — including Sumner on the way.' He had touched the boy's shoulder: 'And, God, wouldn't I like to protect you from the whole bloody lot!'

That had been several days earlier. Now Walter was alone, seeking Miss Rose. Beyond the tram-lines the road curved round the base of the hill, skirting the beach, then began the steep ascent to the new houses, the upthrusts of reddish rock, the unfledged cement of garden walls. With one backward look at the tram conductor, Walter sped along the road to where it flanked the sands. The surface here was damp from the seepings of the rock face above; so damp that footprints were clear in the clay between the dressing of shingle. Like an Indian the boy bent down in scrutiny, but the marks were scattered and presently he gave up the hope of distinguishing Miss Rose's trail. He felt drawn to follow the road up the hill: he had yet, he reminded himself, to apologize to Mr. Macaulay for his eavesdropping on the Garnett's veranda, to assert that he had not really listened . . . He hurried forward and upward, his eyes on the blue lake-like sheen of the bay below, where a few sails whitened in the sun from the west. He would go up to the house.

There were footsteps in front of him, at the turn of the ascent: a woman advanced quickly, almost stumbling, down the shingled roadway, her hat-brim darkening the pale oval of her face. Without timidity Walter called ahead:

'I came to look for you, Miss Rose.'

He thought she was about to pass him in silence, to ignore him completely. Then: 'Take my hand,' she said in a queer muffled voice, turning back. 'Take my hand, Walter. Give me some human contact at least.' She leant against the rock face beside the road, clutching his fingers in a hot grasp. 'Give me some sanity. I need it.'

'I came to look for you,' he repeated.

'Why?' She began to laugh, her face contorted towards the rock, a few strands of brown hair straggling free on her nape. 'Why on earth?'

'I thought you might be lost.'

'I'm certainly lost . . . But you owe me nothing, you know.'

He was puzzled. Was she ill? And quickly he glanced up the hill at the house above the turn of the road. 'Shall I fetch Mr. Macaulay?'

'What?'

'Shall I tell Mr. Macaulay you're not well?'

'I'm perfectly well.' She relinquished his hand, laughter again shaking her as she pressed her fingers to her mouth. 'You know so much, Walter — more than anyone — that you'd better learn at once: Geoffrey and I have parted. It had to come and it's come now. I've told him.'

Walter uttered the first words that came to his mind. 'He's going to marry you. I heard him tell Miss Muriel.'

'Oh, you little fool, you little fool . . .' and suddenly she sank down by the road, her dress spreading round her, and with her face hidden from him began to smooth and pat the rock in front of her knees. 'Hilda fell here,' she whispered. 'She'd reached here when she fell. They found her at this very spot. Do you hear that, you innocent Walter?'

'Yes,' he said faintly and stared at the rocks. 'Yes.'

'Do you know why she fell?'

He began uncertainly: 'Because her heart — '

'Oh, more than that. A lot more.' And caressing the rock before her, talking as though to the hill itself she went on: 'Hilda had been to see me in town that day, Walter. Somebody had told her . . . she knew what was going on . . . some note of mine to Geoffrey had given her the address. I don't know. At any rate, she came to face me, to fight me, to beg me to give him up.

We had a terrible, stupid scene.' Miss Rose shuddered. 'A shocking scene. If she'd dared she'd have hit me, and I her. She fought me like a wild animal, fought me for Geoffrey — but because I was in the wrong I wouldn't budge, I wouldn't give way an inch. I'd won Geoff back from her — or at least she thought it was as simple as that — and now she said I must let him go because of the baby. I refused, Walter; I said the baby had nothing whatever to do with it. Nothing. It was wrong of me, of course, but she'd wrought me up to such a state . . . Are you listening?'

Without waiting for his answer she drew him down beside her against the rocks.

'She threatened me, Walter. She said she'd try to stop her baby, make it miscarry. I just didn't believe her, it wasn't in her nature. It wasn't like Hilda, and I told her that women simply didn't do those things. I even laughed at her; I told her to go home and sleep; I went so far as to offer her sleeping-pills. She threw them out of the window. I knew she was bluffing, trying to frighten me, and I told her so. All the unkind things we'd ever said to one another since we were children were said again. Only sisters can flay one another as we did that afternoon — and Hilda and I were twins, remember. All our old scores came up like ghosts between us, again and again. I'd never seen her so angry.'

The excited, flurried voice ceased for a moment, the hands fell listlessly to her knees.

'When she'd gone I was horrified at what I'd said and done, Walter. I'd been fighting for the greatest happiness I'd ever known, but now it all seemed selfish, utterly wrong. Besides, it struck me that she might have been serious about the baby after all. I didn't know what to do. In a panic I tried to get hold of Geoffrey at his office, but I was too late, he'd left. Then in the evening I brought myself down here to Sumner. I suppose I seemed crazy, I don't know. You met me on the beach. I didn't know what I meant to do, except to see Geoffrey before it might

P

be too late. And too late it was — I knew it at once from the things you told me. My sister was already dead.'

Walter stared at the gloves she had let fall beside her on the road. Now she took off her hat and leant her forehead against the volcanic rock of the hillside.

'Poor Hilda. She didn't kill the child: we know now that what happened was due to heart failure. Only that. But she did kill something else, everything between Geoffrey and me. All that passion we had . . . it was wonderful to both of us, dreadful and wonderful . . . she killed that. Now it's simply no longer in our blood. Hardly a spark left, none. Tonight we looked at one another and saw . . . only two ordinary people, almost strangers. We'd become separate animals again; he was simply the son of a patient I'd been unable to save, I was simply the nurse he'd met in his mother's house eighteen months ago . . . Just like that, you see. And we both knew it. Only his conscience and stubbornness made him try to forget it and ask me to marry him — marry him in a year, two years, some time. I wouldn't, I won't do it. We're finished. He owes me nothing.' She paused, her lips trembling. 'Men are cowards really. Despicable, conventional. All my brother Mark says about women applies to men more. I'd rather try to save others' lives now, for ever, than tie myself to a man.' She nodded. 'I've left Geoffrey, Walter. I'll never marry him and he knows it. If we meet it'll be as friends, even if that. We've parted, and there's an end.'

Breathing deeply she licked her lips, hunched herself silently for a minute, then raised her over-bright eyes to glance at the boy. He had not stirred from beside her: his fingers tugged at the starveling grasses between the rocks.

'I called you a little fool,' she said with a kind of regretful softness, 'but it's I who'm the fool, telling so much as though I hadn't a soul in the world to confide in . . . Do you think I'm a very strange person, Walter? So discontented?'

But, trembling, drawn into her mysteries, he had his own questions to ask. Of all she had told him — and he had become more and more apprehensive as he'd listened — one remark had pierced him to the quick: 'Somebody had told her . . . she knew what was going on.' Yes, somebody had "told" Mrs. Hilda. And now, his face twisted away from Miss Rose, he began:

'If Mrs. Hilda knew, if somebody'd told her —'

'Yes?' she asked absently.

He tried to work it out, striving towards some flash of logic almost beyond him. 'If somebody'd told her . . . I mean about Mr. Macaulay and you . . . wouldn't that be the person who'd killed Mrs. Hilda? Wouldn't it?'

She looked at him sharply in the twilight. 'There *was* somebody. Hilda would only say she'd been told in malice, as an insult. Until then she hadn't known it was me.'

'Then . . . this person . . . she killed her . . .' From the shadow of a bridge, of dark water and dread, he withdrew in fear. 'Did she, Miss Rose?'

'Yes,' she brooded, 'I suppose you could say that was true, Walter.' In some curious way her voice lightened itself of guilt. 'Malicious gossip could be a poison, a shock, indirectly fatal.'

He drew in his breath. The dark water suffocated him and he could not speak.

Again Miss Rose looked at him sharply. 'Was it you, Walter?'

'No,' he said, terrified.

She searched his eyes then shook her head. 'I believe you. It wouldn't have been you.'

He watched her get wearily to her feet and dust the gravel from her skirt. 'If I knew who that person . . .' she murmured and did not finish. She took up her hat; planted it slowly on her head. 'If I knew I would kill her, if it was a woman. I'd do that.'

He could not tell her — not even reveal that he had followed her and Mr. Macaulay that evening from the Square. He could not bring out the name of Mrs. Nelson: Mrs. Nelson who had thrown him into the dark water to drown. He would fight out the battle in his own way, in expiation.

'Come, Walter, we must go home.'

Chilled, silent, he walked beside her down the hill towards the lights of the township. He would kill Mrs. Nelson. He would wait for his moment and then kill her.

Miss Rose rested a hand on his shoulder. 'You're very quiet, Walter. I'm sorry I talked so much. I've tired you.'

CHAPTER X

THE crowded morning tram had only one empty seat. Geoffrey Macaulay, arriving late, sat himself beside Walter at the rear of the trailer, the black band on his arm touching the boy's sleeve. Until they had passed the road under the cliffs and the tram had begun its long run beside the estuary, the young man did not speak. Then:

'Well, Walter, how are you?'

He jumped. 'All right.' And he added presently: 'Thank you, Mr. Macaulay.'

The other ran a cupped hand over his nose and mouth. He no longer wore a moustache: the skin of his upper lip and chin was freshly shaven, raw in the morning light. Walter ventured a glance at him sideways — at the sandy jut of the brows above the brown eyes, at the straight short nose and the red lift of the mouth.

'My son doesn't keep you awake at nights, Walter?'

He took a moment to work out the question. 'No,' he said. The baby slept in Miss Muriel's room. 'No.'

'Good . . . Still collecting stamps, are you?'

Walter warmed, shyly. 'I've got a new one, French,' he said to the satchel on his knees. 'With a flying woman on it. A swop.'

'Where's the woman flying to?'

He did not know. 'I think she's just a figure, like Britannia only French.'

Mr. Macaulay nodded. 'Aye, Marianne maybe . . . Do you read the war news?'

'Mr. Garnett tells us at school when there's anything. Or Miss Threplow does — her brother's a corporal in Egypt.'

'Miss Threplow?'

'Our mistress. Mr. Garnett's mistress.'

'I see.' The other winced. For a minute he contemplated the open salt flats of the estuary, the water reflecting the clouded sky. A hot wind blew through the tram, carrying swirls of grit and dust under the seats. 'Do you know what I intend to do today, Walter?'

The boy glanced at the set lines of his lips. 'No.'

'I intend to take myself to King Edward Barracks and sign myself on for the army.' He folded his arms. 'At least that's one action not to be despised.'

'Are you going to the war?'

'I'll reach the war eventually no doubt.' And the soft Scottish burr in his voice hardened: 'My junior partner can keep my business alive. And this country won't miss an architect or so for a while. So it's a soldier's pay for me.'

Walter hesitated. 'Does Miss Muriel know?'

'Muriel? No, nobody knows at the moment, except you.' His hand strayed suddenly to the inside pocket of his jacket. 'I've a note here. I suppose you wouldn't care to take it back with you this evening and deliver it?'

Walter accepted the square white envelope. It was addressed, in a slanting neat hand, to Miss Rose.

'I'd meant to post it,' said the man's voice, 'but you'll see her tonight . . .' Then, as suddenly as he had given it, he took back the letter. 'No, I'll post it. Never mind. I'll do something properly for once.' With a savage thrust he replaced the envelope in his pocket. 'I've made mess enough. Aye, Walter, you wouldn't know. Mess enough.'

Walter kept quiet. The tram passed over the iron bridge of the estuary: he did not look up.

'Mess enough,' the other repeated. 'You wouldn't know.' Again he passed his fingers over his face, brooding. 'You wouldn't know the tangle a decent educated man can get into over so simple a bunch of trouble as his own instincts. My God, I'm not a monster — most of me's the same as other people!' He shook his head, lowering the richness of his voice in the crowded tram. 'A man's a man. He doesn't look for trouble if he's a decent fellow. And then . . . he's in the mess before he knows what he's at. His scruples are gone, burnt away like paper.' He sought for his pipe, found it and bit on the stem. 'And don't ask the women — any woman — to accept you for what you are, with your own life — oh no, they shove you up on a pedestal, want you to be something like a god, a father, or even a brother. They'll draw the soul out of you to satisfy some illusion of love that never existed. Aye, I know it now . . . I'm not so young or so brash as I've been over this past year — I've come face to face with the weak joists in myself, or some of them, I can tell you, Walter. If I marry again it won't be for smooth arms and soft eyes and all that. I'll get back my self-respect as my own mother knew it.' He touched his pocket. 'Well, Rosie'll read it all in the letter here. I needn't spout it to you.'

He sighed, his voice sinking to silence against the rattle and zoom of the tram as it neared the city and the Square.

Walter had been watching the young man's white collar as it had moved against his neck in speaking. 'What sort of uniform will you wear?' he asked now.

'What? As a soldier? Khaki, I suppose.' The other pulled himself together, gave a dry smile. 'It will not be the kilt anyway, Walter.'

'Will you be an officer?'

'No. I'll try for the ordinary ranks. That's what I want.'

Walter parted from him in the Square.

'Certain of you younger boys,' remarked Mr. Garnett in the middle of the hour given to History, 'assume that the war is a sufficient excuse for neglecting your homework.' He wrote the word 'war' in tall capital letters on the blackboard and drew a deliberate chalk line through it. 'Let that convey something to your brains while you work for me.'

The class had reached King John and Magna Carta.

'Was Magna Carta a smack in the eye for the king, sir?'

'More than that, Bascomb. It was the freedom you know at this moment, as the son of one of England's colonies. The Charter, I assure you, was not — to use the phrase of a contemporary tyrant — simply a scrap of paper.'

'Did the Kaiser really say that, sir?'

'We seem to be back on the subject of war,' said Mr. Garnett sadly. 'Let us dismiss it. Will you all open your exercise books, please, and write a short essay on Magna Carta? In ink.'

'Was Magna Carta written in ink, sir?'

'Larrikins' questions, Collins, mean detention after school.'

The class, sweating in the heat, sighed over its task. The master's beard sank slowly to his waistcoat: he dozed. The north-west wind whistled through a ventilator in the roof and brought a dry scent of grass into the city. Walter lifted his head: in the state of anxiety in which he was living the thought of the fortnight ahead, before the end of the term, was almost unendurable. He had not seen Mrs. Nelson.

'Are you writing, Blakiston?'

'Yes, sir.'

The ink was black, like dark water. His head ached. He put down his pen.

'May I leave the room, sir?'

'You may. Two minutes.'

The playground was empty. On the lavatory wall somebody had written 'There was an old man of Cape Horn . . .' Walter rested his forehead against the cold bricks and thought of what he must do, his sacred revenge.

'I've got sixpence saved up out of my Navy League money,' said Marriner after school. 'We could buy some Tobler chocolate. The card might have a peccary on it.' They were on the way to the tram. 'What say, man?'

'No. I've got to hurry.' Walter ran ahead towards the Square, his satchel bumping against his shoulders as though to push him on. Directly after dinner, he decided, he would go straight to

232

Mrs. Nelson: he would kill her as he would kill a pigmy, a turtle in the sand, a rebel chief in the jungle.

'I want you to pick those apricots in the yard for me, Walter.' Miss Muriel placed the wicker basket on the table before he could escape. 'Do your homework, dear, then pick them.'

It was not until the following afternoon that he found himself knocking, breathless, at the back door of the Nelsons' kitchen.

CHAPTER XI

'CAN we play for money, ma?' Jimmy's eyes searched his mother's face above the grubby cards in his hand. 'Can Walter and me play for money?'

'And who's to provide the money I'd like to know?'

'You are. We'd pay you back, ma. Honest.'

She flicked cigarette ash towards the coal-scuttle. 'No. Nobody gambles on Old Maid, anyway . . . Keep your cards up, Walter.'

'I'm sick of cards, ma,' Jimmy sighed. 'Can't we go out?'

'You'd get yourselves sopped with rain. No, give your mother a little pleasure for a change. She's feeling depressed.'

Heavy summer rain splashed on the back porch and blurred the windows. The half-grown pine trees and macrocarpas against the paling fence at the end of the yard shook in the wind, their green tops whipping at the grey clouds over the township. The hills hung dark, as though they had been dipped in the sea. In the kitchen Walter's Burberry hung over a chair, with rounded shoulders that dripped to the linoleum of the floor. He had been in the house for twenty minutes and had been drawn into the card game before he could find words to protest. For twenty minutes he had watched Mrs. Nelson across the table as she lit and smoked her cigarettes.

'Do the kings on the cards always have white faces?' Jimmy asked his mother.

'I suppose so.' Her broad coarse mouth fell a little open. 'Why?'

'I just asked why. No Maoris on them?'

'No.' Her bosom suddenly swelled behind the cards. 'And don't you go throwing that up at me again,' she said.

'I wasn't throwing anything, ma.'

'Too right you were. I won't have any whippersnapper like you casting coals of fire or whatever it is. Do you hear? Go on now, both of you, play your cards.'

'Can't I go out?' Jimmy insisted. 'My rabbits'll be wet.'

'Darn your rabbits.'

Her son looked at her with baleful eyes: the wet Saturday afternoon had exasperated him. 'I know why pa's in prison,' he said distinctly.

Mrs. Nelson slapped the cards from his hands to the table. 'You say that again and I'll flay every strip of skin from your backside.'

'Well, I do know.' Jimmy backed away. 'I know because the policeman came here. See?'

Mrs. Nelson stood up: she flung a finger in the direction of the door into the passage. 'You go to your room,' she commanded. 'You go to bed and I'll take a strap to you later.'

'It's true, anyway.'

'Go! Put your head under the bedclothes for shame.'

'And I'm glad pa did it, so there!' Jimmy, after a glance at Walter's startled pale face, disappeared with a slam of the door that shook the house.

Mrs. Nelson gathered up the cards from the table, shuffling them absently while ash fell on her wrists. 'That child of mine.' She stared at the cards, then slumped heavily down in her chair. 'I don't know — I don't know, Walter. The way things have worked out . . . Nobody could have guessed.'

He watched her, holding himself taut. The moment had come when he must speak, yet no words would come.

'Do you want to go on playing cards?' she asked.

He shook his head.

She spat on a card, rubbed it with a finger and dried it on her apron. 'All right.' She bit her lip. 'How's the baby?' she inquired after a moment. 'Miss Muriel looking after him?'

'Yes,' he muttered.

'I saw him out in the pram the other day. Red hair, I see. Or sandy, rather.'

Walter said nothing. For a second he glanced out at the rain: the clothes lines in the yard tossed like the ropes of a ship's rigging. The captain would be on the bridge . . . and he stared back again at Mrs. Nelson, tightening every muscle in his body.

'And our Miss Rose?' she pursued.

Walter did not take his eyes from her face. He did not answer. He was going to kill her.

'She's left home again, I hear,' said Mrs. Nelson. 'She's working in this Red Cross depot-place up in town, the one in Hereford Street. Well, she's used to that sort of thing. It'll suit her for a time.' Her voice flagged. 'And then I suppose she'll be Mrs. Geoff Macaulay, with a Red Cross trousseau. Off with the old and on with the new, you might say.'

Walter opened his mouth to speak. But at that moment a plaintive shout came from the far end of the house: 'I'm undressed, ma.'

'You go to bed as I told you.'

'I'm hungry, ma.'

'You get nothing till you've apologized.'

'Can't Walter come and talk to me?'

'Walter's busy talking to me.'

Along the passage a door shut.

'Poor young devil,' sighed Mrs. Nelson. 'But he's quite right about his pa, about Rahi.' She got up, opened a tin on the dresser and piled biscuits on to a plate. 'It's worse than Jimmy knows, Walter. And now I've got the job of keeping the kid straight for the rest of my days.' She offered him the plate. 'Here, take a biscuit.'

He refused.

'Cream wafers,' she insisted.

'No,' he said, staring at her.

She munched a biscuit herself. 'Well, I've taken a lot of knocks from the world already. I'll get my own back, one way or another. I always have.'

And at last he spoke. 'You told Mrs. Hilda,' he said in a strangled voice that he couldn't hear properly himself. 'You told her about Mr. Macaulay and Miss Rose.'

'I did what?'

'You told her. I know you told her.'

'Here,' she said sharply, crumbling the biscuit in her fingers, 'what's this?'

He stood up. 'You told Mrs. Hilda — '

'I never did any such thing.'

'You did.' And summoning a sort of mulish strength from inside him he cried out again: 'You did! It was my secret and you — '

'Stop it.' Her strength was equal to his, more. 'What do you know about it?'

'You told her, Mrs. Nelson. You killed her.'

'Now you be careful with your words, young man.'

'I know you did! Nobody else could have — ' he stopped, trembling. 'It was you.'

'Shut up!' She flung her cigarette into the hearth and began to walk slowly round the room, her hands on her hips. 'All right,' she threw at him at last, angrily. 'I told her. I'd a score to settle with Mrs. Hilda. Always sneering to people that I'd married a filthy Maori — that was Mrs. Hilda, the snob she was. I'd stood it for five years, longer. I'd had enough.' She paused, breathing heavily, her nostrils working. 'Too right I told her about Rose! I told her her precious Geoffrey was keeping her sister like a tart, in town. Oh I didn't blurt it out straight, like that, but I told her all right, I gave her hints enough. We had a fine rumpus, I can tell you. She shoved me out of the house, out on my elbow.' She paused again, leaning against the edge of the kitchen table. 'Well . . . I didn't know then that she'd do the crazy thing she did, of course — start shifting things round the house like a looney.'

'You killed her,' he cried, holding his back against the dresser. 'It was you!'

To his amazement she sank down at the table, moaning. 'Who says that?' she whispered. 'Who?'

He did not answer. He was climbing out of the dark water, pushing it away, struggling for the bank.

'I'm not well, Walter. Not today. I can't battle with you. I've my own troubles.' Her thick lips quivered. 'A part of my life's smashed on me. You heard what Jimmy said about Rahi, that bastard I married. It's true.' She groped for her yellow packet of cigarettes. 'I've waited all these years, knowing he'd come to a bad end, one way or another. He was that sort of a man, dangerous. Now he's gone and hit somebody — a sergeant or an instructor in camp, I'm not sure. The chap's died and they've got a conviction against my husband: they'll have to hang him or shoot him. The policeman came here to tell me.' She lit a cigarette, her face crumpling. 'My name isn't Nelson really, Walter. I've called myself Nelson for Jimmy's sake, but Rahi's name is Napira. I'm Mrs. Napira. "Napier" would've been too close, so I hit on "Nelson".' Her smooth face grew haggard with recollection. 'Rahi was a shearer, you know, when I married him — or rather, when he got me into trouble like that,' she murmured to her cigarette. 'A wild devil, always after the girls. I was working in that house down south I once told you about. I couldn't resist him.' She shook her head. 'I loved that plurry man, that damned savage. And yet when the papers'll say, as I suppose they will, that Rahi Napira's been hung, nobody'll know now that he was mine — or not many people. Your Garnetts may, if they read it; but precious few others.'

Walter had not listened. His anger, saved up, was still hot inside him. He had yet to kill her.

'I don't like you,' he said, his voice coming out shrilly as he advanced upon her at the table. 'I hate you.'

She drew back, surprised, her hand going up protectively in front of her face. 'You keep away from me,' she said sharply.

'I hate you.'

'You've got some spark in your guts, anyway.'

He shouted, close to her, his face contorted: 'I'm going to kill you.' He looked at her throat.

'You what?' Alarmed, she was suddenly on her feet and coming amply, hugely towards him. 'You stay where you are, young man. None of that.'

'I'm going to kill you, I am.'

She made a clumsy grab for his arms. 'A kid like you — '

'You told Mrs. Hilda!' Fiercely, frantically, he fought for her neck, the brown flesh below her chin. 'You killed her!' He beat at her with all his strength. 'I hate you — you tried to drown me — '

'What rubbish is that! Drown you!'

'You told my secret — '

She burst out laughing, then slapped him hard across the face with her open hand. 'You and your secrets, you little pale-nosed whippersnapper — you keep away from me!' But suddenly her shout rang towards the passage: 'Jimmy! Jimmy, come here!' Tears of alarm were in her eyes. 'Jimmy! This kid's gone crazy!'

Walter drew away. He would let her go, he would not kill her. He snatched his coat from the chair and ran, small and bent over, to the door. Sobbing, he rushed into the yard, the rain, and thence to the road. He had saved himself: the dignity of his own heart was intact. He would never see her again.

CHAPTER XII

'Six more days and no more school, I'm a dunce and you're a fool.' And Marriner made what he called a Chinese face at Walter in the playground. The Chinese face meant tilting up the corners of his eyes with his fingers, splaying his mouth long-wise.

'If the wind changes you'll stay like that,' Walter told him, laughing.

'I'd like it. I'd go to China and eat birds' nests.'

Presently they began to talk about Chinese stamps. At five minutes to nine Miss Threplow arrived at the gate on her bicycle, one hand controlling the wide brim of her hat.

'How many Turks has your brother captured?' Questions were fired at her as she dismounted. 'Has he won a V.C.? Has he sent you a bit of the Sphinx?'

'He's in a Cairo hospital,' she told the crowd of boys, sadly. 'He's ill with enteric.'

Blank faces gaped at her.

'But where was he wounded? Tell us.'

'Enteric's a sort of fever, boys, not a wound.' She propped her bicycle in the shed. 'He may be sent home in a Red Cross ship.' She disappeared into the school corridor, followed by puzzled eyes. If a soldier went to war . . . yes, Miss Threplow's brother had let them all down. They turned to other news: Collins had heard that a German dreadnought had been sunk, some weeks before, at a place named Cocos Island. The name was a pleasure, a find in itself, straight out of adventure.

'Please, sir, could the crew live on coco-nuts? Could they fire coco-nuts from a naval gun?'

'No,' grunted Mr. Garnett, after prayers. 'And the island, I believe, is uninhabited.'

'Would it be Robinson Crusoe's place?'

'That was Juan Fernandez, off South America.'

The end-of-term examinations were delayed while atlases were searched for Cocos Island. New Zealand itself looked small enough, a floating leaf or two on the blank blue of the Pacific. Cocos Island was lost in the Indian Ocean, unmarked, a teasing myth. Walter wrote a note to Marriner under the desk: 'Only pirates have found it.' For the rest of the day they lived in a dream of Cocos Island. Nobody knew if the island had stamps of its own . . . Marriner was given detention for writing on the blackboard: 'Cocos Island is barmy.'

Walter walked alone to catch the tram after school. Only the recognition of a face in the street as he drifted along in his trance, his vision of the island, brought him to himself. His awakening was as sudden as it was unexpected.

'Miss Rose. . . .'

She was walking beside a young soldier in a khaki uniform, a slouch hat on his head. The man, Walter saw, was not Mr. Macaulay. 'Miss Rose,' he said again as she passed.

She glanced back at the sound of his voice: and at once her smile stiffened, her oval face grew solemn, then embarrassed: she blushed.

'Walter,' she said, so softly that her escort did not hear. And she gave a light flick of her left hand glove as though to warn the boy in secret: 'Not here, not now, some other time.'

A moment more and she had hurried ahead, her fingers resting on the soldier's arm. At the corner she looked back: smiling, she lifted her glove again like a flag, then held her hat against the wind. When Walter waved in return she had already vanished.

'What your mother'll say when she sees your clothes I can't imagine,' Miss Muriel chided him that evening. She sat on the veranda, holding out one of his jackets of which she had patched the elbows and let out the sleeves. 'This is really a job for a tailor, not for me.'

'Yes,' he said without interest.

'Hold yourself straight, that's a good boy.' She glanced at him, stiffening her own shoulders. 'Are you listening!'

He nodded. 'Yes, but it's too hot to stand straight.'

The sun threw a glowing band of orange across the scorched grass at the side of the house. On the veranda the baby's crib was shadowed by a sagging rattan blind. On one side of the crib was Miss Muriel's deck chair; on the far side old Mrs. Garnett had propped herself upright with cushions on the bleached cane sofa that occupied the right-angle of the veranda and that had one leg supported on a flower-pot. She dozed. Presently Miss Muriel put aside Walter's jacket and took up a bundle of stockings.

'Really, you must have toe-nails like a chicken's.' She held up one of the stockings. 'If you ask me, grandfather's permanently out of prison.'

'Whose grandfather?'

'Your big toe. Haven't you ever heard that expression?'

'No,' he said, preoccupied, watching the baby. The child's eyes were open, the forehead was moist below the reddish duck's-tail of the forelock. 'Malcolm's too hot, Miss Muriel. He's sweaty.'

'I'll take him up in a moment.'

The baby began to whimper. Old Mrs. Garnett stirred, pushing up the spectacles on her nose, her tongue running over her shrunken lips.

'Grizzle, grizzle,' she mumbled vaguely in the child's direction. 'Always grizzlin'. Don't tease him, you, Walter.'

'I wasn't. I didn't touch him, did I, Miss Muriel?'

'I didn't notice, dear.'

The old woman sniffed. 'His father a common soldier,' she remarked to the rattan blind and the lawn. 'No gentlemen left in the world . . . no ladies either.' She peered across the crib at her daughter. 'Why ain't Geoffrey here, Muriel?'

'He's in training at Trentham, mother. You know that. We'll see him after Christmas.'

'A common soldier . . . He ought to have asked me first.'

Miss Muriel laughed, put aside the darning-basket and bent over the crib. 'Who's too hot?' she asked the child softly. 'Who wants a bit of attention?' With careful hands she lifted the baby, to clasp his cheek against hers with a fierce longing. 'Who's that stranger?' she crooned, nodding towards Walter. 'Eh? Who is it?'

'You spoil that child, Muriel.' Mrs. Garnett groped for a small bottle on her lap, selected a pill and swallowed it. 'If you're seein' Dr. Thomson tell him these things taste like mothballs. I want the sweet kind . . . Let that child alone,' she continued. 'No good molly-coddlin' children. Treat him as I treated Mark.'

'Yes, mother. Though I wouldn't say that's a fair example, frankly.' Miss Muriel carried the baby indoors. 'Bring the crib for me, Walter, would you? By the way,' she told him as they reached the kitchen, 'I saw Mrs. Nelson today at the store. She asked after you — she thought you might have been sickening for a cold or something. I soon disillusioned her: I thought you've been looking remarkably well for a day or two.' She glanced at the clock before setting down the baby. 'I'll just get this youngster settled then we'll have dinner.'

Walter took himself off to bed earlier than usual. The wooden acorn of the blind tapped on the open window of his room: the evening light still lay across the lawn below. He did not at once get undressed, but lay curled on his bed, a book spread before him on the blanket. After so long (could it be years?) he would return to his old companions, the boys of Longmeadows.

The Lower Fourth, he read, *could barely control the pained amazement that accompanied their fate for the afternoon. No cricket for them. The sounds of bat and ball might drift through the windows from High Field, the calls of the players resound from the greensward, but the*

Upper Fourth were firmly barred from such joys. Even the cheerful mug of Magpie Melkington. . . .

'Walter, are you in bed?'
'Just going, Miss Muriel.'

CHAPTER XIII

'I WANT a talk with you, Blakiston,' Mr. Garnett began mildly. He sat himself down beside Walter on the narrow tram seat, stowed his dispatch case under him and folded his hands over the lower buttons of his waistcoat. 'I want to talk to you, and you must not be too embarrassed to answer me.'

The tram passed a water-cart spraying the dusty road out of the city. Sweat pricked the boy's spine under his shirt: he stared at the satchel on his knees. What had he done, what was coming? Had Mrs. Nelson spoken of assault, injury, murder?

'We shall talk as friends, I hope,' the schoolmaster continued. 'I have much on my mind, Walter —' he had never before used the Christian name so directly ' — both as a mentor and a man. And, as both, I have noticed that you are among those boys who find difficulty with the work you do out of school. In my house, in fact. You're intelligent but you're distracted, you won't concentrate, and it has struck me that the fault mayn't be yours. Or not entirely yours. And I do not mention the war.'

The tram rattled past a factory-like building in the suburbs. 'Carrageen Irish Moss', a daily puzzle to Walter, was written along the front in black letters. (Another puzzle, 'Cats Neutered Here', graced a green gate further down the line.) Now he withdrew his eyes from the Irish Moss. He waited.

'Not wholly your fault, I fancy.' The old man's voice softened. 'The vicissitudes of my household may well have upset you. They've certainly upset me. Pain and tears are all men's lot, as the Greek said; nevertheless —' he collected himself ' — nevertheless, they should not be visited upon a pupil of mine if avoidance were possible ... Has my household disturbed you, Walter? Has a mind as expanding as yours been disorganized by events which have overtaken my family during these past months? I should be glad to know.'

The tram, coasting easily out from the last houses of the suburb, ran now between hedges of gorse and broom. Gaunt blue gums stood scattered across the marshy paddocks away from the road. 'Do you mean about Mrs. Hilda?' Walter asked in confusion.

'Partly that; and other things.' Mr. Garnett smoothed the fall of his beard. 'You mustn't force yourself into an answer,' he added presently. 'Do not speak from what you do not feel.'

Walter was bewildered: a pulse beat in the roof of his mouth. The underlying question was too subtle, too searching, for him to tackle without thought.

'Have my family disturbed you, Walter?'

'No,' he said at last. 'I don't listen, much.'

'Very well . . . then perhaps we are after all on the side of the angels. Perhaps we have no need, any of us, to reproach ourselves with corrupting the young. Our world hasn't — ' he paused to clear his throat ' — has not impinged upon your innocence.'

The tram, buffeted, shaken by the wind, reached the approach to the bridge at the head of the long estuary. Walter lifted himself a few inches from his seat to peer through the window at the water below the bridge's rusty parapet. This was the place, this the source of terror. Today, however, there was no dog upon the bridge; only — and Walter looked again — a young boy on a bicycle. The boy leant over the parapet, gazing into the slow river below, sitting idly astride his propped bicycle. He was not aware, Walter saw at once, that the tram could not pass him: the space, on that side, between the outer tram-line and the railing was too narrow. The bell of the tram clanged once, twice, the brakes groaned against the wheels, a muffled shout sounded from the driver's window. And only then did the boy look up: he half-fell, half-stumbled across the track to safety, dragging his bicycle sideways, his fair hair ruffling over his forehead in an untidy fringe. Walter saw his face twist upwards in a grin of embarrassment at the driver as the tram passed on its way unhindered. For a second their eyes met, Walter's and this stranger's of his own age, and a signal of escape flashed from one to the other like a greeting or a blessing: nobody but they, the two of them, could understand or share this impish shiver of triumph, nobody but themselves. The recognition was immediate and it vanished. The tram zoomed over the bridge. Walter sank down on the slatted seat beside Mr. Garnett.

'I brought up this question today,' the schoolmaster resumed, oblivious of the boy on the bridge, 'because your mother has written to me, Walter. She has been thinking of your future, apparently, or is at any rate concerned about you. Mine, as you know, is only a preparatory school for boys from eight to twelve. Your parents are thinking of putting your name down for the College in Christchurch. In fact your mother may want to keep you at home for a year first — she would engage a tutor, I gather — before sending you to that larger school. Are you listening?'

'Yes, Mr. Garnett.' His face, indeed, was screwed up intently. He was certainly listening. 'Yes.'

'Good. I am writing to your mother tonight. I may suggest the tutor. You need somebody, obviously, who can improve your powers of attention. . . .'

The tram began to run along the road beneath the cliffs, the approach to Sumner. A chill wind whistled in from the sea across the waters of the estuary, freshening the stuffy air of the trailer. Mr. Garnett shivered, one eye on the boy beside him.

'You'd better turn up your coat collar, Blakiston. You are too young, and I am too old, to die yet, I fancy.'

After dinner the old man called Walter into the dining-room. 'If you'd be good enough to take this letter to the post.' He turned majestically from the desk and licked the envelope. 'To your mother, as you see.'

Walter, the letter in his pocket, ran up the road. He felt as excited as he had ever felt in his life: he might be at home for a year, a whole year. But why? Was there a reason besides that of his mother's love? He took out the letter, inspected the address written in Mr. Garnett's Greek-formed script, then pencilled six crossed kisses on the flap of the envelope. His mother would be surprised. And he began to sing to himself at the top of his voice, slashing at the palings as he hurried along the footpath.

'Hey, Walter!' It was Jimmy Nelson and his bicycle in the dusk. 'A penny a ride. Kapai!' But he did not seem to want Walter to cross the road: he was teaching a small girl to grasp the handle-bars firmly while she planted her shoe on the pedal. From the fair hair on her shoulders Walter knew that the pupil was Ivy Dakers. She gave him an interrupted hostile frown across the road, tugging her skirt primly round her knees.

'I'm busy now,' Jimmy threw at Walter. 'Go in and see ma. She's washing her hair.' He turned instantly back to Ivy. 'Come on, Ive, hop up. I'll hold you.'

Walter watched them. Fearfully crouched over the handle-bar Ivy Dakers squealed as she was propelled along the grass verge of the road.

'Keep your bottom flat on the seat,' Jimmy advised her loudly, mercilessly.

'Don't be rude or I'll go home.' But an airy giggle flew from Ivy Dakers's lips as he held her by the slack of her dress. 'See?'

'I'm only trying to teach you, Ive.'

'I'll fall off if you don't prop me.'

'Gosh, you're all the wrong shape . . .'

'Somebody'll come along. Oh!'

'There's nobody, only Walter. Go on, Ive, shove.'

Walter left them, without so much as a glance at the veranda of the Nelsons' bungalow. Jimmy and Ivy Dakers were already far from him; shouting, squealing, down the road in the greenish evening glow. Walter did not look back. He had loved Jimmy and now Jimmy was no longer his absolute friend. He might never see him again.

'Wa-wa-wa,' Jimmy's voice drifted from far away in the ultimate distance, growing ever fainter. 'Wa-wa-wa.'

Walter ran on, posted his letter, then slowly took himself towards the beach. He searched for the compass in his pocket, found it and watched the steel needle quiver towards the sea. Far out gleamed the tide; the breeze smelt of kelp and the cool floors of sand round the Cave Rock. On the Scarborough hillside, far along the crescent shore, the windows of the Macaulays' empty house were dark, deserted. Walter blew on the glass of the compass, wiped it with his sleeve, then dawdled homewards along the dunes, kicking at the sand.

'Where have you been, so late, Walter?'

'Posting a letter.'

Miss Muriel was heating milk in a small saucepan above a methylated-spirit flame, the baby held swaddled in the curve of her arm. 'Talking of letters,' she said presently, 'I heard from Mark today, Walter. He sent a message to you, though I can't say that I understand it.' She put down the saucepan and fumbled for the letter in her dress. 'Here, you can read it. At the foot of the page, a postscript. Read it out.'

Walter read aloud, haltingly, from the page: ' "Before I understood this place, appointed for my second race ..." ' He turned the paper over. 'Is that all?'

'I imagine so.' She laughed. 'But what is it — what race?'

'It's poetry. I don't know.'

'Neither do I.' She bent her head to grin down at the baby in her arms. 'Malcolm doesn't understand either. Do you, lovely? It's simply Uncle Mark making jokes in his lighthouse for the seagulls and the fish. He's lonely, I suppose.' She straightened the child's clothes. 'Time you had your last bottle,' went on her absorbed voice. 'You're a handful, you are.' She glanced down at the purple flame of the spirit stove and took up the saucepan. 'By the way, Walter, have you let your mother know you'll be catching the morning train on Friday? I told the carter today to collect your trunk in advance: you can't take it with you on the tram and we don't want you to leave anything behind.'

Part Four

HOME

CHAPTER I

'A FOOT taller, quite a foot taller.' Mrs. Blakiston stood back the better to take him in. 'But how *thin*. You look half-starved, darling, like an orphan out of a home.' Her voice broke into a nervous laugh, so that for a moment Walter feared she might shed tears on the station platform. 'You might be a young telegraph-pole or a walking-stick. Look at your wrists!' And with mock despair she clutched at her husband's elbow. 'George, did you ever see anything like it in your life? He's a scarecrow.'

'Don't fuss. He'll fill out in time. Won't you, old chap.' Mr. Blakiston turned aside to dip a match at the bowl of the blackened pipe in his mouth. A moment later he had stalked off, frowning, along the platform to collect Walter's trunk from the luggage office. Seen from behind, his narrow riding-breeches made him appear wirier than the boy remembered, the set of his shoulders squarer, the back of his neck severer, browner, more rigid.

'You horrify me, Walter — you quite shock me.' Mrs. Blakiston stared at him with tender unbelief. 'Those Garnetts have sent back the wrong boy by mistake. They've simply picked the thinnest one they could find, hoping I wouldn't notice or object.' And laughing, on the edge of tears, she led him arm-in-arm across the yard of the small yellow station, among horses, gigs and buggies. '*That*,' she said at last, pointing into the heat and dust, 'is your father's new car. He loves the beastly thing.'

The small upright motor had a dark green bonnet like a flattened nose: the mudguards arched high above the wheels.

Walter was delighted. 'It's as long as Mr. Macaulay's. It's longer than a horse.'

'It smells far worse than any horse. Or so I think.' His mother wiped her eyes, then looped a veil over her flat grey hat and tied the ends under her chin. 'Still, I suppose it's progress, of a sort,' she added. And as they stood before the door of the car she drew Walter to her, suddenly and delicately kissing his forehead, his cheek. 'Walter, is it really you? I can't quite believe it — not after all this dreadful time.'

He pulled himself away, embarrassed. 'I wish you wouldn't snatch — '

'Snatch? You might at least kiss me.'

Her cheek, against his nose, had a faint whiff of fresh eau-de-Cologne. It was her scent, he remembered, and loved her again as though he had not been away.

'That's better,' she said, comforted. 'I have missed you, you know. So very much . . . Did you enjoy gran's, last holidays?'

He swung open the low door of the car, watching the hinges turn. 'I went fishing, every day.'

'So her letters told me. Father thought you liked being by yourself too much, for a boy.'

'I didn't mind.' The hot leather of the seat burned through his trousers as he took in the car greedily with his eyes. 'What would happen if we ran over something? What, mum?'

'I don't know, Walter. Your father hasn't tried yet.'

'How many horse-power?'

Mr. Blakiston, carrying Walter's trunk high on one shoulder, strode stiffly across the yard. 'Those fatheads in the office,' he exploded. 'Because there's a war they think they can loll about day and night doing nothing. I'd show them.'

'You're always so abrupt with these people. What do you expect?'

'Respect for their jobs, for one thing.'

'Oh,' she laughed, getting up beside Walter, 'that. I must say, they're always polite enough to me. Walter, you'd better sit between us, dear. If you put your arm round my shoulder — '.

'No.' He stretched out to touch the dashboard.

'Now don't be difficult.'

'All right,' he said after a moment and snuggled against her.

'I see you haven't really changed, after all.'

Mr. Blakiston jerked at the starting-handle below the car's bonnet: the engine spluttered, roared, died into a clicking aloof silence. 'Damn the confounded thing,' he said sharply.

'You see,' said his wife, and shrugged . 'No horse does that. A horse has more respect for its job.' She glanced down at Walter's profile beside her. 'That turned-up bit at the end of your nose, child — '

The engine roared.

They drove slowly through the sun-blinded township. Dogs roused themselves from languor on the footpaths to bark at the strange, popping carriage without a horse. At the Post Office Mr. Blakiston collected the newspaper and the day's letters, both of which had arrived from Christchurch by the same train as Walter, then strode back to the car.

'Do you want anything at the store, Caroline?' He spoke to his wife without looking at her.

'No. We can go home at once.'

The road beyond the township wound almost immediately into the hills, with tawny paddocks of tussock on either side sloping up to outcrops of limestone against the sky. Sheep grazed among the tussocks or panted in shelter from the sun beneath isolated blue gums and spindly half-grown pines. Whenever a gap in the hills opened to the east Walter could see the horizon of the bay rising from the immense curve of the coast southwards. Nothing, he told himself, had altered since he had driven with his parents down this same road on his way to school and the Garnetts, ten months before. Even the larks, singing as they hovered in strange leaping flight overhead, might be the same birds — might have watched his disconsolate departure from home.

The car halted. 'Hop down and open the gate, old chap.'

Walter hadn't forgotten the gates either: there were three,

breaking the road into the hills. He hopped down, and back.

The car resumed its chugging progress between upland paddocks. And now, behind a fringe of pine plantations ahead, the boy could see the white roughcast front of the house itself, with hills and gullies rising beyond, against the hot sweep of the sky. Home.

'Mum, am I in the same room?'

'Your own room, Walter. I've even left most of that appalling museum in the cupboard. Did you want it all, still?'

He was dismayed to think that any fraction of it might have been destroyed. 'I want the coins . . . and the moa-bones . . . and the eggs.'

She laughed, studying his face again in stolen side-glances. 'I still can't get over your appearance, Walter. In another ten years you're going to look exactly like early pictures of granpa — the Graces themselves — '

'Leave the child alone, Caroline,' Mr. Blakiston intervened from behind the wheel. 'I can't say he looks to me so vastly different.'

'Oh, you! He could come back disguised as the Wild Man of Borneo and you'd notice nothing,' she remarked with reserve and gave a small elegant touch and tilt to her hat. 'This is the first time he's ever come home from school, after all — no thanks to you.' She bit her lip, twisting her face aside.

The car threaded a shingle drive through the plantation and drew up at the side of the house. While Mr. Blakiston took the machine away to the garage Walter and his mother went indoors. The boy held his breath until he had reached the hall, then inhaled a deep satisfied sniff: here at once was the cool unforgotten savour of home, different from any other scent in the world. He had returned at last. Meanwhile, behind him his mother had lifted her veil and hat and was patting her hair before a brass-framed glass on the wall.

'I'm hungry,' he told her. 'What's for lunch?'

'Wait and see, dear.' She stuck her hat-pins into the back of a chair, drawing her delicate body in at the waist. 'What did Miss Garnett give you for your lunches?'

'Sandwiches, mostly.'

'No wonder you turn up looking such a young clothes-horse . . . I want to hear about the Garnetts, later. And the school. I want to hear everything that's happened to you. Everything.'

He began to run his hands over the chairs he remembered. On the wall by the stairs was a blank space. 'There used to be a picture . . .' he observed, dismayed. 'The one of the boy on the deck . . . Casabianca.'

'I put it out in the apple house while you were away.' She laughed with a small sad shudder. 'Every time I went upstairs I used to pass it and think of you.' She came to him and made him face her. 'Do I look older, Walter?'

He was too occupied to decide. 'No,' he said indifferently. 'I don't think so.'

'We must talk as we used to, some time. Tonight perhaps, when you go to bed. You used to tell me everything — remember?' Her fingers brushed the hair coolly from his forehead. 'You must tell me your secrets and I'll tell you mine.' Her voice trembled. 'All this past year . . . but no, that can wait, all of it.'

He ran upstairs. His room across the landing was as he had left it, but cleaner. Above the cotton counterpane a mosquito-net was bunched-up, a ghost, under a hanging hoop: a pink linen mat lay on the dressing-table. The oak trees surrounding the lawn at the back of the house threw a green clouded light on the ceiling. And in the cupboard, spread out on an upper shelf — a shelf that he'd always had to stand on a chair to reach — was his museum: the flints and bits of lignite and pyrites, the birds' eggs in a tobacco tin, the bones, the skeleton of a dog-fish, the Chinese coin, the shell of a crab. Now they were on a levet with his eyes. As he had gathered these treasures in the past he had thought they might be worth a thousand pounds, a million, more perhaps. Now he turned them over, one by one:

they might be valueless but they were still his own, part of him.

'What'll you do this afternoon?' His mother piled cold beef and salad on to his plate at lunch. 'Will you rest?'

'No,' he told her with scorn. 'Explore.' There was in fact everything to do. And by the evening he had made his excited round . . . a fresh oat-bin beside the harness room, a new vane on the windmill in the gully, a few Jonathans still lying shrivelled among straw in the apple room. The rich world he remembered had not altered: its charm was eternal, unforgotten.

'What are the names of your friends at school?' His mother's face studied his over the dinner-table. 'Tell us.'

'Well . . . there's Marriner.'

'A nice boy, is he?'

'All right. He was in my class.'

Mr. Blakiston lit his pipe. 'I suppose old Garnett dusted the seat of your pants for you, occasionally?'

He murmured a vague reply: school, he remembered, had not been quite like Longmeadows in the book. Far from it.

'Don't mumble,' said his father, more sternly. 'We want to hear. You've told us nothing that I've heard.'

But what was there to tell? 'School's just ordinary,' he vouchsafed at last.

'A rest cure no doubt. At twenty guineas a term.'

Walter looked at his father. In a tweed jacket, his grey hair neatly brushed above the ears, Mr. Blakiston sat at ease after the day's work. The boy was afraid of his sarcasm, his hardness; of something rigid and unyielding in his father's character. He said nothing.

'Very well,' his mother sighed and began to clear the table. 'We'll ask you about school some other time. I think you're over-tired.'

Upstairs he dawdled over his undressing. He did not light the lamp, which attracted mosquitoes from the garden, but lay in bed listening to the thrushes and magpies still singing from the plantations. Presently he heard the rustle of his mother's skirts in the passage. She seated herself on the counterpane, her long fine hands folded on her lap.

'You seem so reluctant to talk about school, child . . . I wondered if you'd been unhappy? Have you?'

'No.'

'Then . . . you're angry with us, with me, for not letting you come home this past year? Is that it?' Her soft voice spoke in breathless spurts, then died. 'Walter, listen — it was partly my fault,' she whispered, 'but not all.'

'Gran said you'd been ill.'

'You wouldn't be any wiser if I . . . yes, I have been ill, in various ways. Dr. Lester's been looking after me.'

His eyelids began to droop: the warmth of the bed was lapping him round in security. 'Did you run down a hill and hurt your heart?' he asked after a moment.

'Run down a hill?' She thought he was dreaming.

'Did you have to take drugs and pills?'

'No. Or not often.' She patted the counterpane, hesitantly. 'Have you ever thought that you're an only child? . . . I mean, without brothers and sisters?'

'I don't mind.'

'No, but I do.'

'Why?'

'I have minded, always. And because I had only you I'd always wanted to keep you at home, not send you away to school. You see? Your father thought differently, largely for reasons of his own. He and I don't always see eye to eye, you know, to put it mildly . . . Are you listening?'

'Yes,' he said from the first mists of sleep.

'Last year he thought I was making too much of you, spoiling you. He insisted that it was time you should grow independent of me . . . not tied to my apron strings. He thought a year's separation would do you good. I disagreed — in fact he and I nearly came to a parting of the ways — but he won. Against all sense, I let you go: I said I wouldn't see you till the end of the year . . . Your father's very strong-willed, Walter. He always has been, ever since we were married. Many a battle's been hidden from you.'

'Did he marry the wrong woman?'

'What? Now you really are dreamin', my dear.' Smiling, she shook him gently. 'What a thing to say — '

'Why have you been ill then?' he murmured.

She became serious, withdrawn. 'I hated being without you. Hated it. It was terribly lonely here, with your father out all day on the station. We're so isolated, somehow.' She smoothed the sleeves of her muslin dress. 'Having let you go like that, you see, my mind couldn't rest or be still. It seems to me I almost lost my reason, some days: and then I developed all sorts of physical symptoms, headaches, pains . . . In the end it was really better that you shouldn't come home until I recovered. You wouldn't've liked an ill mother, not at all.'

'Would gran have adopted me if you'd died?'

She was shocked. 'Wouldn't you have missed me?'

'Yes. I only wondered.'

'At any rate,' she said, and got up, 'I didn't die. But all this has meant that I've had to pull myself together. For ten years you'd been my baby, my possession. Perhaps I'm a slightly wiser woman now, I don't know. More stable, at any rate. Of course Heaven knows what would have happened if I had died — I can't imagine — '

'Dad might have married someone else, different.'

'Walter, you're saying the oddest things.' She looked down at him, puzzled, reflecting. 'What do you know about marriage? Very little, I hope.'

His eyes sought drowsily for the looped mosquito-net over the bed. 'Must I sleep under the net? It's so hot.'

'Wait, I'll let the window down further.' Her shoulders were outlined against the orange-green of the sky. Far away beyond the window the wekas, more than birds, called their panicky cries from the gullies in the hills. 'Yes,' she said, 'you'd better

260

have the net round you. The mosquitoes are fiends this year.'
And she resumed as she tucked the net about his pillow: 'The odd
thing is that it's your father who's now chosen to keep you at
home for a while, before we send you to College. He wants
you to help him on the farm here: we're losing so many shepherds to the war, you see.' She hesitated. 'Even your father's
still young enough to go to the war himself, if he has to.'

'Would he go as a common soldier?'

She laughed. 'I don't know about "common", I'm sure,
child. At all events, if he did go we'd have to run the place
somehow, you and I between us. However, that's unlikely. He
simply wants you with him for a bit, to help in the meanwhile.
We'll have to see about a tutor for you later. Mr. Garnett said
in his letter to me this week that you might profit from a tutor.'
She peered at him through the mosquito-net. 'What are you
laughing at?'

He had smiled, remembering the crosses for kisses on the
envelope — a secret he had not told her. 'I was thinking about
Christmas,' he murmured drowsily, already in dreams.

She lifted a corner of the net and kissed him. 'What were you
"thinking about Christmas"? Something as odd as the things
you've been saying to me?'

'No.' He looked up at her sleepily from the pillow. 'What
presents shall I get? Anything decent?' His eyes closed. 'A
gramophone . . . ?'

CHAPTER II

'RAIN—that's what we want, Walter. The whole place is as dry as kindling.'

Walter held the gate open to let his father through. The hot sun baked the tussocks of the hills behind them; the parched grass in the gateway threw a white glare under their chins. From where they stood the homestead among its tufted plantations of pine and oak below looked like a toy house or a Noah's ark with a red roof planted on the seaward undulations of the tawny landscape. The tilt of the land seemed to cant the whole countryside towards the waters of the Pacific. The blue sea curved powerfully south along the sweep of the bay and was confined at last by the finger of a frail peninsula on the further tip. Walter, screwing up his eyes against the glare, glanced now across fifty miles of ocean towards a place he remembered, a dot not distinguishable in the furthest heat-haze of the bay, a mere fleck at the foot of the peninsula, almost infinitely distant.

'Sumner's over there,' he remarked to his father. 'The Garnetts.' He turned to shut the gate on the hillside.

Mr. Blakiston nodded. His own attention was fixed nearer home, upon the almost sapless pasture of the slopes and upon the sheep clustered together in the gully directly below, a gully like the course of a creek long since parched. 'Too dry,' he murmured, and in a fit of reflection or memory added: 'I should never have burnt the bush out of these gullies, Walter. It gave shade and held the moisture of the hills as it came down . . . I've learnt a lot, these past fifteen years — in fact I've never stopped learning.'

'Since you came from England?' the boy asked idly.

'More or less.' Mr. Blakiston stood looking down across the

country, the rich slopes of the nearby land he owned. He pushed his hat back on his forehead, thinking of England. 'My father packed me off from Devon to make a man of me,' he said presently. 'He sent me half way round the world to put some sense into me and make me fend for myself and by myself — make me stand on my own feet. A man's got to find his own independence, the earlier the better. He's got to go through the mill.' He withdrew his eyes from the landscape and looked down almost apologetically at the boy. 'That's how it is, Walter, in case you wondered.'

Walter turned his head aside. In his shyness with his father he bore neither dislike nor malice: his year's absence was over and now he was home. He was even pleased to be with his father, his companion on this sun-parched hillside in the morning. He too looked at the sheep in the dry gully below.

'Couldn't we shift them?' he suggested after a moment. 'There's water in the dam, further down.'

'Yes, we could ride up tomorrow and do that, I suppose.' But Mr. Blakiston had withdrawn himself: he preferred to make his own decisions. 'Though the grass is better here,' he said with a return of the stern tone in which he so often spoke to his son.

They went together down the hill. 'Could I ride my bike if I came with you to shift the sheep?' Walter asked.

'No. Keep your bicycle for flat country.'

The bicycle had been Walter's Christmas present from his parents, a month earlier.

'A horse is more useful to a farmer,' Mr. Blakiston told him. 'However, the bicycle was your mother's idea.'

'Mr. Garnett had a penny-farthing bike,' Walter said presently. 'He rode it one evening and it bust all over the path.' He laughed, then bit his lip and looked away from his father. 'No,' he murmured, 'I made that up. I invented it.'

With his walking-stick Mr. Blakiston tested the wires of the fence outside the homestead plantation. 'Always remember,' he advised the boy, 'you can tell a good farmer by his fences. A fine tight wire, no sagging — '

'Yes,' said Walter, preoccupied.

'You listen, but I doubt if you take in what I tell you. It's no use dreaming your way through the world, you'll find.'

They went between the trees, past the greener leaves of an orchard. The house was cool, the sun-blinds down over the veranda.

'If you must go about with bare feet, Walter,' said Mrs. Blakiston, 'you ought to wear shoes or sandals in the house.'

'Why?'

'Because I have to wipe grubby footprints from the floor, that's why.'

'All right. Yes, ma.'

'And don't call me ma.' She frowned. 'Oh, and another thing — don't leave your bicycle in the hall.'

'I want to keep an eye on it.' He ate his cold lunch, hungrily. 'It's the first bike I ever had.'

'I notice you've already worn out the bottom of your school pants on the seat.'

'They were worn out before. Miss Muriel mended them.'

'Muriel Garnett?' Mrs. Blakiston ran a finger over her forehead. 'She was good with your clothes. I should have written to thank her when you sent her that card at Christmas. I meant to.' She glanced at his torn shirt. 'What you really need of course is a complete new set of clothes. You're in tatters.'

'If I'm to work with dad . . .' He knew that his father scarcely ever bought new clothes: his wardrobe upstairs was stuffed with relics. 'I can wear his old ones.'

'You'll do no such thing,' his mother objected. 'A good bonfire is *their* appointed end.'

Mr. Blakiston moodily pushed away his plate. His security was threatened and he recouped himself by a mild attack on Walter. 'You'll have to perk up a bit, my lad,' he gloomed, 'if you're to make a farmer. It's not all chatter and bicycles, you

know.' The attack widened. 'Didn't old Garnett teach you dis-
cipline at school?'

'Yes.'

'It's not obvious to me then. I can't make out what you did
learn, except how to bury your head in a book.'

'Leave him alone, George.' Mrs. Blakiston intervened: she
took up the challenge on Walter's behalf. 'He wasn't sent to
school to be trained as a sheep-farmer — unless that's what you
so oddly mean by a gentleman.' She rose, collecting the plates
together. 'Walter, you can get down now, dear, if you've
finished.'

He escaped, seized his bicycle from the hall and rode twice
round the house, the pedals crisp and cool against his bare soles.
With luck he might have a whole free afternoon before him: he
must ask his mother. And he presently pulled up the bicycle
under the window of the dining-room, bending down to
scratch at the mosquito-bites on his ankles.

'Only monkeys learn anything "instinctively", as you call it,'
his mother's voice was saying to his father indoors. 'Boys have
to learn.'

'That's bunkum.'

'Indeed it isn't. And social education's something quite
different from mere schooling — '

Walter leant across the sill. 'Mum, can I ride down to the
township for the mail?'

'Yes, . . . if you want to.' She looked from the window at
his flushed face. 'But put on your boots first. And your cap,
or you'll get sunstroke.'

'I'll tie a handkerchief round my head . . . like a pirate.'

At four o'clock he was back, having pushed his bicycle up the
long hill, the leather mail-bag bumping on his shoulder. The
afternoon had grown cool, almost chilly, with clouds sweeping
from the south across the plains: a hint of rain. In the mail was
a letter for his mother, also a second letter addressed (he had
discovered the fact with surprise) to himself — a letter on cheapish

white paper like rice-paper, written in a steep up-and-down hand he did not recognize. He ran up to his room to read it, stretching himself out on the counterpane, his eyes puckered in the sultry light from the window.

Dear Walter:

Your kind card came at Christmas and I should have thanked you before, but so much has been happening, with my mother suffering in the heat and the baby growing fast. We had a quiet Christmas here, just five of us including Rose who came for one night and asked after you. My brother Mark could not get home.

My father is at last thinking of giving up the school and retiring, which would please us. He finds the tram-journeys fatiguing after so many years. Not that the school would disappear, but somebody else would take it over. Father thought Mark perhaps, but Mark has his own ways and theories and would alter father's English pattern. We shall see. We live in awkward times.

How are you, Walter? You grew so fast with us, became a little stronger too, I hope. And I don't think cold baths harmed you. Now your mother will be keeping your neck and ears clean and mending your clothes, as I tried to do. Already it all seems a long time ago.

I must add something before I close. Mr. (now Corporal) Macaulay was here soon after Christmas, on his first leave from camp. He tells us that he will be sent abroad later, to where N.Z. soldiers are needed. And then, at the end of the war or when he returns to Sumner, he and I are to be married. This makes me very happy. Some day, when you have finished. College, you must come to see us again.

Enjoy yourself in this summer while you are young. Time enough later for sorrows. I think of you often. Yours affectionately and sincerely   MURIEL GARNETT

Walter folded up the letter. Without knowing why, he

wanted to hide it. He got up from the bed, opened the cupboard door and slid the envelope between the tin of birds' eggs and the crab shell, in a corner of his museum away from the light. Presently he went downstairs. The letter, he told himself, had been for him alone, not even for his mother.

'I've heard from gran, Walter.' Mrs. Blakiston sat beside the tea-tray in the living-room, fanning her face with the open letter in her hand. The room itself was almost an extension of the veranda beyond and of the baked untidy grass of the garden. 'Was your letter also from her?'

'No.'

She spoke absently, from the distance of her own thoughts: 'From some friend at school then?'

'No,' he said again.

She watched him scratch at the lumps on his ankles then snatch at a slice of cake from the tray. If he wanted to be secretive . . . and she went back to her own letter. In the silver tea-pot and jug on the tray Walter saw his face balloon at him as he munched the cake in his hand.

'Your grandmother writes,' Mrs. Blakiston broke the silence, 'that you seemed very concerned about some dog . . .' She flicked over the page. 'No, not "concerned" . . . I don't understand. Her writing's become so difficult.' She propped the page against the tea-pot and glanced at the watch tucked in her belt. 'Your father's late for his tea, as usual.' And she returned to her letter. 'Tell me about this dog,' she said.

'I've forgotten.' And suddenly, almost without meaning to speak, he added: 'My letter was from Miss Muriel.'

'From Muriel Garnett?'

He sat hunched up in his chair, his confidence withdrawn as soon as given. He did not answer.

'Really,' his mother exclaimed, 'you can be the most *exasperating* child that was ever born! You tell me nothing, nothing at all. You've hardly mentioned the word Garnett since you came home; I've had to drag every word out of you, literally.' But after a moment, repenting, she sat herself on the arm of his chair. Her tone softened in her throat. 'I don't think you care about me at all, Walter. I'm beginning to think just that. Or don't you understand what it is to love?'

Again he was silent.

'Answer me, Walter. I'm asking you an important question.'

'I don't know,' he said slowly and was aware of the odour of his own sweat rising from his open clothes.

'What don't you know?'

What was it? What was this secretive, all-important fact that had, it seemed, been forcing itself up like a blade of grass, a leaf, a bud, for months, inside him — an uncoiling of ignorance towards knowledge?

'What don't you know?' his mother repeated slowly. 'Is it love itself you don't understand?'

He nodded, crumbling the cake in his fingers, while he struggled for words. All he could manage at last was a string of broken phrases: 'I don't understand why people — men and women — why they behave like that.' And he twisted away from her, abashed by the impossibility of explaining. 'Are they just crazy?' he brought out in a burst. 'Are they just mad or — ' and he remembered the school-word ' — or completely barmy?'

'What on earth's put that idea into your head?' She began to turn the wedding ring on her finger, looking down with compassion and tenderness at the young growing body of this son she had brought into the world and whose coming-into-being she must now try to explain. 'You don't imagine, surely, that children are born because two people happen to have gone off their heads, do you?'

'No, but — '

She laughed. 'But what?' And when he did not answer she went on: 'How often have you seen people in love — anyone at all?'

'The Garnetts,' he said at last.

'Ah, the Garnetts — those girls, I suppose.' She bit her lip,

268

smiling. 'I see. I thought I should hear about them sooner or later.' She touched his hair. 'Well, tell me, tell me everything.'

'No.' The word came out like a detonation from the immense guilt of the past few months. He had 'told' once, and it had led to panic and anxiety in his secret soul. Love was something one did not tell about, ever: it was mixed up with his own blunderings into an adult world and the mystery of his own physical existence: it was the secret, the pain, and the guilt he could not resolve. And from his chair he glared up at his mother's smiling face above him. 'I'll never tell you,' he said.

'But, Walter, listen — '

'*No*.' She was remote from him, involved in all the things he did not know. 'I'll never tell you,' he repeated, his heart in conflict.

'Then let me tell you something.' She put out a hand to stop him from rising. 'I suppose you think love's something very dreadful — I suppose you think that your father and I were never in love because we happen so often to quarrel. But it isn't like that, you know.' And her voice took on a calmness and dignity he had seldom heard in it before and that was like a cool hand on his forehead. 'Your father and I had a very true love — a physical love — for one another when we were married, Walter. He loved my body and I loved his. It's quite simple, and nothing to be ashamed of. And it isn't what you call crazy, either, though it may lead people to do crazy things sometimes.' She looked down at him suddenly. 'You don't feel angry or ashamed or guilty because I was in love with your father when I conceived you, do you?'

'No,' he said presently, his head bent. It seemed to him that walls were falling away from him on every side, leaving him exposed and strangely happy. By her confession that she too had been a party to those mysterious emotions that had so agitated Miss Rose, his mother had released him from his guilt and his pain. His own parents had not been exempt from that madness that had puzzled him and through which he himself

269

had been begotten. He glanced down at his hands and his body as though only now did they belong to him, the individual Walter that would eventually perhaps create his own image. 'No,' he repeated to his mother, 'I'm not ashamed or angry. I'm not, really I'm not.'

'You're growing up. I knew it would happen.'

There were footsteps on the veranda outside. Mr. Blakiston strolled into the room, wiping his forehead with the back of his hand.

'Rain,' he remarked and nodded towards the tossing trees of the garden, 'rain at last. And every drop of it worth a shilling to us farmers, Walter. To you and me.' He planted himself down in great good humour before the tea-tray, throwing his hat negligently across the room. 'Tea,' he said and touched his wife lightly and affectionately on the arm. 'And none of your rain-water and milk for me.'

For a moment Walter watched his mother and father together. He felt he had never before seen them properly as one: a unity to which he too belonged. Peace and an odd excitement seemed to stream from them towards him, as though the rain rustling in the garden had created some special minute outside time. The moment passed. He jumped up. In a wild scattering movement of arms and legs he hurled himself towards the veranda door. 'My bike,' he flung back at his mother. 'I left it outside. The rain'll rust it.' He was gone.

'That bicycle,' said Mr. Blakiston and shook his head. 'Any-one'd imagine he had nothing better to think about.'